The Necklace of Zedan

BY MARK GREENLAW

RoseDog Books

PITTSBURGH, PENNSYLVANIA 15238

RoseDog Books
585 Alpha Drive
Suite 103
Pittsburgh, PA 15238
Visit our website at *www.rosedogbookstore.com*

ISBN: 978-1-63661-575-2
eISBN: 978-1-63764-977-0

PROLOGUE

The Gohwarf craftsman finishes his latest project with a smile of extreme satisfaction. Coming from a Dwarf father and a Gnome mother he was strong, smart and skilled.

Zedan puts away his tools. His hands are calloused from using them. The smell of sulfur from the forge hits his nostrils. "Finally!" he sighs."I have created a necklace of great power. My buyer will be quite pleased."Clutching the necklace into his vice-like fingers, he heads to the strongbox. He knows it will be safe in the box and retires for the evening.

Two days later, the Gohwarf is traveling to the marketplace. Zedan swigs on his ale flask. After wiping the residue from his lips onto his sleeve, he starts to scan the vast area set aside for people's haggling and dealings. The Marketplace is the ideal place for any deal, shady or legal.

"He's supposed to be the third tent on the right," he thinks to himself. His roving eyes spy the tent, not too far away. "Aha! There it is!" Traveling as fast as his short, stocky legs will allow, he makes it to the tent and heads inside.

Inside, he sees his buyer awaiting him. He is sitting down on an expensive and elaborate pillow arrangement. A display of white teeth greets Zedan as, he closes the tent flaps. The tall human stands up and greets Zedan with the customary handshake.

"I was hoping you would be punctual," he replied matter-of-factly. "And in that, you did not disappoint me, Zedan."

Zedan nods in understanding. He takes a swig of courage from his flask. Motioning for the human to sit, he begins his narrative of the necklace.

"This necklace will enhance a magician's ability to use magic. If used in a fighters' hands, it can create special magical tricks to go with the weapon. For instance, it could allow a sword to shoot fire or electricity. However, it is more powerful in a mage's hands as it allows them to enhance what magical power they already have. It won't cause instant death, but if you use your imagination right, people will wish you did kill them outright." All the talking causes his lips to dry out, so he finishes off his flask of ale. Quickly, he puts the empty bottle away and opens a new one. It seems his supply of ale is unlimited. "It does cost a person a price; it is going to want to take a piece of you with it; it can properly channel its power. For example, it would lop off the finger and replace your finger with a hard green crystal. I am unsure as to its magnitude or what it will want, but be warned it will want something." He chuckles as that was the most challenging part for him to incorporate. "I am a genius!" he gloats to himself.

"I also have," he resumes. "Done a lot of studying on you and concluded that you are a generous, honest, and kind-hearted man. So it is for this reason that I am selling you this necklace. Somebody should use this necklace for the good of all races and not for evil purposes. A weapon of this power in the wrong hands will cause a loss of many lives and much destruction."

The tall man nods in agreement. "I have the 1000 gold pieces you requested!" He speaks. His voice is gentle yet purposeful. Zedan smiles at the purse of gold. He dreams of the life this kind of money will give him and his family. His son Vlim, only six years old, is already studying blacksmith's craft and ax fighting. His wife would thrive and be content with a more oversized kitchen and more space in a bigger home. With one swift motion, he scoops the money purse up and hands over the necklace.

"It's a pleasure doing business with you!" the human smiles. Zedan takes a swig and exits with the money safely in his pack.

~ ~ ~

He is a few miles from his homestead when he spies two beggars shuffling along in front of him. Their tattered remnants of clothing and dirty skin tell the tale of their life of poverty and misfortune. Feeling the strings of sympathy and pity tug at his heartstrings, he slows his horse down and approaches.

"Hello!" He greets the scraggly strangers. Their cold, hateful eyes stare back at him. He turns to get his money from the pack. Thoughts of generosity invade him as he prepares to give the beggars some of his fortunes. These thoughts are quickly interrupted. In the split-second it took to turn his back, he is yanked off and thrown roughly to the ground. One of the beggars is already on him, holding a dagger to his throat. The other ruffian is rummaging through his pack.

"Whoa!" the ruffian cries out. His wicked grin spreads to his eyes as he holds out the money sack to his companion to view. Zedan tries to throw the bandit off of him, but he discovers he is a lot stronger than his disguise of a beggar indicated.

"The guild will be pleased with this haul!" he states. Seeing nothing further of interest, they take the helpless Gohwarf off the main path and interrogate him immensely. As they beat him with fists, and clubs Zedan thinks of his family. He won't be able to bless them with this money after all. His family will probably be destitute. He imagines his sons begging in the street each time he gets hit. His heart aches for his family's future. Satisfied, they stab Zedan in the gut with a knife then leave him to die.

~ ~ ~

Zedan can make it back to his homestead and relay his tale to his son Vlim before dying in his son's arms. Thus begins the strange twist of events that unfold involving the Necklace of Zedan.

CHAPTER 1

Footsteps cut the silence of the cold, fresh winter air; as snow crunches under the feet of a hapless sentry. His repeated curses and mumbling carry into the chilly night.

"Why must we have guard duty on top of a castle where no sane human would even try to climb the sheer-faced wall? Besides," he adds as a point only to himself, "it's too damn cold for anyone even to be out." He turns around and retraces his footsteps. "That damn crazy wizard is always making us do strange, useless chores. Maybe someday I'll get a transfer and be in the army. That's where at least some action is. It's hard to be cold when you're in a fight with an enemy soldier. Yes! That would be nice" he walks in a dreamy daze. "Even death will be a lot better than freezing your ass off, retracing your steps, and waiting for somebody to appear on top of a castle wall that's damn near impossible to climb." He turns. Just then, the wind picks up. The cold rips through his armor, clothes, skin and finally pierces his bones and grabs hold.

"Brrrr!" he shivers. "Blasted wind, it's chilling me to the bone." He turns. His shift is almost over and he dreams of sitting in front of the fireplace. This dream cheers him up for but a second. He turns. In his path sits a black cat. Seeing only a cat, he sees no need for alarm.

"How did you get up here, fella?" He asks as if expecting the cat to answer his question. The sentry begins to approach the cat.

The cat stares at him innocently. His tail swishes back and forth.

Cautiously the sentry picks up the cat. Answering his own question, he follows the cat's footprints. "Aha!" He says triumphantly. The prints stop at the ledge. "That's peculiar. Can you fly, cat?"

"Swish"! "Swish"! The tail answers. "Purrr"! "Purrr"!

He releases the cat as he peers over the edge. Smash! A fist sends him reeling. Blood trickles down from his nose and into his mouth. He can taste his blood.

Standing before him is a figure in black. He notices the cat walking away. The figure is taller than him with a muscular build. A rapier gleaming in the moonlight is waiting in his hands. The sentry tries to regain his pride rather than yell for help. The figure in black smiles mockingly. Enraged, the soldier rises to his feet with a scimitar in his hand.

"You want to play, huh?" he asks boldly. "Well, let's have at it. I want to be near the fireplace roasting your cat on a spit." He charges. The scimitar, curved, wicked, come arcing down at the intruder. "Clang"! The scimitar strikes the rapier. With a look of dismay at the parry, the sentry rethinks his plan. He thrusts his scimitar. "Clang"! The blade parries and comes at him. "Clang"! Parries. The sword fight ensues.

"Clang"! "Clang"! "Clang"! Back and forth, they fight. The sentry realizes his mistake. His more massive weapon is tiring him, while the black figure has a lighter weapon by far. With grim determination, he continues his attack. "Whoosh"! His weapon slices air.

Rolling to the side, the intruder thrusts the rapier, it penetrates the armor and pierces the heart. The thief salutes the sentry as he gives his last shudder. "It's been a long time since I encountered somebody good with a blade. It's a shame we met as enemies."

He strips the body quickly and, with a heave, rolls the body off the wall. Seconds later: "Sploosh"! It hits the moat. The thief changes into sentry clothes.

The second watch begins his way, grudgingly up the flight of steps. He isn't looking forward to his duty. Already he can feel the chill coming from outside the door at the top of the steps. He is late too. Thinking quickly, he begins to come up with his excuse for his tardiness. Satisfied with what he comes up with, he continues his way up and opens the door to the roof.

You're late," the thief replies sourly.

"I know, I know. I uh," The sentry tries to remember his lie but fails miserably. "I overslept. "It won't happen again."

"You don't want me to tell Belghar, do you?"

"N-n-no, I don't." His eyes bulge in fright with the mention of the name.

"Well then, let's say that you give me 20 gold, and I'll forget that you were even late."

"O-ok," he agrees as he begins to shake, not due to the cold.

"I'm waiting," the thief holds out his hand.

"N-n-now?" the sentry looks puzzled.

"Yes, now! Hurry up; it's getting cold out here." The sentry starts fumbling with his pockets. Finally, he brings out some gold.

"I only have six gold on me. Can I give you that and pay you the rest when I get paid at the end of the month?"

"Yeah! That's fine," he rolls his eyes. There is a slight "Meow." "What was that?"

"I dunno. The noise came from over there," the sentry points into the shadows.

"Well, check it out, imbecile. It's your shift now." Warily he creeps over to the corner of the wall. Unbeknownst to him, the thief is silently following behind him. A dagger-sharp, deadly, is in his hand. From the shadows, a black cat emerges.

"Oh! It's just a little kitty." He smiles. "Hi, kitty!" he begins to scratch the cat. "Purrr-Purrr" "Swish-Swish". Faster than the sentry can react the thief, brings the dagger across the poor sentry's throat. A quick boot and the guard's body falls to join his comrade. "Sploosh"! Having served its purpose, Thadden removes the sentry garb. He is sure he won't need the disguise anymore tonight.

"Well, Feacon, let's finish what we came here to do. We have five hours until the next sentry shift."

"Purrr-Purrr" is the cat's only response.

Without making a noise, he heads down the steps and into a well-lit hallway. Some bright burning torches are the cause of the illumination. Looking ahead of the rows and rows of doors, The thief can see his destination.

"It's nice to have the map of the place that you intend to rob," he chirps. Preparing to react should a door open, Thadden continues forward. He makes it to the door without incident. He presses his ear against the door and listens. Not a noise can he hear from the room. With a shrug, he opens the door and enters the room.

Thadden enters into a world of darkness when he shuts the door behind him. He moves forward to his final destination; he turns the knob. It's locked. "Naturally," he replies. Working a little quicker, he retrieves his lock-picks. Within a matter of seconds, there is a "Click," and the door is unlocked. He laughs heartily.

"Now entering the room of Belghar Haffen cruel King to all his subjects." He opens the door and sees the object of all his evening's efforts. The room basks in a green hue. It is coming from the item he came to collect. Just as he is about to reach for the glowing necklace, he hears voices.

"Pig Slop!"

With catlike reflexes, he is under the bed. The blankets are huge and ruffled. They descend to the floor. Sucking in his breath, the thief listens as the door opens.

~ ~ ~

"And in here, my sweet is my bedroom he continues his sentence. "This is where you will be spending most of your time." Belghar brings her hand to his lips. She shudders, a reaction more of distaste and fear rather than of love or the up-coming lovemaking.

"You fear me, don't you, Menecha?." He produces a giggle. "It does not matter. For all that matters is that your father owes me, and you have to pay that debt severely." Glaring eyes burn into her face. "So come in. Make yourself comfortable. I shall get the wine." With that remark, Belghar strolls out of the room. He closes the door behind him. Menecha sits down on the bed. Before long, the tears start flowing. Her sobs are enough to bring the intruder out of hiding, but only for a brief moment.

"Excuse me!" he speaks.

"OH!" she replies, startled. She quickly starts to remove her tears in a vain hope that he won't see them.

"Try this; it works better." He hands her a handkerchief.

"Thank-You, ah?"

"Thadden," he finishes for her.

"Menecha," she flutters her eyelashes.

"I couldn't help but overhear you crying. What kind of debt do you owe that you have reduced yourself to that of a common whore?"

"What kind of job do you have where you have to hide under people's beds?" she counters.

"Good point." I'm just taking a castle tour, incognito style. He winks at her. Thadden hears footsteps in the other room. He darts underneath the bed.

"Tomorrow, when you wake up, go to the Wolf's Paw Tavern and ask for Menecha. I will talk to you then." With a thump-thumping heart, he mulls on what is said and daydreams about tomorrow.

"Did I hear voices, my dear?"

"No! I was just talking to myself."

"Oh! Well, here's the wine."

"Thank you!" she blushes convincingly. Belghar pours the wine into the glasses. Just as he is about to drink his, she stops him.

"Wait! Why don't we make a toast."

"A toast? Of course! Where are my manners?" Belghar slaps his knee. "Well, my pretty, what shall we toast to?"

"Why lust, of course."

"Lust? Very well then, to lust."

"To lust," she repeats as they bring their glasses together. Then they engaged in their lustful activities after many, many toasts. Two hours later, the mighty magician waves Menecha away. She leaves abruptly. Belghar wants to play with his newly acquired necklace, but exhaustion takes over. Within minutes all is quiet except for Belghar's snoring.

Thadden waits five more minutes to make sure that the magician is genuinely asleep. "It just won't do to get myself blasted by a fireball before I even get to see Menecha again" he thinks to himself. Finally, he is in front of the dresser and has a powerful necklace in his clutches. Silently, he leaves the room with the snoring mage. "Another time, perhaps?" he calls back to the room and it's sleeping, inhabitant. It is then that he hears a familiar sound. "Clump"! "Clump"! "Clump"! It is the sound of boots on wood. "The sentry," he hisses through his teeth. Wasting no time, he puts his back-up plan into action. "Just stall him, Feacon. I'll be there shortly."

~ ~ ~

The sentry arrives at the top to find no-one at the post. He is about to raise the alarm when he spies a black cat sitting directly across from him. The need to know how the cat got there overrides his need to raise the alarm. Curious, he approaches the purring cat. His sword is unsheathed. The cat continues to purr. When he gets within two feet, the cat arches its back. The hair stands on end. It issues a hissing warning. The sentry looks around to see what is bothering the cat. When he looks back at the cat, it is out of sight.

"Huh!" "Where did it go so fast?" He begins to backtrack warily as a shiver runs up and down his spine. "Maybe I'll go get help now."

"Rrrowrrrr," the cat screeches as he steps on its tail. Terror grips him; his heart raced in his chest. The soldier drops his weapon as he looks behind. Again, the cat disappears. A definite feeling of needing help assails his senses. Quickly he reaches for his sword. It is not quick enough; he discovers as a claw scratches his hand.

"Bladder!" he yells as he bolts for the door for safety. The cat appears again to foil his attempt, as he trips and crashes to the ground. Tired and sore, the sentry gazes at the doorway only a few feet away. He begins to crawl. Slowly he inches his way forward. With aching, throbbing hands, he reaches for the door. It swings open. "Safety," he mutters as he sees an image through his fear-filled haze.

"Not safety," A voice corrects, "but close." Thadden, seeing no need to kill, brings the pommel of his rapier down on to the sentry's head. His teeth slam into his tongue as Thadden knocks him unconscious.

"Nice job, Feacon. Let's get the hell out of here." Smiling, he prepares for his long climb down.

Chapter 2

Music, merriment, and the sound of haggling pursue Thadden as he walks among the multitude in the Gena market. Kids giggle as they begin their snowball war. Occasionally, they'll throw a snowball or two at the clerks, customers, or even the soldiers hired to keep peace at the market, which causes a scowl from the latter, so the kids brave another throw later on. Thadden is in no rush. The necklace buyer can wait a little longer as the thief is in the mood for a little mischief. It isn't long until Thadden finds the object of his merriment. Up ahead, he spies an apple merchant trying to cheat a customer. He shakes his head in disgust. The argument is still on when he arrives.

"Four coppers and not a copper less for one apple!" The apple merchant says obstinately.

"I'll give you two coppers. Surely that is a fair enough price for one meager apple."

"Four is what I said," he says finally. "And four is what it shall be. These apples happen to be the finest in all of Gena I have them imported this time of year. Either buy an apple or get the hell away from my stand." Just as the man is about to leave, Thadden interrupts him.

"Excuse me!"

"What?" the merchant glares.

"I couldn't help but overhear your conversation. Is it true that you are charging four coppers for one apple?"

"Yeah! I guess your ears heard correctly."

Thadden surveys the crowd that is forming. "Perfect," he says to himself. "The bigger the crowd, the harder it is for the soldiers to get here." He swoops up three apples.

"Hey! Put those back!"

Pretending not to hear, Thadden begins to juggle the apples. "So, these apples that I'm holding in my hand are worth twelve coppers?" He asks skeptically—the merchant nods. "Oooops!" he lets one of the apples go as it hits the merchant on his foot. "Your apples have bruises, mister merchant. And you want to sell these for four coppers an apple?"

The other apples fly as the merchant puts his hands up to protect himself from the barrage. Thadden notices that one of the soldiers has given in and begun throwing snowballs back at the naughty kids. The apple merchant removes the leather guard on his ax.

"That's going to cost you either twelve coppers or your life. Which method do you plan to pay?"

"You see that people," he looks at the crowd. "First, he tries to cheat you all by selling bruised apples at four coppers a whack; then, if you refuse to pay his outrageous prices, he threatens to kill you."

"Arg," the merchant yells as he runs at the troublemaker. His ax comes down. "Clang"! Before he has time for another blow, Thadden's rapier finds the target. The merchant's belt shears in half. His trousers drop to his knees.

HA! HA! HA! HA! The crowd laughs at his demise. He lunges for the thief. His pants won't allow it as they send him crashing to the ground. Thadden tosses two apples to the haggling customer, who, in turn, salutes him. With another slash of the rapier, the cart's leg is gone, and the apples spill out onto the snowy ground. "I'm slashing all of your prices, merchant. Next time treat your customers with a little more respect." With that parting remark and a laugh, Thadden leaves before the soldiers arrive; and heads for his destination.

~ ~ ~

Whistling softly, Thadden walks on until he comes to a sign that says: Xibnar's Magic Shop. This message follows: CLOSED. Ignoring the warning, Thadden proceeds to step up to the front door. Without wasting a single second, he pounded on the door. A sound of shuffling feet, lock turning, and a face is peering out from the door. It is an old pinched face with frazzled gray hair and an unkempt, scraggly gray beard.

"Oh, it's you," the cracking voice speaks. With that, the door opens just enough for Thadden to squeeze his body in. Looking both ways, the aged man quickly closes the door.

"Do you have the necklace?"

"Let's say I was able to obtain the necklace and quite possibly have the item in my backpack; what exactly was the reward?"

"Hmmm." He says. "Hmmm." He repeats as he stares at the ceiling. "I believe it was 75 gold. Yes! That is what it was." He nods his head to confirm it.

"Hmmm," Thadden says mockingly."Hmmm." He mimics the wizard as he too stares at the ceiling. "My memory seems to recall it was more like one hundred gold, and three of your healing potions. Or maybe that was a different wizard that had made that proposal." He starts for the door.

"No, No, that was me. Ha! Ha! Ha! Now I remember. It was 100 gold and three healing potions." He stammers. "My memory isn't what it used to be." Xibnar produces a stack of coins and three potions. Thadden counts 100 gold. Xibnar's withered fingers prepare to snatch the necklace as soon as Thadden brings it out. With deft quickness, Thadden has the necklace in his hands but just out of the old wizard's reach. The wizard's greedy eyes stare at the chain, entranced. He seems to drool at the necklace as a dog would a bone.

"You know, maybe I will see the wizard in the next town. He did seem to want it an awful lot." He motions to put the necklace away. Despair fills the wizard's heart as he witnesses this act of cruelty. "On second thought," Thadden argues with himself. "I did make a deal, and I wouldn't want to go back on my bargain." The wizard nods in agreement. Finally, Thadden hands the necklace over to the slobbering mage. "Enjoy; I hope we can do business again sometime." No sooner do the words leave his lips when he feels rushed out the door. Thadden finds himself on the doorstep with the door already being bolted. "Well, so much for gratitude," he remarks to the door.

Thadden wonders why the mage was in a hurry to get him out of there. With a shrug he remembers the young lady he met last night. The image of

Menecha explodes into his brain. Frantically, he searches for the Wolf's Paw Tavern. He is about to give up in despair when he sees a man stagger out from an alleyway. With excitement coursing through his veins, he breaks into a run toward the alley. He amazes himself when he gets there, to see that it is far from being an alleyway. Turning the corner, he sees that it is indeed The Wolf's Paw Tavern. His heart begins to beat a little faster. "It's just beating from my fast run," he almost convinces himself. Thadden walks in.

The tavern is well-kept. A fireplace, far in the corner, is roaring and crackling. Most tables are empty as all the patrons seem to have flocked near the warmth of the fireplace. "Obviously," he notes to himself, "this is a bar that hardly has fights." Its atmosphere is that of friendliness and homeliness. As much as it tempts him to sit down, he knows he'd rather be with the warmth of a woman. "Not just any woman," he thinks. "This woman is named Menecha." With that thought in mind, he heads over to the bar. At first glance, a bartender is a fellow who would seem to want to kill someone rather than speak to them, but underneath the overlying toughness, Thadden can sense kindness and friendly fellow. "I'll just be sure not to get him upset," he warns himself. Putting on his best smile, he summons up his courage and speaks.

Excuse me, sir," the bartender looks up. "Do you know where I can find Menecha Rebish? I need to speak to her."

"And why would you like to see my daughter?" He folds his arms across his chest.

"Y-y-your daughter?" he asks, dumbfounded. "She could have at least given me some warning." He thinks, a little annoyed.

"Yes, Menecha is my daughter."

"Well, I met her the other day in the market, and she wanted me to come by here. She wanted to talk to me."

"Oh, she did, did she?" He glances at Thadden, a little skeptical. "Menecha," he yells to a room behind the bar. "Somebody's here to see you. Somebody from the market?" There's a thudding of feet on wood.

"Stairs," Thadden guesses at the sound. Menecha enters through the back room.

"From the market? Who am i..." The words die out as she notices Thadden. "Oh! Hi Thadden," she begins to smooth her dress. "Daddy, this is Thadden. I ran into some trouble in the market, and he rescued me. I figured you'd want to see him and congratulate him or something," her voice whispers the last two words. Thadden glances at Menecha, thankfully. He begins to relax.

"Well! Thadden, You should have said something earlier." His face brightens. "Would you like something to eat?" He nods his head. At the mention of food, Thadden's stomach begins to rumble. He hasn't eaten all day. The food statement suddenly brings out Thadden's feline companion, who begins to rub against his leg repeatedly.

"And where was he hiding?" Menecha asks, surprised.

"Oh, he comes, and he goes. You'd be surprised at how easy it to miss such a small beast. If you'd be so kind, could you get some food for my cat as well? I'd be willing to pay for both of us."

"You can forget about paying, son; this food is on me. It's me who should be paying you for rescuing my daughter."

Thadden blushes.

Soon a piping hot meal of ham, potatoes, gravy, and a glass of mead sits in front of him. For Feacon, there was a little slice of chicken with a bowl of milk. Together they eat in silence. With their stomachs sated, they sit back and languish in Menecha's attention. While she is petting Feacon, she talks and smiles at Thadden, who struggles to keep from stumbling over his nervous words. Soon, it is time for bed. "So Thadden, whereabouts do you live?"

"Somebody raised me as an orphan in The Shondell Guild. I usually go there if I don't find a place to spend the night."

"In Shondell, huh, well as long as you don't go stealing anything, I suppose I could let you spend the night. You and your cat can sleep on that couch over there near the fireplace. It's the best I can do."

"Thank-You! It'll be just fine." Thadden moves over to the couch. Just as he lies down and prepares for sleep Menecha's father throws in one last comment.

"My daughter likes you, Thadden. I guess I do, too. Be sure to keep an eye out for her but don't go out of bounds. You do that, and we'll get along just fine. Pleasant dreams!" Thadden listens for the footsteps to go up the steps. When all is quiet, he places Feacon on his lap and falls fast asleep.

~ ~ ~

As soon as Thadden rushes out the door, Xibnar is making his plans. Eagerly, he rubs his hands together. He puts the necklace around his head. The emerald hue ebbs in and out, waiting for its commands. With fumbling hands, Xibnar opens up a dusty, ancient book. In it, there are all the ancient chants to some of the most potent magic. The magic that Xibnar is about to release through his twisted means. At last, he finds the words, and slowly he begins to recite them:

Oh! Mighty Necklace of Zedan.
Place all your power in my hands.
I will destroy all that's in my path.
In the end, they will know our wraith
When they reach their final breath,
They'll know we came, for we bring death.

With the chanting of the last word, the necklace becomes unbearably hot. A stench of burnt flesh fills the air as Xibnar's skin begins to bubble.

"Ieee," he manages to scream as the fire seems to consume him. Green-light dances about the room. It strikes the counter and the shelves. Xibnar's potions begin to boil. Although none of the wood catches on fire, scorch marks remain to remind Xibnar of its presence. With a simultaneous explosion, all the potions and vials explode, hot liquid showers onto the floor, and shards of glass fly across the room.He is still screaming when one sliver penetrates his eye. He pays the price of the spell. Xibnar slumps to the ground.

Chapter 3

"Arg," the scream, angry, seems to send a chill up and down every resident of Belghar's castle. Pontew, Belghar's aide, rushes into the bedroom of his master. He waits for the berating. A scream like that does not mean good news for the aide. Belghar is sitting on his bed, staring wide-eyed at a space on the dresser.

"What is wrong, master?" He doesn't want to ask, for fear of his wrath, but he knows he must.

"What do you see on top of my dresser?"

"I see nothing, sir."

"Nothing," Belghar screams in anger. "You see, nothing." He breathes heavily. His chest moves up and down rapidly. Never has Pontew seen his master in such a frenzy. "Why do you suppose you see nothing on top of my dresser Pontew?" At this point, Pontew is not sure which answer, if any exists, would be correct. He decides to go with the obvious one.

"Because there isn't anything there, sir."

"Imbecile!" He knocks the dresser over with his hands. The finest robes, sandals, and undergarments spill out onto the floor. "Get me the sentries from last night's duties."

"At once, sir," Pontew leaves as fast as his legs can carry him.

Fifteen minutes later, he arrives with one sentry. Pontew carries him in. There is blood drying on his hand with some around his mouth. Pontew notices the dresser is back in place. Someone had put away the clothes. Pontew remembers seeing a servant leaving just as he was entering with the wobbly-legged guard.

"I assume you have a reason for being so late?"

"Well, sir, I've just got done reviving this guard."

Wanting to hear nothing more, Belghar motions Pontew to stop. "Now, sentry, what is your name?"

"K-K-Kyle DuVac, s-s-sir."

"Kyle DuVac?" He says the name with acid dripping off his mouth. "Well, Kyle DuVac, what do you see on top of my dresser?" He wonders where this question leads him, but like Pontew, he can only come up with one answer.

"Nothing, sir," is his reply. A slight giggle comes out of Pontew's mouth. One glance from Belghar cures him of his need to laugh, and he resumes his silence. Belghar restrains himself from having another eruption.

"So, you see, nothing." He seems to be calmer. "And for once in your entire, miserable life, you are right; there is nothing on my dresser." The sentry begins to breathe a little easier. It doesn't last long. "Now, let me ask you another question. Maybe you can be two for two, and that would make my day. Since you see nothing on my dresser, what did you see on your sentry duty? Or did you indeed see nothing then as well?"

"W-w-well, I did see a cat, sir," he stammers.

"A cat?" Belghar begins to pace. "And how did this cat happen to get on top of the castle?"

"I don't know. It was there when I arrived for my shift. I didn't see another sentry, just a black cat."

"You see a black cat, but no sentry, and you did nothing?" he asks, his voice showing signs of anger.

"Well, actually, sir, I was on my way to do something when I ended up tripping over the cat."

"There were two of them?"

"No, it was the same cat. One minute it was in front of me. The next, I'm tripping over it."

"This is a very amusing story, please, do go on." Belghar interrupts.

"I then tried to attack the cat, but it was once again gone. Somehow, I lost my weapon because I remember trying to pick it up, and that's when it scratched me."

"Disarmed by a cat! This just keeps getting better." He begins to chuckle. "Pontew, are you hearing the same story that I'm hearing?"

"Yes, Belghar, I believe I am."

"Good, I was just making sure. Continue, Kyle," he motions with his hand.

"Well, at that point, I wanted just to leave and get help, or something. I don't know, and I just wanted to get away from that creepy cat. Before I got to the door, I was tripped up once again by the cat. I started to push myself back up to my feet when the door opened, and I thought someone was saving me."

Belghar looks at Kyle incredulously. "Saved from a cat! Now, that is funny. You seem to have had more excitement last night than I did. I sure hope your story gets better."

"It's almost over with, sir, I assure you."

"Good!"

"When I looked to see who's coming out the door, I saw a figure dressed in black. My vision was a bit hazy, sir, so I didn't get a good look at his face."

"Oh! Of course." Belghar replies, his voice riddled with sarcasm.

"Before I could react, he hit me on top of the head with the pommel of his sword. I just came to when Pontew came and got me." There is a pause.

Belghar inhales deeply. With a voice that could freeze hell, he replies. "Pontew, put this man in chains until I sort this mess out. A cat disarms him? Rubbish! He's in league with the very man who stole my precious necklace."

"B-b-but, sir, it's the truth, I swear." Kyle begins to whine incoherently. Belghar's fist silences him.

"Pontew, I said get him out of here!" Pontew instantly drags the screaming sentry out the door. He hears a crash.

"You there, servant," he points to a boy in the hall. "Go immediately to Belghar's bedroom. Carry out any orders he demands of you, and stand up his dresser," he adds, remembering the crash.

One hour later, there is a knock on Belghar's door. "Come in," he replies with a booming voice of authority. Pontew enters the room again. As always, he carries about him an air of knowledge and cunning. Many times Belghar has relied on him, and every time he has passed. Belghar motions for Pontew to sit, who does so immediately.

"What's the news on the sentry's story?"

"Before you send me to the cells to rot with Kyle, you must first hear me out. I believe the sentry's story." He waits for a reaction. Belghar does not stir. Instead, he sits and waits to hear Pontew's argument. He is not a fool. I have given Kyle a truth serum and have questioned. He still gives the same answers in exact detail. After that, I sent a few spies into town. Who came up with some interesting answers. It seems there was a thief, dressed in black, in the market today. He has black cat as a companion." At this news, Belghar clenches his fist. He nods his head. Pontew continues. "The thief hassled an apple merchant , a fight ensued and the thief left victorious. He was missing for about an hour, and then he turned up at the Wolf's Paw Tavern. He has not left."

"What is this thief's name?"

"Thadden, master Belghar."

"Thadden, what?"

"It's just Thadden. That's it. No last name." Belghar, for the first time this day, smiles.

"You have done very well, as usual, Pontew. I want constant surveillance on Thadden until I can find a means with which to destroy him."

"It's already being done, sir. What about Kyle?"

"The sentry! Let him rot for one day, as punishment for his sloppy work, then send him to me. I have special plans for him." He smiles. "Is there anything else?"

"I've been thinking. Maybe we should put a bounty hunter after this Thadden character. We'll offer more for him to be returned alive. Once we get him, it won't be long until we get your necklace back. Then we'll throw him in the arena. He will be a lesson to any other would-be thieves who have dreams of robbing the Magnificent Belghar."

"Pontew, I am once again in your debt. Set all of those things in motion. Keep me posted on ANY changes." Belghar's day has just gotten progressively better. With a bow, Pontew exits. Belghar's evil laughter is all that anyone hears.

~ ~ ~

Sunlight filters in through the windows of Xibnar's Magic Shop. Its beam of light shines upon the man on the floor. The figure seems to awaken with a groan as if he was in a deep, deep sleep. Xibnar opens his eyes, well, one of them anyway. All the memories of yesterday's events come instantly flooding back to him.

Slowly, painfully, he rises to his feet. His eye, blinded, wounded, is throbbing. He staggers to the counter for support. When he feels strong enough, he makes his way towards the back of his shop. Slowly, he opens the door and thrusts himself forward. He almost falls but manages to grab onto the doorknob. He is home. It is a small home, but adequate for a single male. Still, in a daze, he finds his way, on steady feet surprisingly enough, to his bathroom. "Nooooo!" he screams, horrified at his appearance. His hair is in shambles. Blood streaks all over face. A shard of glass is in one eye socket. Before he can stop himself, Xibnar grabs the shard of glass. A quick yank and he removes it from his eye. "Ahhhh!" he screams in pain. Blood oozes out of the hole that was once his eye. Working quickly, he opens his cabinet. Various potions line the cabinet shelves. He retrieves the one marked Healing. With shaking hands, he uncorks the bottle. Bracing himself for the pain, Xibnar splashes the potion on the wound.

The blood starts flowing, as miraculously, the wound closes. Xibnar stares at himself in the mirror. Although his hair is a little singed, it seemed to take the least of the punishment. Huge blisters cover his chest, where the necklace still rests. The chain, however, is no longer ebbing. It is as still as a chair bolted to the floor. His one eye that used to be brown is now a bright amber. A theory, insane, illogical, but a theory nonetheless, pops into his mind. "I have suffered a great deal, but I now, at last, have power. I already feel it coursing through my veins. As soon as I've rested, I shall find out exactly what I can do. The loss of the eye was worth it." He cackles madly. Xibnar heads off to bed. In the morning, he shall wake up to become the mightiest wizard in all the land.

~ ~ ~

Belghar sits upon his throne. He peruses over a stack of papers. With a huge smile on his face, he signs one. Happily, he throws another away. Such is his job day in and day out. In front of him is his monetary advisor, Ragan.

"But sir, that paper you just threw away is from the Duke of Millings' Dale. He is very influential and has enough money to increase our army to monstrous proportions."

"The Duke is a nobody. Nobody listens to him. Nobody wants anything to do with him. And nobody certainly wants to take his dirty money. Besides, I need to save our money for other more important matters. If this Duke is so rich, why is he asking me for 1000 gold to pay for his daughter's wedding?"

"But, but, my lord," Ragan begins to protest.

"Enough! I have thrown the paper away." His voice is final. "I don't have to answer to the Duke, and I especially don't have to answer to you." "Have I made myself very clear?"

"Y-y-yes s-s-sir, you have," he gulps.

Belghar begins his signing ritual again. He throws another paper away. Ragan looks as he's about ready to protest but instead keeps quiet. Pontew enters the room.

"Excuse me, master, but I have a visitor for you."

"A visitor?" Belghar asks?

"A Mister Romeelus Delgoth."

"Who?" he asks.

Pontew approaches Belghar and whispers in his ear, "the bounty hunter."

"Oh! Him! Of course, let the man in here." A smile worms its way to the surface of Belghar's sinister face. "That is all for now, Ragan. I'll send someone to fetch you when I'm available." Ragan slinks away like a dog who's just lost a fight. Pontew returns with a man in tow. The man wears a black plate mail. He carries a wide assortment of weapons. A shield, dagger, longsword, net, and a whip are just a few of his visible arsenal. He instantly impresses Belghar, and he doesn't impress easily.

"My lord, allow me to introduce Romeelus Delgoth, the finest bounty hunter in the entire kingdom of Belgharia." Pontew addresses Belghar. Romeelus makes a slight bow.

"Did my aide inform you of your target and the payment?"

"Yes, he did."Romeelus' speech is short and to the point.

"Businesslike," Belghar notes quietly to himself. His liking of the man grows. "I want to get that thief and his mysterious black cat. I want him alive. The cat you can do with as you will. You'll get 1000 gold for the thief. Once you have him, bring him to me. You will get nothing if he is brought back dead. Is everything to your liking?"

"It suits me just fine. I prefer them dead but, I look forward to collecting the money very soon." Romeelus turns and walks away, leaving a very stunned Pontew and a much impressed Belghar to stare after him.

"When he's done this assignment, see if you can't persuade him to be my bodyguard and hitman. If he refuses to remember one thing, if he's not working for me, he's not working at all."

"Yes, sir," Pontew responds as he too leaves the king to his throne.

Chapter 4

"Whoossh"! Thadden wakes up to the sound of a roaring fire. With his uncanny reflexes, he jumps out with his rapier held in front of him. Menecha's father is staring at him, perplexed.

"Is everything alright?"

"Yeah, I just forgot where I was. I'm not used to sleeping indoors. I'm sorry if I surprised you." Thadden says with a grin.

"No problem, it's understandable."

"I have to be going soon, is there anything you need? Wood, for the fire, or maybe the floor needs to be swept?" Menecha's father's face holds one of shock. He had never had anyone ask that before.

"Well, if it's no trouble, could you bring in some wood from the back?" Thadden nods. "Good, just go out that back door; you'll see a stack already cut. Just bring in a few armloads. When you finish, I'll have Menecha cook you up a meal. You might as well take a bath before you leave. If you don't mind me saying so, you could use one."

"The bath would be great. Don't worry about the food, though; I have plenty of money to buy some later on."

"Oh, I guess I'll have to tell Menecha not to bother cooking breakfast. She enjoys cooking, but I'll tell her you don't want anything." He throws the comment into the air as a fisherman would throw a line in the water. Like a greedy little fish; in Thadden's case, his conscience, he takes the bait.

"No, on second thought, maybe I'll have a little bite to eat," Thadden replies. He leaves to get the wood before her father can convince him to stay for another week.

"That's what I thought," Menecha's father comments with a cunning smile. Thadden retrieved three stacks of wood. It wasn't too hard to find. He passes by the set of stairs that he had guessed was there the previous night going out the back door. He then walks by the kitchen and out another door that leads him to a vast woodpile. When he finished, he instantly goes upstairs to the bathroom. Menecha's father, Jake, throws him a washcloth and a lump of lye to wash up.

"You have to be clean if you expect Menecha to cook you up a meal. It isn't my rule, you see. I rather wish I didn't have to bathe every night, but my daughter is stricter than her mother. Come downstairs when you're finished. Your food will be ready by then. Enjoy yourself," Jake responds. He closes the door. Thinking about how foolish kids are when they're in love, Jake begins to laugh. Thadden can hear the laughter as he begins to wash.

Feeling clean and refreshed, for the first time in weeks, Thadden descends downstairs. "Those made me feel good." A smell of cooked eggs, bacon, and toasted bread slams into him as a cannonball would break a castle wall. He begins to drool. "MEOW" Feacon speaks as it joins him before he enters the bar-room. "Where do you always take off to? And why do you only seem to come back whenever food arrives?" he asks, annoyed at the cat. "PURRR-PURRR" was the response he received. An image of beauty slapped him around and sent him reeling. He was at a loss for words. Menecha was wearing a low-cut dress that seemed to cover very little of her well-endowed breasts. Then Thadden thought for sure his heart had stopped. Senses reeling, he staggers into his seat. Two pairs of eyes stare at him peculiarly. Taking a few quick gulps of water, he revives himself from his previously dead state.

"I-I'm sorry," he exclaimed out. "I just suddenly didn't feel well. I'm fine now."

"That's okay; we all feel dizzy at times. Especially if we are surprised by someone or something's appearance," she teases him. He blushes and takes another swig.

"Ahem!" Jake clears his throat. "Now, it's time for a little grace, and, then we can begin our meal."

He says grace for about five minutes. Thadden is getting hungry as Jake thanks everybody from Belghar to the tax collector and finally to a nail whose very existence wouldn't have provided them with a roof over the head. Thadden's stomach lets out one final growl as a hint when Menecha's father finally finishes grace. Soon, everybody ends eating; even Feacon got to eat as endless scraps land his way.

"Menecha," her father speaks to her when they finish. "Could you please pick up these dishes and wash them?" Thadden starts to rise as if to help. Jake grabs on to Thadden's arm. "Not you, Thadden, you and I have to have a little discussion." Eyes sharp, unnerving, let Thadden know that the conversation is a serious one. Seeing no choice in the matter, he prepares himself for the worst. Let's go over near the fireplace. It's more comfortable."

With a scraping of chairs, the two men walk over to the couch. "How old are you, son?" Thadden had expected a father disapproves of son liking daughter routine, but he hadn't expected the third degree right away. "He could have warmed up to the subject." He tells himself.

"Twenty-one!" He finds that his voice is surprisingly firm. He is as ready as he'll ever be.

"Good." "Now, I know you and my daughter like each other." Thadden nods. "No point in trying to deny that statement," he thinks.

"As her father, I feel I have to tell you something. A little while back, I ran myself into a little financial trouble. There was a man who helped me clear it. You've seen my business; you know that I don't bring in a lot of money. I make enough to pay my bills and keep food on the table. The man who paid my debt is demanding payment for his loan." At this point, tears start to well up in Jake's eyes. The conversation is ending up being nowhere near the topic that; he thought it was going to be. He remembers where he met Menecha and that Belghar had said that she had owed him. Thadden is beginning to see exactly where this conversation is leading. "H-h-he made my daughter perform s-s-serv" he tries to finish, but he begins to cry hysterically.

"Services," Thadden ends for the distraught man. Jake buries his head in his hands and weeps as no being has ever wept before. A thought, a plan enters Thadden's creative mind.

"How about if I take Menecha with me when I leave," he asks. I have 100 gold on me now. You can use that as part of the payment. She'll be safe with me. I'll bring her back when she and I obtain enough money to pay off your debt. I just don't know how to tell her" He knows that her father was thinking similarly but was too ashamed, or too sad, to mention this plan. With numb horror, Thadden realizes he has thought about and cares for someone else other than himself. This stranger, who took him in, fed him, let him spend the night, fed him again, and let him take a bath, has been more like a father to him than anyone else. His parents he doesn't remember. All his childhood life contained was a life in the Guild. Tears form in his eyes as he, too, cries. The men hug each other in understanding. In the doorway stands Menecha, who has been watching the scene for a few minutes already. With tears in her eyes, she sneaks away, being careful not to interrupt the crying men.

Thadden leaves Jake in search of Menecha.

"Hey! she says. He stares at her and she beckons him into her room. I need to talk to you. I need to find a way to pay my dad's debt without doing it in the bedroom. I don't think my dad can handle the bar without me but I need a way to leave. Can you help me?"

Thadden smiles. Jake needs Menecha to leave to protect her and she needs to leave to save her dad. Both are too prideful to talk to one another. I will make sure your dad understands. He tells Jake he made Mencha understand and then tells Menecha the same. Without actually doing anything he solves their problem. With that taken care of Menecha makes her way upstairs. She has much packing to do.

~ ~ ~

Xibnar wakes up, feeling very refreshed. He opens his eyes. He sits up with a bolt. "Both eyes!" he screams joyously. "I can see out of both eyes." With sudden agility that belies his old body, he springs out of bed. There is a mirror on his bureau. Excitement shooting throughout his body, he lifts the mirror to his face. With a gasp, he almost drops it. The necklace is no longer on his neck. All that remains is a scar, hideous and foreboding. His first thought is to panic. It is then that he remembers the reason for the mirror. He looks at what should be an empty, black socket; instead, he finds an amethyst eye. His replacement IS the necklace. His body, too, he notices, is younger. With his more youthful face but gray hair, he knows he's now a real mage. In his mind, he sees the thousands of spells he has at his leisure. "It is now time to become a legend; to become a God!"

All of his life he had been a has-been mage. Full of parlor tricks that fooled no one. He was a joke in the community and was only good for selling items that magicians needed. His goal to be known, to be powerful is about to be a reality.

Ha! Ha! Ha! His evil laughter reaches his ears, and like the sound of angels singing in heaven, he relishes in its melody. He dresses in his finest robes and is out the door.

His destination, he already plots in his mind. "Snap"! He snaps his fingers. "Teleportation is a wonderful thing." He thinks as the spell whisks him away to a destination only he knows. He hopes he knows where he'll turn up...?

~   ~   ~

The cell is cold, lonely, depressing. It is a place where only criminals belong. "Certainly not a place where a mage's sentry is to be in for telling the truth. It was the entire stupid cat's fault, and the man in black." After only a day in jail, he is already beginning to hate the thief who knocked him unconscious. Like a bitter aftertaste that won't ever go away, he thinks back to the night of his duty, the night that caused so much trouble and put him in his current predicament. "All I want is one chance to get even at those two." His mouth is parched, he looks for some water. His search is in vain. Rather than waste all of his saliva talking to himself, he remains quiet. Sitting with his back to the wall, he hates quietly. He does this by dreaming of another encounter with the thief and cat who caused him to be in here. It is in this silence that he can hear the other noises in other cells. Mutterings, curses, and a lot of shuffling feet carry into the silence. From one section, there is a groan. These noises don't seem to cure him of his thirst or help his mood. He is about to strike up a conversation with himself when there is a cell noise beside him.

"Pssst!" he starts. "Pssst!" it repeats. "Hey! You in the cell, what are you in for?" His first reaction is to bust down the wall, grab the owner of the voice by the throat, and beat him repeatedly until he dies, but then reality hits him, rebounds a few times in his skull, and comes out of his mouth in the form of speech.

"I murdered a thief," he replies. "It's a lie," he rationalizes with himself, "but it does have a nice ring to it. Besides, this idiot isn't going to know I lied if I told him." A dry chuckle comes from the other cell.

"I hope it was worth it. I can't stand the buggers myself. They're always trying to put their nose into other people's business while at the same time lightening their pouches. Me, I'm in here for refusing to pay my taxes. I have no money, no kids, and no wife. Just me, and my cow. How can I pay if I don't have any money?"

"How long have you been down here?" Kyle asks, keeping the conversation going.

"Who knows? I've been down here for a long time. I know that much. There hasn't ever been any light down here, or any windows. I assume they feed us once a day." Silently Kyle nods in the dark. "If that's the case, then I've been down here for two months and four days. Lord only knows when I get out of here. So, what did the thief you killed take anyway?"

"He didn't try to take it. He did. He took my pride and publicly humiliated me. What else was I to do? I did what I thought was right. While he was still laughing at me with the crowd, I buried my sword into his skull." He starts to believe the lie existed.

"I bet he wasn't laughing anymore." There is another dry chuckle.

"You can bet he wasn't," Kyle replies as he too starts to laugh. "What's your name?"

"Lawrence Vimmura, what's yours?"

"Kyle, just Kyle would be fine."

The sound of a door slamming brings silence to the cells again. Footsteps walk over to the cages. They seem to stop at each section. There's a sound of scraping, then a chittering noise. The footsteps start up again, and the procedure repeats.

"What's going on?" Kyle asks in whispers.

"Dinner," Lawrence's voice whispers back. A slight chuckle is dry like Kyle's mouth. Footsteps approach Kyle Lawrence's cell. As the scraping noise occurs, Kyle tries to remember what the prisoners eat. He doesn't recall ever knowing as he was only a sentry.Cell duty was never one of his jobs. His food arrives "maybe it's leftovers from the mess hall," he thinks, trying to be optimistic. Then there is the chittering noise. Just as his curiosity can stand, no more the guard approaches his cell.

"Give me your bowl, prisoner!" Kyle's fingers fumble blindly in the dark and find the bowl. He slides it forward. The sound of heaven reaches his ears. "Water, thank God," he cries as the bowl slides back to him. Kyle notices that the guard didn't speak to the other prisoners. It strikes him as odd when the Guard replies:

"Here's your dinner. I hope it's to your liking." Ha! Ha! Ha! The guard laughs as he throws the food into the cell. The laughter and footsteps recede. With just water on his mind, he ignores the food and lunges for the bowl. It isn't until he drinks his last drop that he hears the chattering noise in the corner of the cell. His stomach growls as a reminder of his neglect. The noise from Lawrence's cells is enough to make him shiver. Eyes searching, he sees movement in the section. Kyle quickly grabs the creature in the small confines of the cell. The word's dinner, mockingly, creates a flashback in his mind. "A rat!" he says in disgust. "GROWL"! His stomach reminds him. Is it desperation that causes him to do his next deed, or is it just insanity?

"Go ahead!" The voice from the other cell goads him. "It's your only meal tomorrow. Don't worry, it's not too bad, as long as you got water to wash your mouth out."He"! "He"! "He"! "Ho"! "Ho"! "Ho"! Lawrence cackles, obviously mad. Kyle opens his mouth. The rat begins to squirm. It starts to scratch at his hands, looking for an escape.

"Slam"! He throws the body against the wall. The body just twitches then is still. "growl"!

Finally, with the creature dead, he again lifts the crushed, furry body to his mouth. "crunch"! His teeth sink into the head of the animal. Fur sticks in his teeth. Blood dribbles down his chin. "growl"! Quickly he takes another bite. "crunch"! "dribble"! "bite"! "crunch"! "dribble"! Over and over, he eats his meal until he finishes the rat, leaving nothing but the bones. His stomach seems satisfied.

Slowly he picks the fur out from his teeth. Without thinking, he reaches for his water bowl. He brings it to his lips and drinks nothing but air. The tastes of flesh and blood invade his mouth. He can do anything. Suddenly his stomach doesn't quite feel that good. It begins to churn and buckle, like a soup about to boil. He runs to the corner. Slowly it starts in his stomach. It picks up speed as it shoots up to his chest. As something alive and wants release, it speeds up and reaches the throat. The blast comes out like a geyser. It hits the wall and starts to drip off. His mouth tastes chunks, very similar to rat flesh. His throat begins to burn. Then it starts again. As his stomach begins to heave, he is ready. "Hruggh"! He sprays the wall. "Hruuggh"! As soon as he wipes his mouth with his sleeve, it starts for the final time. "Hruuggh"! "Hrruuggh"! "Hrruugh"!

Finally, it subsides until he just coughs. Kyle stops throwing up.

"It always happens like that the first few times. But you'll get used to it." Heh! Heh! Heh! He laughs again. Like a nasty disease that will never go away, the hate builds up inside him. He hates the man named Lawrence. He hates the thief in the night and his black cat. He hates Belghar. He hates the guard, but worse of all, he hates himself.

It doesn't take long until Lawrence begins to babble. But this time, Kyle notices he isn't talking to him. Curious, he comes out of his dreamy, hate phase.

"W-w-who are you?" Lawrence's voice is panicky.

"I am a friend of Kyle's." The voice responds. It sends a chill through Kyle's heart, with more pain than a dagger would if it thrusts in profoundly.

"What are you doing?"

"Saving him!" The voice sends another blast of cold air at Kyle's heart. As Lawrence cuts loose a scream as dry as his laugh, the darkness shatters by a green light. Darkness again surrounds the cells. Kyle is cowering in the corner when the chilly voice, right in front of him, commands him to rise. He does so willingly. A pair of green, glowing eyes stare out at him from the darkness. "Hello, Kyle. I wish to save you from your current position. But my services don't come cheap. I need you, and you need out. You need to be free if you wish to make those who put you here punish. Isn't that what you want to do?" There's a pause. "Get revenge?"

"Yes!" Kyle says with authority. He stands up. "Take me with you!" He is a man on the verge of losing his sanity. "Get me out of here!"

"That's the spirit, Kyle. Take my hand, and Trust me!" he holds his hands out to Kyle. He grabs them. Freezing numbness spreads throughout Kyle when he clutches at the hand. "SNAP"! The two men disappear. All that remains of their presence is a dead body and chunks of rat flesh on the wall.

~ ~ ~

Pontew answers the summons to the throne room. "Yes, oh, mighty one!" the aide replies with slight sarcasm.

Belghar stares at Pontew. His eyes seem to narrow and then brighten. "Pontew, can you fetch that miserable sentry from the dungeon. I'm sure he has learned his lesson. And prepare my chambers; I'm expecting a visit from my lady friend tonight."

"That young girl from the tavern?" Pontew inquires.

"Yes, Why?"

"My spies reported to me earlier today that the same tavern was where the thief had been seen after he robbed you. At last the gears in Belghar's head begin to turn forward. "Pontew, that night of the robbery, I had the girl in my bedroom. I left to get some wine glasses. When I returned, I thought I had heard voices. I had asked her, but she said she was talking to herself. And I found the door unlocked when we first entered. You don't suppose?"

"I do, sir. It seems the bastard was in the same room with you and just waited for you to fall asleep. Also, we noticed two sentries didn't report in last night. Someone killed them and threw their bodies in the moat. I think if you send a squad over to the tavern, you will get your answers."

"Thank you, Pontew. Now go and fetch me that sentry!"

"At once, sir," Pontew bows then leaves.

A half hour later there is a knock on the throne room door. "Come in, Pontew, you don't need to knock. You should know that by now." The door opens, and in steps Pontew, alone.

"Where is the sentry?"

"I don't know, Belghar. The cell was empty. The cell next to his had an occupant, but he is dead now."

"Dead?"

"He was burned to a crisp. The guard remembers seeing Kyle when he brought the food to him. It was after that when he must have escaped."

"And how is it that a sentry that gets outwitted by a cat can escape from my dungeon?"

"I don't know, master. He just did."

"Pontew, let me ask you one more question."

"What is it, sir?"

"Do you have any good news to report?"

"No, not yet."

"Then, please return to me when you do have some." He rubs his temples.

"Yes, Belghar." Pontew exits the room. Seeing a servant waiting for instructions, he hails him. "You bring Belghar some water and those head pain tablets, and be quick." Pontew shakes his head. It's just another day in Belghar's castle.

Chapter 5

Just as the Wolf's Paw Tavern is getting its first customers, Thadden and Menecha are sneaking out the back door. Tears salty, wet, were rolling freely off of Menecha's cheeks. She is going to miss him and strong demeanor, but mostly his hugs. She gives him a good-bye kiss on the cheek. When she steps away, Thadden steps forward with his arm extended. Jake grasps it firmly, then pulls Thadden forward for a farewell hug.

"Please, take good care of my daughter. I'll do all I can to stall Belghar. I hope to see you again soon. I must go inside now and check up on the customers. May God grant you luck and speed. Good-bye!" he quickly turns away. He does not want Menecha to see him cry. He must appear to be strong. Jake makes his way into the bar.

"Good luck to you too, Jake. Don't worry; Menecha will be safe with me." He yells to Jake's back... holding hands, Thadden and Menecha head off for the next town. The tears are still falling as Menecha, for the first time, walks away from her home, from her father.

~ ~ ~

Romeelus sits silently in the corner and casually checks out the customers. He notes the merchant who jingles as he walks. There's a man dressed in chain mail armor drinking heavily and ogling a female customer. The woman doesn't seem to mind as she too flirts back. He sees the woman who purposely leans over to pick up the handkerchief she dropped. Her breasts struggle to stay inside her top as she does so. With a grin, the soldier begins his ogling again. He finishes another ale. Near the fireplace is a figure wearing leather armor underneath a shirt and hood. The model is eyeing the merchant. He also can hear the jingle of money. Quietly, he waits for the bartender to return.

Romeelus is no fool. He knows what is transpiring outside. "As soon as the bartender comes in, I can sneak out back and follow my contract." He cherishes this thought. Wiping his eyes, Jake does indeed return. "Now, all I need is a diversion." Patience is a characteristic that Romeelus always exhibits. He never rushes into anything.

For this reason, Romeelus is one of the best bounty hunters. While sipping his water, the bounty hunter watches all activity. It doesn't take long, however. The door swings open. Soldiers bearing the crest of Belghar march imperiously into the room; they fear no-one. All activity stops. Romeelus takes another sip. The thief casually walks near the bar; he stands next to the merchant. Romeelus studies the soldiers' movements. With cocky arrogance, the guards swagger over to the bartender.

"Are you Jake Rebish?" A lieutenant asks.

"Yes, I am." His expression is blank. He waits for what he knows is coming.

"Then you are under arrest. This establishment is now, and forever, Closed!" The lieutenant stares at the individuals at the bar. The merchant gets up to leave. The thief bumps into him, apologizes, and then leaves hurriedly. Wanting no trouble, the soldier picks the woman up from his lap, whispers in her ear, and then they go together. "Probably for a night's pleasure," Romeelus remarks to himself. Jake doesn't put up any fight. They search him for weapons. Finding none, they escort him out of the building. No one had seen him hiding in the shadows. Patience has again brought him his reward. He briskly walks out the back door and follows his target's trail. "Soon," he thinks to himself. "Soon, I shall have him. Once I get paid, I'll move on to another town, another hunt. I love my job. The hunt, the chase and the capture."

~ ~ ~

The lieutenant brings in Jake.

Pontew gleefully smiles for the first time that day. "Finally, some good news for a change. Guards, follow me with the prisoner!" They silently obey. Pontew reaches Belghar's bedroom, way ahead of the soldiers and their cargo. He almost knocks on the door and then thinks better of it. "He did say I didn't need to knock," he remembers. Just as the guards come around the corner, he barges into the room. "Ohhhh!" he seems shocked. "I didn't know your majesty was er, entertaining one of the servants." Belghar thinks nothing of his current disposition as he puts on a robe and sends the naked servant out the door. "This had better be good." Pontew does not flinch from his master.

"It is, sir." He pauses. "I wouldn't be here if it wasn't." There is another pause. "You did tell me only to return when I have some good news."

"Yes, I know, Pontew. Would you please get on with it?"

"Well, the soldiers we sent have brought in Jake Rebish."

"Jake Rebish?" he says. Pontew rolls his eyes at Belghar's inability to remember names of any sort; he often wonders how Belghar can remember his without having to be told.

"Menecha's father! The owner of The Wolf's Paw Tavern."

"Ah! Yes, I remember now, Jake Rebish" Belghar seems pleased with himself as if it was he who produced the name.

"Shall you speak to him here or in the throne room?"

"Where is your head today, Pontew? Put him in the dungeon. We'll let the torturer deal with him for a bit, and then we'll go down and question him."

"As you wish, master." Pontew opens the door and leaves. The guards are waiting in the hallway. Their faces still register shock at seeing the naked boy come out of the room and run down the hall.

"Bring Jake to the dungeon. Let Drekkar handle him for a while. Tell him to leave the tongue intact, though, and we still need him." The lieutenant nods, then quickly they depart. "I hope all the excitement has completed for the day; I need a little rest." He talks aloud too no-one in particular. Tired from the days' events, he retires to his quarters. He closes his eyes and prays for sleep.

~ ~ ~

"So, tell me again, Kyle! The cat was in front of you, then suddenly it was behind you?" Xibnar speaks. They are both seated in front of a campfire. One hundred feet away is the roadside leaving Gena. Both men seem absorbed in their conversation.

"It was right in front of me. I turned around and tried to run, and then I tripped over the cat." Xibnar's glowing left eye stares deeply into Kyle's soul. It knows he is telling the truth.

"Do you know what it is you faced?"

"A cat?" he answers, dumbfounded by the question.

"Yes, but what kind of cat?"

"A black one!"Kyle answers easily. Xibnar swears under his breath. He cannot believe that any human could be so idiotic.

"Let me explain, Kyle. hat black cat is familiar. Which, in your slow, numb mind, means that the cat once belonged to a magician. A magician can summon it and give it certain powers—the familiar and the wizard link as one mind in two separate bodies. The panther has gotten the power of teleportation. Which means it can move forward or backward in a second. One minute it was in front of you; the next, Poof, it's behind you. Do you follow what I am saying?"

Kyle nods.

"Good!" He, at last, begins to see hope for the former sentry. "Somehow, that cat has separated itself from its master and joined up with that rogue." The same rogue that got me that necklace, he muses to himself. "Your job Kyle is to get me that cat. I don't care what happens to that thief, just get me that cat. In exchange, I'll grant you magic so powerful you could defeat all of your enemies. You know, the ones who caused you to degrade yourself in the dungeon. You could even kill that thief. So, what do you say?" Xibnar holds his hand out to Kyle.

"It's a deal, wizard." He shakes the hand. Kyle can see the wizard's eye flash amber for a second in the firelight, and then it's gone. A twisted smile appears on Kyle's face. The hate that has never left him grows more robust. "I'll be able to strike out at those I hate. They better be prepared."

~ ~ ~

Meanwhile, before the sun has set, Thadden and Menecha are making significant progress. "Which town are we going to?" Menecha asks.

"To Fentias," the thief responds. "It's two towns over, but we will have to stop and rest in Wobb's Hill first. Cutting through the forest should save us a little time. Plus, we can escape from a hunting party easier in the woods. We should be entering the woods soon. We'll rest there for the night. In the morning, we'll start again. By midday, we'll be at Wobb's Hill. I say that in two days, we should be in Fentias."

"It's there where we should make some money; that town has the biggest market in all of Belgharia." They continue in silence.

Roughly half-hour behind and gaining is Romeelus. He jogs along the path. He's sure they won't stray from it until nightfall. It is then that he will begin to look for signs. Knowing that he is close to his prey, he smiles as he jogs.

~   ~   ~

"Crunch! The fist pounds into Jake's face. His body, Drekkar, ties to a post. Drekkar stretches Jake's arms out in front of him and connects them to a second post. Only his face is free, for obvious, painful reasons. "snap"! The thunderous punch of Drekkar, the dark-skinned torturer breaks Jakes nose and blood gushes out. Ha! Ha! Ha! "That was some punch. I bet I could have heard your nose break over there." He points somewhere behind Jake. "And I'm just warming up."

" Thoomp"! "Thoomp"! "Thoomp"! Three more blows find their mark. Jake's eyes barely remain open. They're puffy and swollen.

"Go to hell!" Jake manages to utter. "Thump"! This time its jaw.

"It's too bad they told me that I can't cut out your tongue because that would be a real nice thing to do right about now. Oh, well!" He shrugs his shoulders. "I guess I'll have to do something else." Drekkar looks Jake up and down. Nodding to himself, he reaches his answer. "Hold on, Sweetie," he taunts. "I'll be back in just a minute. "Har! Har! Har"! The footsteps recede. Jake closes his eyes in prayer. "Please, be safe and far away, Menecha."

Footsteps arouse him out of his prayer. Slowly, methodically, teasingly, they approach. Each step is loud, slow, deliberate, for this is the kind of fear that the torturer loves to inflict. Mental anxiety will always do in his victims, a lot sooner than any physical pain. As Jake will regrettably find out, the torturer is extremely good at his job.

~ ~ ~

Knock! Knock! Knock! Pontew groans as the knocking on his door persists. He was just about to go to sleep. "Knock"! "Knock"! "Knock"! "I'm coming,"he yells at the door. Slowly he rises out of bed. With a sigh, he opens his door. A servant stares at him expectantly.

"What is it?"He asks irritably.

"Lord Belghar wishes to speak to you."Pontew, recognizes the servant. It is the same one that was in Belghar's bedroom. It's the same one that is always hanging around Belghar's room, waiting for instructions.

"Belghar has his favorites."Pontew remarks with distaste. "Is he in his bedroom or the throne room?" Pontew knows the answer. He just wants to patronize the servant. It works. The servant blushes.

"The b-b-bedroom," he replies as he lowers his head.

"Good!" he replies. "Now, get out of here. Unlike Belghar, I do not like young boys." The servant runs away, very much afraid of the aide. With a devilish smile, Pontew heads for Belghar's bedroom.

Chapter 6

A pair of eyes watch Thadden and Menecha as they wake up from their night's rest into a sunny, winter day. Menecha untangles her arms from around Thadden's neck. Cold ashes indicate that the fire has been out for a long time. Their only source of warmth has been each other. Thadden gets up and surveys the area around him. The silence in the woods gives Thadden a false sense of relief. "Purr"! Feacon regards the couple curiously. From whence he came from neither of the two know. Thadden, by now, has gotten used to this trick, but Menecha still seems very much impressed. Walking side by side, the trio heads toward Fentia; one bird flitters away as they depart. This time, Thadden pays no heed. A face smiles in the bushes. The face seems to revel in the stalking. It eagerly waits for the capture. It is no fun to capture them sleeping; the fun is in the look of terror in their eyes.

~ ~ ~

A moan comes from out of Jake's lips. His hands rest on a block. There's no way to move his arms. As his fingers rest upon the block of wood, there stands a grinning man holding a hammer.

"It's too bad you can't move, 'cause this is going to hurt..." "Slam"! "Crunch"! Two fingers break as they can offer no resistance. Belghar will be coming down here to interrogate you. It would be easier for yourself if you answer his questions." "Slam"! "Crunch"! Two more fingers buckle and break. The bones poke through the black and blue skin. Jake, however, does manage to stifle a scream. Hearing footsteps coming into the dungeon, Drekkar decides to speed up his work if they spoil his fun. "Slam"! "Slam"! "Slam"! "Crunch"! "Crunch"! "Crunch"! This act sends waves of pain too much for Jake to bear. His fingers are bleeding, and the throbbing sensation is enough for Jake to know how much trouble he is in.

~   ~   ~

"Well, hello, Belghar! It's a pleasure to see you again. Shall we go interrogate the prisoner?" With a nod and a smile, Belghar follows Drekkar to the prisoner. Belghar looks upon the tortured man with a smile. Pontew blanches at the sight of what is no longer the same Jake Rebish they'd brought in last night.

"So, you are the father of Menecha Rebish? And how is your daughter today?" The sarcasm is very obvious.

"Fine, I guess," Jake speaks through cracked lips.

"You guess? Don't you know where your daughter is?"

"No, I don't." His tone is defiant and protective. "Crack"! A fist careens into his mouth. Jake surprisingly finds that the fist came from Belghar, not his pet Drekkar. Belghar is the only wizard king around. That is why he is so powerful an enemy to have.

"You owe a debt to me. Your daughter has yet to finish paying it off. Furthermore, you harbored a criminal in your inn the night before last, and she is presumably with him right now. You can ease your pain this very second if you tell us where that thief took your daughter. I guarantee that no harm will come to your daughter. I'll ask you again. Where are the thief and your daughter?" His voice bellows in anger.

"I told you. I don't know."

"Crack"! "Crack"! "Crack"! An angered magician strikes the poor man repeatedly in the face. Drekkar laughs aloud. "Drekkar, do what you want with this man." There's a smile. "Be sure to keep him alive. I do want to show his daughter the cost of her action. By the way, Jake," he sneers at the name, "your daughter wasn't too bad in the sack. I look forward to meeting with her again.

I'll try to be gentle this time. It won't be a problem, and I'm sure that once the thief finishes with her, she'll be ready for us." Belghar's laughter Jake hears from up the stairs. The comment enrages the prisoner, but he is helpless to do anything. Jake sighs and waits for the pain to come. Pain is always temporary the emotional pain of loss of a loved one will live forever. It is this mindset that keeps Jake focused on one thing; his escape.

"I will get out, and I'll get my revenge. It's only a matter of time." He plots and smiles inwardly. When the pain arrives, Jake can't feel it. His thoughts focus on one thing, freedom.

~   ~   ~

Kyle sits cross-legged near the coals of last night's fire. His eyes close. In front of him is the wizard. His eyes, too, close. The sound of chanting is like a melody to Kyle's ears. He's eager to receive his newfound powers. The powers that Xibnar is about to bestow upon him. Sweet, sweet music floods his ears like a bursting dam:

> Almighty God of Wildqernog,
> Let me see through the fog.
> I ask permission to give some power,
> To a man who does not want to cower.
> He asks for our help. He is all alone.
> He wants to be able to win on his own.
> Let's make his spirit, strength, and willpower stronger.
> Our enemies approach, we can't wait any longer.
> He is going to be our darkness, our light.
> Through him, we shall win the final fight.

Gusts of wind, strong and quiet, swoop and swirl around the two men; it's a fury stronger than any house. A spark of lighting shoots out of Xibnar's fingertips and wraps itself around Kyle. It travels through his legs, his abdomen, and his chest. It continues to his arms, his lips, and enters through his eyes. Kyle screams once. His body starts to spasm and then stops.

Kyle opens his eyes and stares at Xibnar. A smile, devious and malicious, plays across his face. With an aching body, he rises to his feet. "It is done, Xibnar. Now I shall get you your cat." Powerful, purposeful strides carry Kyle out of Xibnar's sight. Xibnar, too is smiling. Xibnar's smile brims with pride. He looks at Kyle as a father would when his son becomes a hero. Xibnar, however, does not quite know what he has unleashed. Xibnar snaps his finger, and he, too, disappears.

~ ~ ~

"Crack"! The sound of the whip carries through the room like a thunderclap. A piece of flesh tears to ribbons as the whip finds its mark. A slight murmur of pain escapes from Jake's lips. The pain rips into his very being and shakes him like a rag doll.

"Ha"! "Ha"! "Ha"! "Ha"! Drakkar's taunting laughter, coming from behind him, feeds the burning fire called hate creeping into Jake's soul. "Crack! "Crack"! "Crack"! "Crack"! Repeatedly the whip strikes the flesh—blood cascades down Jake's back. The meat just hangs in loose strands. Occasionally, one of the pieces will fall to the floor and add to the collection. Ha! Ha! Ha! Hee! Hee! Hee! Ho! Ho!

"What's the matter, sir? Are you in a little pain? That's too bad because I'm enjoying myself. Don't worry, though; there's more fun coming up.

~ ~ ~

Thadden and Menecha are three-quarters of the way to their plotted destination. Remarkably, Thadden notes, there is no sign of pursuit. This knowledge seems to give him great delight. Menecha squeezes his hand in affection. Off to the side, just twenty feet away, stands the bounty hunter. He aims his crossbow directly at Thadden. As his fingers start to squeeze the trigger, a row of teeth, stained and crooked, indicates his smile. "Shoop"! The bounty hunter fires his shot. At the last second, a black streak barrels into the two targets, knocking them over. The arrow flies into the trees.

"Feacon, you bumbling, idiotic cat, watch where you're going?" Thadden's curses drift to the bounty hunter. The cat seems unconcerned at the rebuke.

With its head held high, the cat walks forward. Once, it turns its eyes in the direction of the shot. Green, cold eyes freeze the bounty hunter in his tracks. He notices the hair on the back of his neck is standing on end. Cowering before the gaze, he places his crossbow back in his sack. Feacon has bested him in the staredown.

"To get the thief, I must first get the cat." He studies the cat as it turns around the bend and out of sight. Its master, still cursing at the mysterious beast, follows behind. Soon, he, too, is out of sight. Romeelus remembers how it's always fading in and out. "How to capture a teleporting cat, now that truly is, a good question.

~ ~ ~

Meanwhile, unbeknownst to the bounty hunter, watchful eyes have studied him, as well—these amethyst colored eyes, narrow with hatred. Without knowing why, Romeelus' skin begins to crawl, and his hairs stand up on end. He waits for it to pass, and then starts his stalk again.

~ ~ ~

He laughs so much his throat is sore. Now there is only a giggle coming out of Drekkar's cruel mouth. Body limp, bleeding, and hurting, Jake slumps over his whipping post. What used to be his back is now a mass of shredded skin and blood.

"I whipped you a good one that time, yes, sirree!" A childlike grin looms in front of Jake.

"The torturer lacks any brains," Jake mumbles under his breath. He laughs insanely at his joke.

"You thinking you're funny now, are ye?" The face becomes a mask of rage. "Well, good, give me some fight, 'cause I'm sure ready for phase two." Jake watches Drekkar as he walks over to a cabinet. He opens the doors, seems to be trying to read, then grabs a bottle of liquid. The chuckle is the sure sign that Jake isn't about to be laughing. "You know what I'm holding in my hand?" Jake refuses to answer. "It's a healing potion." Drekkar starts to pace back and forth as he explains his next idea. "I'm going to pour this all over your bloody little back. Now, it's only going to hurt for a second as it begins to repair the damage. But why am I doing this, you might ask?" He thrusts the bottle under Jake's nose. "After your back is nice and healed, I'm going to start whipping you again. It looks like we're both in for a long day." Jake's last thought before Drekkar opens the bottle, is that dumb or not, the man before he is a master in his field. He braces himself for the pain as Drekkar's hand begins to turn the cap...

~ ~ ~

As a thief and his damsel walk wearily towards Fentia; their tired footsteps drag on the path. They hope that they are almost there. Their traveling companion, Feacon, is absent from sight.

"Time to play cat catcher," Romeelus replies to himself. "But first, I need a little distraction." His eyes quickly scan the forest. He picks his spot, then moves into action. With a whirling motion, he sends a rock flying out of a sling. It barely misses the thief. He smiles when he sees the cat appear as if to protect the thief from harm. Romeelus laughs.

Thadden pushes Menecha into the trees as he turns to face the assassin. He spent too much time, however, on rescuing the girl, as three pebbles imbed themselves into his skull. He flies back and bangs his head into a tree. Lightheaded and dizzy, he tries to stand. He gets to one knee, and then another, with an extraordinary effort, he gets to his feet. Just as he tries to move forward, his wobbly legs give, and he falls to the ground. A pair of hands grab him and gently yanks him into the forest. As the cat leaps at Romeelus, he reaches behind him and throws a net. It snares the cat before it has time to react. Acting quickly, the bounty hunter knocks the cat unconscious. He keeps the net wrapped around the cat and places it in his sack. "If I know the teleportation effect correctly, that cat won't be able to teleport if it can't see where it is teleporting. It's too bad I don't have time to get the thief, but I'll get him next time." The bounty hunter runs back into the forest. He marks this as a round for him. "And seeing's how the cat isn't in any position to threaten me, I think I've already won the battle." Satisfied with his day's progress, he finds a place to camp.

42

~   ~   ~

A feeling of cold, wetness wraps around Thadden like a blanket. He opens his eyes, thinking he's bleeding. Instead, he finds Menecha staring back at him. She has a wet cloth and is applying it to the three lumps on his forehead. The look of concern leaves her when he opens his eyes. His head is pounding like an earthquake.

"There's a stream right over there; I figured we could refill our water flasks. Then I got the idea to put a damp cloth to your forehead to ease the pain and reduce the swelling." She smiles. It warms him up and gives him strength.

"Feacon, what about Feacon? Have you seen him?"

"He was taken by the man who hit you with the stones. I caught a glimpse of him taking the cat and putting him in his sack."

"What did the man look like?"

"He was tall and dressed in black armor. He seemed to be carrying a lot of weapons on him. I missed his face. He had a cowl covering it."

"A bounty hunter!" he gasps in surprise. "Obviously, he noticed our escape. He had to have been very good to have to take me out so quickly."

"Come, these woods are no longer safe. We must travel quickly to Fentia. I shall try and get Feacon back as soon as you are safe." They gather their things then quickly depart.

~   ~   ~

A feeling of elation overwhelms Romeelus. It's the feeling he always gets whenever he has maintained a victory. Humming softly to himself, he builds his campfire. He knows he is safe. "The thief won't come after me yet. If he's as good as they say, his first concern will be to get the girl safely to town. Then, and only then, will he come after me to claim his stupid cat? By that time, I'll be waiting for him." He continues to go about his preparation for his nightly lodging. His hair on his neck again stands up in the air. He turns around with fantastic speed.

"Alright, come out of hiding. I know you're there. If it's you, thief, you're better off running away because I'll kill you quickly." Romeelus begins to yell into the trees. Without warning, a figure emerges into the campfire light. "Who are you, and why have you been following me?" He challenges the figure.

"My name is Kyle. You have something I need. Give it to me, and I'll let you live. Keep, and you will surely die." The voice is guttural. It speaks short, quick sentences and gets to the point faster than Romeelus likes. He surveys the situation. In a calm, unwavering voice, he replies.

"Well, what is it that I have that you want?" He takes out a colossal battle-ax. It shines red in the firelight.

"All that I ask for is the cat. Give it to me, and we'll forget we ever met."

"Then you'll have to kill me because I'm not giving up this cat for anyone." The two men circle each other in the moonlight, like a pack of wolves, circles, and growl. The intensity of the two would be too much for any bystander to perceive. Both men want a prize; neither will refuse. A battle will be the decision...

Chapter 7

As the sun begins to set in Fentia, two figures stumble into the town. Their exhausted bodies nearly collapse into the dirt. Dirty, disheveled, and looking like they've had better days, Thadden and Menecha look warily at the locals, who stare at them in wonder. None, however, have the courage to neither speak nor offer the pair any assistance. With a sigh of relief and disappointment, Thadden supports Menecha as they trudge along through the vast, gathered crowd. Murmurs and whispers buzz in the air. Paying no heed, they keep on walking. Only occasionally do they look up, and that's to read the signs. The Smelly Goblin Thadden reads. Without any words spoken between them, they enter.

The looby area, as they called it then, was neat. A checkered tile floor that was clean and shiny caused a slight gasp from Menecha.

"It's beautiful," she replies in awe. Thadden doesn't respond. Instead, he puffs out his chest and then saunters over to the innkeeper, with long, elegant, regal strides.

"Good evening, sir!" He replies with a bow. A puzzled look portrays itself on the innkeeper's face. Never before has any customer been this nice to him. With a trace of suspicion lingering, he ensues the conversation.

"Good evening to you and your pretty companion as well." His beaming smile shows that he, too, can flatter. Like gladiators facing each other in an arena, they stare at one another. Each one is trying to pinpoint and spot a weakness. The innkeeper, much to his dismay, can find no flaw in the figure before him. Thadden continues his stare down, sees the innkeeper flinch, then smiles. He has won. The conversation continues.

"I was wondering if you have any rooms available?"

"Rooms, Uh? He thinks for a minute. "Yes, we do!" Menecha notices that the innkeeper flusters and flounders as if something is wrong. Seeing no-one else, she shrugs her shoulders and waits patiently.

"Well, which one is the cheapest?" Thadden already can see the inn-keeper's defenses weakening.

"The common room is the cheapest but has Absolutely no privacy what-soever. You look like the kind of people that could use a little privacy. How about I give you the third classroom, for the price of the common room?"

"Is there a bath included in the third classrooms?" His gaze shreds the last of the innkeepers' defenses. His smile, cocky, and mocking, sends the sword home.

"O-o-of course, I shall give you the keys to the bathhouse. There's a cord with a bell on it. Pull-on it if you need anything. Your price will be one copper apiece." The innkeeper gulps at the loss of the money. "It's the same price as the common room." Seeing his opponent down and at his mercy, Thadden gives the poor innkeeper a break.

"Sure, that's fine!" Thadden says as he tosses one silver coin the innkeeper's way. "Keep the rest, sir, and thank you very much." The innkeeper knows that it still wouldn't have been enough to rent one-third classroom to somebody see-ing the silver coin. With a final act of hopelessness, he puts the silver in his pocket. He marks it off as a huge tip from a standard room's occupant.

Heartbeat's race as adrenaline pumps throughout the body of the two men. Romeelus has his ax in his hands; he is ready. It is black, with a slight white haze surrounding its bloodstained edge. Cautiously, he eyes his opponent, who has yet to take out a weapon, and waits for him to make a move.

"Well, stranger, what are you waiting for?" His cowl protects all but the mouth, which is showing a nasty sneer. "If you want what I got, then you have to come and take it."

"That will be fine by me," Kyle replies. Uprooting a medium sized oak tree, he throws it at the disbelieving bounty-hunter. Reacting quickly, Romeelus dives to the side as the tree crashes down into the ground, at the same spot that Romeelus had just vacated seconds before. He cuts the distance to his unknown assailant by half with this move.

"He's still too far for me to do anything with my ax." Romeelus notes in his head.

Kyle wishes to end this. He brings his fists together, interlocks the fingers, and then smashes the ground with a loud yell. A shockwave carries through the mud. A massive wave of the earth comes rolling towards Romeelus.

He runs forward and up the hill to reach the crest of the earth wave. "I'm on to your tricks, asshole," he yells as he dives off the ridge before it can take him any further away. In mid-air, he swings his ax at Kyle. Suddenly, a wall of stone erupts from the ground and creates a barrier in front of Kyle. The ax smashes into the rock. A slight crack begins to form, but that is all. Romeelus lands smoothly and curses under his breath. "Damn, flaming, Magician. If it weren't for his magic, I'd be able to kill him easily."

"Is that what you think?" A voice from behind him penetrates his mutterings. He whirls to face Kyle. A large figure looms over him. The figure has plate mail armor that is black. The armor seems to be a little different. Parts of the armor appear to be moving. "Impossible," Romeelus mutters as he glimpses his new threat. Kyle clutches a mace and shield.

"Ready for some hand to hand, bounty hunter?" The voice is mocking Romeelus.

"Of all the things to do, you don't mock me!" Romeelus yells as his eyes narrow, and his facial expressions harden into that of pure and utter rage. Clenching his double bladed weapon, Romeelus charges the figure. This combat will continue, with only one victor.

~ ~ ~

At the sight of the beds, Thadden and Menecha breathe a sigh of relief; they eagerly yearn to slump down onto the little heaven. Many hours later, Thadden wakes up. He stares at the beautiful woman as she sleeps. A smile is on her face. He thinks about waking her up but decides to let her have her moment of happiness. After all, he is comfortable with this kind of life. She, on the other hand, has lived with her father all her life. "This must be hard for her," he replies softly. Thadden kisses her on the cheek. The sleeping figure turns a little, and then it is still. He rummages through his sack and brings out some paper and a pen. He writes a note and then places it on her chest. With a final examination of the room, he sees that everything is ok. Seeing the rope hanging down from the ceiling, he tugs at it. A slight gong noise comes from downstairs. Within minutes, there is a knock on the door. Thadden opens it a crack. A woman dressed in white stares back at him.

"What can I help you with?"

"Can you please show me where the rooms for the baths are?"

"I'm sorry" She starts to protest. "But the baths are off-limits to people on this floor." She begins to turn away.

"Yes, I know. But I'm an exception to the rule. I have a key to the room, courtesy of the innkeeper. If you would please lead the way, I shall be delighted." He flashes a warming smile—her facade breaks.

"This way," she leads him to the bath-house. Making sure he locks the door, Thadden follows the woman down the hall. They go up two flights of stairs, down another corridor, and taking a right; they reach the bath-house. Disbelieving, she waits until Thadden produces the key. Only when he inserts the key and unlocks the door does she finally decide to leave. The key has a number etched into it.

"Thirteen?" he remarks with an odd expression on his face. Steam fills the room as it seeps from the cracks underneath the doors of the bathhouse. Finally, he sees the door with the number "13" on it. He opens the door with the key and enters the steamy room. Closing the door behind him, he starts to remove his clothing. Naked, he lets one-foot dangle in the water, testing its temperature. Soothing heat overwhelms his foot. "Perfect," he replies with satisfaction. Slowly, he enters the hot water. When all but his head submerges in the water, he closes his eyes. His bones start to loosen and relax. For the first time since the inn, Thadden feels content. It isn't long before he is fast asleep. Sometimes a person needs this to relax the muscles before the next encounter.

~ ~ ~

"Clang"! The noise carries throughout the quiet forest. It is the sound of metal on metal. The breaths of the combatants is loud. The winter air causes the sounds to be sharp and precise. Romeelus utters a few more curses as Kyle begins to get frustrated. Neither man has had the advantage in the entire fight. Both men are equal matches. Romeelus swings his ax, "Clang"! It rebounds off of Kyle's shield. Kyle swings, only to have it blocked by the ax. Nobody can feel the cold, as their bodies are in too much activity to register anything. Romeelus keeps his ax in one hand. While at the same time, he reaches behind him to grab for his dagger. The motion is a blur. Even Kyle fails to notice the blade as it streaks toward his armor. It would have pierced his heart if it wasn't for the armor that he is wearing. As the dagger is about to hit home, a tendril, black and long, snatches it and throws it back at the bounty-hunter. Romeelus, however, will not be thwarted. He does a roll, catches the dagger in mid-air, and then strikes with it on his way up. Sharp pain jolts up Kyle's leg as the blade buries itself deep inside. Kyle temporarily ignores it as Romeelus left himself open and is in close range. "Bong"! A mighty swing and the shield smashes into Romeelus' head with jarring impact. He falls back, temporarily stunned. With perfect timing, the mace slams into the bounty-hunters' chest. He staggers backward from the blow.

A shake of the head and Romeelus is back on his feet. His armor s dented inwards. It's scraping into his skin. "One more hit there, and I'll be in deep trouble," he warns himself. Another plan forms in his mind. Years of experience have enabled Romeelus to be the ultimate fighting human. Faster than the eye can blink, he hurls his ax at Kyle; he knows what the result will be, but that's what he's counting on. Once he releases the ax, he reaches for his crossbow. As planned a tendril, snags the ax in midair, but the ax is too heavy for the tendril to throw. An instant later, two bolts heads for Kyle. He has time to block one bolt with his shield, but the other bolt slams into his right arm. He drops his mace. The tendril releases the ax.

"You are indeed too great a fighter for me to tangle with directly." He glares at his smiling opponent. "But, there's more than one way to dispose of your ilk." Cold, hands reach through the snow and grasp Romeelus' ankles.

"What in hell?" He has time to utter as he tries to free his feet. As he struggles, the hands grip harder. "Crack"! He can feel one of his ankle bones snap. Alarmed at the new threat, Romeelus stops working and reaches for a short-sword. As he is about to attack the hands, there is a rumbling noise in the distance. He turns around to see an avalanche of snow heading his way. Frantically, he begins to beat at the hands with the sword. The backpack on his back loosens. A grinning Kyle waves the prize at him in a mockery that angers the bounty hunter.

"I said don't mock me!" Romeelus yells in anger and with two mighty blows, the hands at his ankles shear in half. As he is about to lunge at Kyle, he sees the wall of snow before him. It slams into him with such a force that it is like being run over by twenty stampeding horses. Kyle watches in amusement as he sees legs and arms flailing in the snow.

"That should carry him miles away from this place. That's assuming he can even survive that much punishment for that long. He was a good opponent; I'll grant him that." Kyle remarks as he rips the crossbow bolt out of his arm. He snaps it in two. With surprise, he notices the ax is no-where in sight. "Must have gotten carried off in the avalanche." He turns his back on the scene and throws the backpack onto his back. "My master will truly be pleased." His feet begin to walk as he laughs maniacally.

~ ~ ~

The pain is much more than Jake could have ever imagined. With a hearty laugh, Drekkar pours the healing potion onto the strands of skin that was once Jake's back. Gritting his teeth, Jake resists the urge to scream out in pain. Strand by strand, the flesh begins to join, becoming whole again. The blood stops flowing. All the while, the pain reaches out with its greedy little paws and squeezes with all its might. Even Drekkar amazes at Jake's inability to scream. Although he never seems to show it, instead, he thinks up more and more ways to inflict pain in the hopes that he will hear one more scream. He never gets satisfaction until he hears the last plea for help. It is then that Drekkar becomes bored with his patient, as he likes to call them, and puts them out of their misery. Thus far, Jake's performance disappoints him greatly. He has thought about removing Jake's tongue, as he once promised to do, but that will be Jake's salvation. He could scream all he wanted, and not even Drekkar would hear him For once in his lifetime, Drekkar is confronting a challenge. A challenge that he knows he must win. "All I need to do is find out what this man fears most. Once the torturer discovers this, he'll be screaming to my heart's content." When he completes these thoughts, he notices Jake's lovely, smooth, unblemished back. "I'll have to take care of that," he muses.

"That's a nice back you have there." His voice floats up to Jake's ever listening ears. Jake shudders when he feels fingers caress his back lovingly. "It's a shame I'm going to have to ruin it." "Crack"! The loving caress turns into a brutal instrument of pain. The whip has again come back to visit Jake Rebish. Whether due to a sore hand or just plain boredom, the whipping has stopped its destruction upon Jake's back only three hours after it started. He begins to go into convulsions at the sudden, rapid changes and being on his backside. Again, the familiar feel of blood pouring down his back and of loose strands of flesh barely hanging on to the remnants of his back re-familiarize themselves with Jake. With the room spinning, Jake barely maintains consciousness. Finally, he can feel the torturer untying his hands. Drekkar lifts him and escorts Jake to his cell. "Thanks for the good time." Drekkar mumbles with a slap on the back. The torturer whips Jake around and pushes him back first into the sand floor of his cell. Pebbles invade his back as maggots flock to rotting meat. Pain's hands decide to take his back and give it a few goods wrings before easing off and giving him a calmer, throbbing sensation. This time, he does pass out.

Jake wakes up in time to hear Drekkar's all too familiar cheery voice say:

"It's time for dinner. Oh, and by the way, go easier on it, then I went on you. You never know when a friend might come in handy." Ha! Ha! Hee! Hee! Haw! Hsw! His laughter echoes throughout the cell. Before he goes away, he puts in one last comment. "Drink your water after you eat. You'll need it." Ha! Ha! Hee! Hee! Hsw! Haw"! His footsteps recede until he hears nothing but silence.

"Scree"! "Scree"! A noise from the corner of his cell puts Jake on full alert. A pair of red eyes stare at him through the darkness. "Thump"! "Thump! His heart beats faster at the thought of having to eat a rat to survive. He grabs the creature and cups it in his hands. He closes his eyes, then opens his mouth. "Scree"! The rat speaks. He opens his eyes to see the little rat squirming in his grasp and staring at him with pitiful eyes. His heart begins to melt. Jake puts the creature in front of his water bowl. It scurries out of his hand and drinks a little water. As if seeking an answer, the rat looks outside its cage, then to Jake. It continues its pattern but does not move from its spot. Slowly, cautiously, he extends his hand out and gently pats the ugly rat on the head. It seems to like this. Its eyes close as Jake keeps scratching. Like a long lost pet, he scoops up the slumbering rat and puts it in his pocket. Jake forgets all pain, closes his eyes, and welcomes sleep.

~ ~ ~

The Smelly Goblin's innkeeper is just about to relax and make plans for the sudden increase in his rates when a silent, figure enters his establishment. Green eyes glow out from underneath the hood that masks the appearance. The eyes scan the room and then decide to look at him, and there they linger. A sudden rush of cold sweeps into the room, causing the innkeeper to shudder uncontrollably. The hooded person walks over to him.

"Excuse me, innkeeper!" Cold breath shoots out from the person. A man, the innkeeper, can only assume, judging by the low, guttural voice. "Have seen a young man; I believe his profession is that of a thief. He is wearing leather armor, and he's almost six feet tall."

"Now is my chance to get even with that little swindler," the innkeeper gloats to himself. "If you have money, then perhaps I have seen this person." The man is taken aback, somewhat shocked, at such an answer.

"Let's say I let you live, and we consider us even." The eyes glow brighter for a brief second. A hand reaches from out of the robes, grabs the innkeeper by his tunic, yanking him towards the counter. In less time than the innkeeper can react; the other hand removes the hood. Death stares back at him. With his whole body trembling, he blurts out the information."The m-m-man you a-a-are looking for i-i-is currently in the bath-house. H-h-his girlfriend is still in their room. H-h-here is the spare key, second floor. He is in bath-house number thirteen. I'll have a servant come down and take you there." Drool flies out of his mouth as he babbles on, trying to save his life.

"I already know where it is." He taps his head with a smirk. "Thanks for the information." The hand releases its hold of the tunic. The innkeeper slumps to the floor. He does not stir until long after the sounds of the man's footsteps on the floor disappear. It has been a rough day for the man behind the counter.

~ ~ ~

A knock on the door arouses Menecha from her deep slumber. She opens her eyes on the third knock. Thadden is nowhere in the room. On her chest is a note. She gets up and walks over to the door. The note flutters to the ground.

"Who is it?" She asks, pressing her ear up to the door.

"I'm just a servant, madam. I am just here to check up on you to see if you need more sheets."

"No, no, I don't. Everything in here is fine."Menecha tries to remain calm,but her spine feels as if an ice flow is rubbing up and down on it. Her only thought is to escape, as she recognizes this sign as one of danger, she starts to back away from the door. She turns in time to see a man's face in front of her. His lips touch hers. A slight puff of air releases as he drives his tongue down her throat, her eyes' flutter; soon, she is asleep.

"I guess I'm a lousy kisser." The voice says with a bit of humor. Laughing insanely, Xibnar hefts the body and quickly throws it over his shoulder like a sack of potatoes. "SNAP"! The room is again empty. All that remains is a piece of paper that rests on the floor, unread.

Chapter 8

Thadden opens his eyes at the sound of the door opening. Squinting through the thick steam from the bath, he sees a figure standing and staring back at him. Through the mist, he can barely make out the outline of a female body. "Menecha?" he speaks to the silent figure. At the sound of his voice, the shape comes to life.

"Oh, Thadden, I was so scared. I woke up to find you not in the room. Thoughts of you leaving me filled me with dread."

"I left a note on your chest." He says, baffled.

"That's why I'm here now. Once I read the note, I felt warm inside. I felt safe." Menecha begins to stride towards him. Before he can respond, she disrobes and displays her beautiful, naked body to him. Her breasts big, supple, jiggle teasingly at him; his gaze travels downwards. Everything about her is perfect. He gazes into her eyes and feels his heart beating rapidly. "Thump"! "Thump"!

"Hold me, Thadden. Make me feel safe."

He stands up as she gets into the tub and stands before him. "Thump! "Thump"! From the first moment he saw her, he has always wanted this. He grabs her in his strong arms and brings his lips to hers. "Thump"! "Thump"! Their arms caress each other as their tongues interlock. Passion sweeps into Thadden and overrides any of his other senses. "Thump"! "Thump"!

Menecha slowly pushes him downward. He is lying down in the water. "Thump"! "Thump"! "Thump"! Her smile, sensual, erotic, tears apart the last hope for any of his defenses. She grabs onto his stiffened member and parting her legs; she begins her descent down.

~ ~ ~

The day is warm, for winter. The sun shines down upon the land and smiles contentedly. It begins its battle with the snow and slowly begins to melt it. Another force is fighting the snow, as a fist punches through. Again a fist punches out. The fists disappear only to come back in a different spot. After many repeated punches, the snow flies upwards, and a man enters a sunny day. He falls to the ground. Scratches and bruises line his face. His left ankle is grossly twisted out of proportion. On his side is a double-sided ax. It appears to be the only weapon on his person. Black, battered, and dented armor shows that he's been in a war. Romeelus looks up into the sun and lets out a laugh.

"I have cheated death. Once I heal my ankle, I shall let that wizard called Kyle to know that he has messed with the wrong bounty hunter. No one steals my prize." He sits down on the cold snow that was previously his mode of transportation and his prison. He's been in many fights. A broken ankle he can quickly fix. Romeelus is not a man known to experience pain. With an expression of utter calm and toughness, he grasps his ankle. "Pop"! The ankle aligns back into its original position.

Romeelus knows he'll walk with a limp for a while, but he can live with it. "It will give me the element of surprise when I next meet that magic using cheater." Getting to his feet, Romeelus hobbles over to a nearby tree. His ax easily cuts the branches that he'll need for his small splint. He curses at the loss of all of his weapons except for his ax. Its magical properties will always make it return to him.

"All I need is one more weapon, and I'll be ready to collect my earnings." With his splint intact, Romeelus begins his long trek, hobbling all the way.

~ ~ ~

The pleasure Thadden feels as Menecha rides him is too intense to describe. But Thadden is finding him getting more and more tired as the event unfolds.

"Thump"! "Thump"! "Thump"! "Thump"! His mind knows he can't be tiring. He was just waking up from his sleep. All the steam in the bath seems to be getting thicker. "Thump"! "Thump"! "Thump"! "Thump"! His heart keeps talking. Her moans of ecstasy are like a sweet melody to his ears. His eyelids start to close, then open. He starts to fall asleep, realizes it, and then snaps his eyes open again. Menecha, he can no longer see as the steam is too thick. "Thump"! "Thump"! "Thump"! "Thump"! Finally, his senses jog back awake. He knows he's not supposed to be sleepy. When he starts to listen, he knows that her hips' rhythm and the moans seem to flow together. As he listens further, he can feel his eyelids getting heavy. "Thump"! "Thump"! "Thump"! "Thump"! As he is about ready to climax, he clings on to his last bit of energy.

"Enough!" He bellows as he stands up and throws the body, which he no longer thinks is Menecha, into the steamy water. All at once, he can feel himself slightly waking up. He is far too sleepy to fight the thing, but he has a different idea.

"I'm sorry, Menecha; I just wasn't prepared for what we were doing. How about we try it again?" The doppleganger Menecha looks at him with suspicion and then concedes.

"It's not on to us yet." It says to itself.

"This time, Menecha, I'll be on top." This action takes the woman by surprise, but it still throws away all caution. It has its prize right where it wants him. The steam again builds up. Thadden prepares to do what he hopes will be the right thing.

~ ~ ~

Along the road to Fentia, the sounds of a horse's hoof prints carry up to Romeelus. Looking behind him, he can see the dust cloud. Knowing that this is his only salvation, Romeelus prepares himself for what he must do. Right before the horse and its rider come into view, Romeelus throws himself to the ground. He lays face down, blocking the road. The horse comes around the bend, and then at the rider's command, it stops abruptly, inches before the hoofs grind Romeelus' body to paste.

"What have we here, Bargan?" The rider dismounts and walks cautiously over to the face-down body. Warily, he checks the woods for the right spots to lay an ambush. Seeing none, he decides that the figure on the ground is actually hurt. He checks the wrists. There is a pulse.

"Ohhhhh!" The man on the ground begins to moan. His eyes flicker open, blink, then look directly at the rider.

"I was just making sure you were ok... I didn't mean to alarm you. What is the problem?"

Romeelus doesn't believe the man cannot see the splint on his leg. As he spies the man's sheathed dagger, he continues with his acting.

"My ankle is badly broken. I managed to get a splint on it. I must have collapsed while I was walking to Fentia. Do you know how much further it is?"

"Yes, it's only two miles from here."

"Only two miles, well, I guess I can make it on my bad ankle. I should be there by nightfall. That is if I don't pass out again." A look of deep pain stabs into the rider's good heart.

"Tell you what fella, I'm going to Fentia. If you want, you can ride double with me. It won't take any time at all. Once we get there, you can get some treatment. I hear they have outstanding healers there."

Romeelus nods his head in agreement as he gets on the horse. His heart feels tormented. He doesn't want to kill this kind man who stopped for him on the road. He isn't getting paid to do it so there isn't much point. As Bargan begins to pick up speed, Romeelus comes to terms with what little conscious he has. He raises his ax and hits the rider in the back of the head with his pommel.

"Ugh!" The rider manages before he falls off his horse. Romeelus, no slouch on the horse, slows the horse down. With quick strides, he stands over the falling rider. A tiny trickle of blood oozes out of the back of the rider's head. The wound's not severe, so Romeelus carries his gaze to the dagger. It is just a straight, ordinary dagger, but it will serve his purpose. Acting quickly, so the rider isn't conscious that the bounty hunter carefully slides the blade into the splint when he gets done. Next, he walks over to the horse. Using soothing words to calm the horse, he slowly mounts it. It starts to buck at the sense of a different rider. Being the professional that he is, Romeelus has no trouble calming the horse down. As he gets the horse into a trot, then a run, the ex-rider regains consciousness. He has time to shake his fist at the horse and rider before they round the bend and are gone from sight.

~ ~ ~

In the steam of the bathroom, two figures engage in a ritual. The smell of sex lingers in the air as they grunt and moan. Thadden knows that what he is doing is disgusting. Well, not really what he is doing, but whom he is doing it with. Even though he knows that it is not Menecha he is doing it to, he doesn't know who or what is sharing this ritual. He does test one crucial theory. If he lets it be in control, it will be his finish. As the bodies collide and join, they create a harmonious rhythm that any other outside forces cannot stop. This rhythm is what Thadden is hoping will win him this bizarre battle? The more he thrusts, the more he can feel his energy return. Strength flows into him. He no longer feels tired. His mind begins to wander. Suddenly, he can sense himself getting tired again. She has tried to alter his plans. When his defenses are down, she, it, had wrapped her legs around his waist and was riding him instead. With incredible speed, she rose and fell and drained his strength, willpower, and eventually his soul.

"Nooo!" He yells as he finds the strength to untangle her legs. Before she can cling on again, the thief forces his mouth onto hers. He begins to drive his tongue deep down the she-things throat. As it tries to counter this move, he parts her legs and penetrates deep into her moist area.

Again, the strength comes back to him. This time he refuses to let his mind wander. "The next time I do, I won't be able to stop it from winning." With grim determination, he carries on with his strange, almost pleasurable, conflict. As he climaxes, she lets out an ear-piercing scream. He does not stop, however, until the body lies still, and the screaming stops. An undetermined amount of energy pours into his body. The steam is dissipating away until there is nothing left; presumably, gone with her, as it arrived when she did? There is nothing that remains of the body except for a dried, withered, gray pile of skin and bones. He shudders at the sight. Realization dawns on him. Fear grips his heart. Menecha," he yells as he runs out the door. The creature had to have a body if it wanted to copy it.

~ ~ ~

"Rise and shine." Jake wake's up to see a smiling Drekkar. "Did you sleep well?" Jake rises to his feet before another boot can find its mark. "Not too many rocks got into your back, I hope." Ha! Ha! Ha! Ha! He grits his teeth as he resists the urge to punch a hole in the blackened squares Drekkar calls teeth. All the pain has gone in Jake's back, as it has reached a numbing stage. He can only wonder what is in store for him if Drekkar is in a happy mood.

"Drekkar must be getting sloppy," he observes. "He's letting me walk out of the cell instead of carrying me." He stores the information for later use. "Do I go to my usual post, or is there another special place you would like me to go." Jake doesn't care anymore what Drekkar does. He might as well enjoy himself. Drekkar didn't seem to care that Jake had spoken either.

"Oh, this place is special, alright." Another fit of laughing hysterics, then Drekkar, leads the way. With observant eyes, Jake notes every square inch of the room. In his map called memory, he marks down where all the cells are, where the weapons are,or torturing and fighting instruments. He also jots down the one exit from the room. He finds Drekkar's stupidity extremely pleasing. Smiling, Jake follows his torturer and prepares to get more details for his living map.

"Here, we are!" Drekkar points to a chair that's in the corner. "Go on, sit on it. It'll be your latest companion for the next few days." Jake sits down in the hard wooden chair. Happy with himself for his latest ingenuity, Drekkar straps his victim's wrists onto the arms of the chair.

"Speaking of days, how long have I been down here?"

"I don't know. Not long enough, though, since you aren't screaming; but you will mark my words." Ha! Ha! Ha! Hee! Hee!

"You don't know? Don't you ever leave the dungeon for anything?"

"Nope. I stay right down here. I have all of the food in the storage room over there." He points to Jake's right. Another useful bit of information. Jake adds it to his collection. "No one up there cares about me. They certainly don't want to talk to me. But that's okay; I enjoy it down here. I enjoy my work."

"How would somebody know if you're dead? They don't check up on you?"

"Nah! They come once and a while, but that's only to give me new prisoners." He laughs. "They know I can handle myself." Drekkar beams with pleasure as he says the last statement. "Now enough talk. It's time to try out my new device. And remember, the only talking allowed is screaming." Jake is happy with his progress. He's gotten all the information he needs. Now all that is required is a plan. Wearing a smile, not often found in here; he awaits the pain.

~ ~ ~

Thadden rushes out of his stall and into the bath-house area. He can see the other rooms. As the thief is about to leave for his room, there is a shuffling of many feet. He can sense many bodies surround him. With his newfound energy from the succubus, he grins. With his rapier in hand, he prepares to battle as his enemies close in.

~ ~ ~

Darkness! It's a strange and disturbing concept that frightens both people and animals. For Feacon, he is petrified. The panther desperately wants to escape, but it doesn't know where the darkness ends or where it begins. It tries to move, but something closes around him tightly. It briefly remembers seeing a man in black. The man had previously attempted to kill Thadden, but Feacon had stopped him. Then the man had tried again. It does not know if he had succeeded with his plan. Unfortunately, he captures Feacon as well. He remembers this feeling of capture from a long time ago. That time then, it was horrible. Feacon can feel movement. This kind of activity, it knows about as well. Someone is carrying him. The cat knows that, in its capture, it can't do anything until its captor lets him out. Eagerly, it awaits the moment.

~ ~ ~

It doesn't take long for Thadden to recognize his current threat. There are six of them. One, the leader, is grunting commands. He is much taller than the thief and appears dense and heavy. His lower canines look sharp, and wicked. He is hairless and has dark, black skin. Thadden laughs as he recognizes his opponents as Scorcs, a vicious breed of creatures that generally follow more of an evil path than good. Though not as big as the leader, the other Scorcs have some hair. They all grunt and growl, then make their way to the thief. Thadden, full of energy, holds his light, and fast rapier in one hand and dagger in the other. The weapons give him a sense of confidence. Five Scorcs close in as the leader sits back and waits for his troops to bring him the corpse. The thief will gladly disappoint him. Thadden screams a primal scream. Startled the Scorcs stop their advancement. That's all the time Thadden needs as he advances on one Scorc. His dagger quickly finds its way in its throat, as the creature drops down dead. "Clang"! He parries the oncoming blow with his rapier. Adrenaline adds to his stolen energy as Thadden launches himself amidst them. Using his acrobatics and deadly skill, he keeps all the blades away from him, as his rapier and dagger continually find a body to stab.

There only stands one Scorc and the leader, who has yet to step forward in the first five minutes of the fray. The last Scorc seems smarter than the rest. He doesn't rush Thadden. He's seen the results of that. Hardly breaking out a sweat, Thadden decides for him. He somersaults over the dumbfound Scorc and lands neatly behind it. With but a flick of the wrist, the rapier strikes the leg, slices open the gut, then finishes it off by stabbing the heart. The creature dies a horrible death.

The leader glances Thadden up and down. He is alone, but he is better than his flunkies. He certainly hopes so as he takes out his whip and short sword. His pointed ears twitch as he slowly walks towards his adversary. Thadden fakes a lunge. The leader doesn't flinch. "At last some competition," he replies with satisfaction. They eye each other up and down.

Wanting to react before his energy wears out, the thief strikes first and furious. "Clang"! "Clang"! Incredibly the Scorc hads blocked both weapons with his sword. "Crack"! The whip lashes out and draws a chunk of flesh from Thadden's cheek. Thadden needs a new plan. "Crack"! In a fraction of a second, the whip wraps itself around Thadden's rapier. A quick yank and his weapon fly from his hand and skitters across the floor. Grinning viciously, the leader awaits Thadden's next action. Thadden blinks. "Crack"! A piece of flesh comes out of his other cheek. Blood runs down the side of his face into his mouth. The taste of it gets him into action.

"I've got to get that whip away from that creature," he realizes to himself. He throws caution to the wind and just throws his dagger. As it sails in the air, he makes a run for his rapier. "Crack"! "Crack"! The whip slams the blade into a wall. It then wraps itself around Thadden's running legs. Just as his weapon is within reach, the thief finds himself falling backward. "Slam"! His teeth bite his tongue as he falls to the floor. The Scorc drops its sword and grabs onto the whip with both hands. He starts to drag the helpless thief towards him. With his eyes on his weapon, Thadden gives one last stretch to try and snag his rapier. His finger almost reaches it. They scrape across the floor, grabbing nothing. All hope seems to disappear for him. He puts his mind into action as the leader drags him towards him. Just as he is within striking distance, Thadden gets his plan. It's so simple it makes him laugh. The Scorc seems baffled at the response of laughter. Heedless, he keeps on pulling.

Using his acrobatic skills again, Thadden lifts most of his body off the floor. He lunges out with his fist, knowing the creature won't be able to block it with its hands full. "Crunch"! It hits the animal in the groin. Thadden grabs hold and begins to twist and twist for all he can. The whip drops as pain flares into the leader's groin. Thadden lets go and rolls for the Scorc's fallen sword. He is on his feet when the creature is still cupping his swollen, sore balls. It howls in utter agony. Helpless, it can't stop the sword from shearing the head clean off. The decapitated head rolls across the floor. The expression of pain is frozen forever on its face. The body falls to the floor, still grabbing on to its last remembrance of pain. The thief drops the creature's weapon and gathers his own. The rapier and dagger match his appearance, bloody and scratched. He staggers out of the room; weary from his past two battles.

~ ~ ~

"Bravo, master thief, Bravo." A familiar voice replies.

He is not sure how much more he can go on in his fatigued state. Thadden glances up to see a man in robes. He has glowing, emerald eyes, and he also has Menecha as a hostage. "That was quite the show you put on for me. I was thoroughly impressed. You probably don't remember me, but then again, you can't see my face. Here let me show you." The man lowers his hood.

"Xibnar" Thadden says with disdain.

"Very good!" He applauds. "It's amazing what can happen when you get a powerful necklace. For that I thank you." He smiles.

"I knew I should have sold to a different wizard. But then again, you looked like such an amateur, and I figured even the necklace couldn't save a has-been mage I guess I was wrong."

"Indeed, Thadden, indeed. I have another proposition for you. I need you to steal another item for me. Before you protest, keep in mind that I'm holding your girlfriend. If you were to try and kill me and end up striking her; that would truly be a shame. The human body, you know, makes a great shield. Besides, you wouldn't want her father to go through all the torturing that he is so that he can find out that you got her killed would you? So, will you get me the item that I require?" Thadden weighs his options; there are none. He can only seethe inwards. He sheathes his weapons.

"Where do I go, and what do I obtain?"

"You go to your old home, the thieves' guild. They have just recently stolen staff and a robe. You must get them both."

"Do you realize what you are asking?" The thief asks, amazed. "You want me to steal from my guild. That's blasphemy. If they catch me, my kind will forever hate me. I need some time to think about this." He tries to stall for the time he does not have.

"You must decide now, young one. If you say no, I'll kill Menecha, escape, and leave you to explain that to her father, who is in the torture chamber of Belghar's dungeon. What is it going to be?" Emerald eyes flare up and glare at Thadden.

"Consider it done." The Thief says. You must release her when I have obtained the items. Where shall we meet?"

"The same place as last time. It was such a success; why change it now." With that, Xibnar snaps his fingers and leaves Thadden alone with his bloody weapons. He knows what he must do. It is the aftermath of it all that he must live with.

~ ~ ~

As Feacon sleeps in the packsack, dreams, familiar, and haunting, keep him from getting any rest. He whimpers as a painful flashback comes back to him...

He remembered when it all began. In the jungles of Pyrgronnese, Feacon was a fierce hunter. His sleek, panther body moved silently and quickly through the dense, cool jungle. He was a terror. Other animals flee in panic at the sight of him. His hunting senses are sharp. He would wait in a tree branch. Before long, an animal, sometimes a deer, a rabbit would come along and ask to be the next lunch. Size didn't matter; Feacon would let loose a terrible roar. The animal would freeze in its tracks, too afraid to move. Big teeth would sink into the animal's throat. The battle was already over. After he ate, Feacon would mark its kill by ripping out the flesh and fur and eat the still-warm heart. A victory roar will show its superiority, and with blood dripping off his chin, the panther would find a spot to rest. Feacon lived his life this way in a repeat cycle. Until, on one fateful hunting excursion, Feacon's life changed.

The day was sunny. Feacon was eagerly waiting for his prey. His tail swished back and forth. Finally, a doe entered into his range. His eyes narrowed. His tail swished vigorously. "Rwooor"! The doe jumped but found itself unable to move from the spot, its bladder had let go, and the feet refused to move. Feacon leapt off the tree. Just as he was about to cling onto the doe's back, he found himself passing right through the creature. The doe's moment of fright was over as soon as Feacon landed; the intended victim bolted away. Feacon stared bewildered at the beast. He was about to give chase when he slowly faded away. His legs disappeared, then his midsection. Feacon sent out one last roar before the head too had disappeared.

Chapter 9

Bargan brings Romeelus into Fentia. It took him longer than expected due to the horse's slow speed. He dismounts the horse, turns it around, and then slaps it on the ass. It bolts away.

"It'll go back to its master if its master isn't already dead." Romeelus, who knows every town since he's had an assignment in every one of them, instantly heads for the blacksmith shop. "Blasted mage, caused my armor to dent. I'll make him pay for that, dearly."

He steps inside the blacksmith shop to hear a series of loud banging. The heat from the stove used in the making of armor, and weapons, blasts into him from the other room. All various types of armor and weapons line the walls. He whistles at some of the prices. Romeelus resists the urge to interrupt the Gohwarf making the loud racket, but he knows the Gohwarf very well. Kram Ironjaw is not one to interrupt. Finally, the banging does stop, and heavy foot-steps come thudding towards the room.

"And what can I do for you?" The Gohwarf asks as it enters the room. Upon seeing Romeelus however, Kram rushes over and shakes his hand vig-orously. "It's been a long time, friend. Who is your target that you have to come over here?" The Gohwarf produces a bottle like magic from somewhere on his person; and begins to take swigs. Kram is a Gohwarf. It's a race known to be very small in height but robust and stocky in weight. They are fierce warriors, great ale drinkers, and expert weaponsmiths, and armorers. He sits on top of his counter and drinks as he waits for Romeelus to spill out his tale. Kram will refuse to do anything for the bounty hunter until he tells a story. It doesn't necessarily have to be accurate, just exciting. Romeelus tale satisfies him a lot.

"You know, come to think of it, there was a thief and some lady who wandered into town just yesterday. They looked tired, and he had a few bruises on his head. The locals didn't trust them, so they ignored them. The Smelly Goblin is where they are currently. I don't believe they've come out yet." Kram takes another swig from his bottle. "I'll get to work on your armor. You go check out the inn and then come back in ten minutes. I'll have you suited in your armor by then. You need weapons as well, I suppose." The Gohwarf eyes him up and down with a frown. Romeelus nods.

"I'll get some from the stockroom. Don't worry; I know your tastes."

Romeelus removes his armor and hands it to the blacksmith. Standing in his breeches, tunic, boots, and gloves, Romeelus feels entirely naked.

"I'll avoid the suspicion this way, at least." He remarks, under the noise of the banging. He exits the building. It takes him three minutes to get to The Smelly Goblin. Seeing the sign, he curses under his breath. "When are they going to change the name of that sign?" He reminisced back four and a half years ago:

The place initially was the seediest inn and bar in Belgharia. There were two or three fights every hour. Romeelus had been hired to murder a man who was sleeping with the wife of Romeelus' client. He had killed the man without a hitch, or so he had thought. As it had turned out, he had killed the man's twin. It was the only contract that Romeelus had ever botched. When he did get the right man, whom he made die slowly, the bounty hunter was only paid half because he wasn't supposed to have killed the original man.

Romeelus thinks of this incident, which leaves a bad feeling in his gut that feels worse than poison, which he has had the misfortune of tasting many times. Then he remembers the reason for the name.

Years before the place was closed down, which happened when the owner died mysteriously, a sudden string of murders in the inn had happened. The murders were kept relatively quiet as the owner didn't want to lose any business. But one day, the murders had gotten out of hand. It turned out that the owner's brother was illegitimate. When the owner was two, his mother had a second child. The second child was said to be a goblin. Rumor had it that the owner's mother was raped by a goblin and had became pregnant. The owner's brother was said to have still been alive and lived in the inn's basement. After the murders became oddly familiar to him, the owner had decided to stop them. He had butchered his brother with a razor-sharp ax. He then closed up the basement and kept it locked forever. He had given it the name The Smelly Goblin, since the smell of his brother's dead carcass had flooded the building. Coincidentally, the owner had died, with a razor-sharp ax embedded into his skull.

Romeelus comes out of his reverie with a shudder.

"I wish they would change that damn sign" He enters the building with sweat covering his body—the innkeeper smiles at him. Romeelus would love to erase the smile as he knows a fake one when he sees one. "He's hoping he has another sucker to sleep at his establishment." The bounty hunter thinks to himself. I don't believe in ghosts," he rationalizes with himself. "But I wouldn't sleep in here if it was the only stop, and there was a pack of demons on my back." He walks over to the counter.

"I'm supposed to meet a friend here. You don't suppose you could tell me if he's still here, and if so, what is his room number?"

"And who might your friend be?" Seeing no profit in the conversation, the innkeeper erases his smile. Now there's just an annoyed scowl.

"He goes by the name of Thadden. He should be with a girl. He just arrived yesterday."

"Ah, yes! the thief! he hasn't checked out yet room 13. You know, that sure is a popular fellow. You're the second man today that has asked for him."

Without a word Romeelus turns away abruptly. He heads back towards the blacksmith shop. His thoughts are on the other man that was looking for Thadden. "Maybe it's Kyle. I sure hope so, because I've got a surprise for him."

The innkeeper burns holes in the bounty hunters back as he stares at the rapidly departing figure. "That thief sure does have strange friends." He heads to bed to take a nap.

~ ~ ~

Jake laughs in Drekkar's face as the torturer places the hot poker into his cheek. It is the laugh of a man on the brink of insanity. There is a slight sizzling noise, then the smell of burnt flesh. The laughter just infuriates the dark-skinned man as he is unsure how to deal with someone that is absolutely and utterly crazy. "He must be crazy. This man doesn't feel any pain; I'm running out of ideas. Drekkar thinks sadly.

'I'm going to leave you to rot there for a few days until I can think of some way to deal with you. I will have the last laugh. I'll guarantee you that." Like a child who gets his toys taking away, Drekkar walks away sulking. As soon as Drekkar turns the corner, Jake stops his acting. He does not know how much longer he can hold out, but he'll go until the very end. He slumps his head and waits for the pain to subside and the hunger to start.

~   ~   ~

Thadden leaves the inn. His departure doesn't go unnoticed. Dark, sinister eyes watch him as he makes his way down the street. A slight chuckle and a figure slips in step behind the thief. Thadden curses at himself for his sudden stroke of bad luck. Things were fine until enemies started coming out of the wood-work. He swears at the amulet, the mage Xibnar, and the bounty hunter, whom he assumes Belghar hired. So deep in thought is the thief he fails to pay attention to anyone who might be following him.

"My plan better work! I don't have a lot of time." He begins to mumble. His feet take him to the stables. The smell of manure snaps him back awake. A stable boy stares up at him, waiting for a command.

"Get me a horse please!" The stable boy breaks off into a run and comes back with a horse.

"This is one of the few horses we have left. The rest other people already own." Although young, the boy looks like he has haggled many times; his father is the best in the business. Not having the time to spare to haggle, Thadden asks for the price.

"Three hundred gold pieces," the boy crosses his arms across his chest as if expecting a haggling contest to begin. Thadden reaches into his pouch; for those who thought it was empty, he is an exceptional thief and forks over the money without comment. He even throws in ten gold pieces as a tip. The boy stares at him with total shock. "Thank you, kind sir."

Thadden gets on the horse and rides out of the stables. He fails to recognize the man in black armor; his mind is on Menecha, and Jake and his own current predicament.

The bounty hunter utters a curse when his target becomes a black speck in the distance. The horse thunders out of town. Romeelus curses some more when he finds out that there are no more horses left.

"I can either hoof it or wait here for him to come back. His girlfriend has not left yet. Maybe, I'll pay her a little visit." A vicious grin comes across his face. Expecting a good time, he heads back to the inn.

~ ~ ~

A foot impacted Feacon's body; his last image was of him attacking the doe. Feacon tried to roar, but it had came out a lot lower than he expected. "Meow"! He roared. He looked up at the figure before him. He was a significantly older man. His beard was all tangled, with wild mangy hair. The man sent a cruel smile, Feacon's way. Feacon' was astonished to see how small and helpless he was as a kitten. His life of dominance and pleasure was over.

"I am your master." The voice had replied. "Thud"! Another kick sent the point home. "You are what's called a Familiar. You will do everything I say."

"Thud!"

"I have bestowed a few powers upon you. As long as you can see where you are going, you can teleport. You also have one more power, but you won't know about it until I inform you of it." "Thud!"

"I have a leash for you. Just in case you have any ideas about teleporting away. It won't work as long as this leash is on. You can't leave anyway. You are my familiar. It means we can read each other's thoughts; I'll know when you want to leave." "WHOOSH"! Xibnar's foot strikes the air. Feacon, had read the mind of the mage and knew the foot was headed toward him. Perhaps, Xibnar had said a little too much.

Inside the bag, Feacon was murmuring in pain as the dream progresses. Long forgotten memories find themselves returning, and Feacon finds himself wondering why.

~ ~ ~

Heavy, familiar footsteps come back around the corner. Jake has only felt an hour or so pass since Drekkar left. He wonders why he has come back a lot earlier than his intention. Drekkar is not in his right frame of mind.

"Hello, my friend! Why don't you have a seat and take a load off?" Ha! Ha! Ha! 'Never mind, I see you're already sitting down.' Ha! Ha! Ha! The jokes begin to annoy Jake as they aren't hilarious.

This must be his latest kind of torture. Telling me bad jokes until I'm sick to my stomach" the prisoner muses. Jake doesn't think it'll take long before he starts screaming. Fortunately for us all, Drekkar becomes serious again.

"I just remembered one more torture method. If you don't scream with this one, I'm going to have to kill you and move on to more pleasurable, agreeable, prisoners." Drekkar starts to drool at the thought of getting a screaming prisoner. He beams with pleasure. Jake clears his throat to remind Drekkar of his chore at hand. He knows Drekkar won't kill him immediately after this latest torture. When Drekkar removes him from the chair, he'll have to make his move. Drekkar hears the apparent noise and comes out of his dreamy haze.

"As I was saying," he continues as though he never stopped talking. "The chair that you are sitting on is my pride and joy. The idea was all mine; I just had to have Belghar help with the finished product. When I crank this wheel, it will release lightning bolts, which will hit the chair. This action will cause disastrous results to the body, especially when I soak you with water first. You might survive the first few blasts, but you won't for long, then I'll turn the machine off and kill you quickly and painlessly. The choice, of course, is yours." Jake follows Drekkar's' big brutal hands as they clasp on to the wheel; with his oh-so-pleasant laugh, Drekkar turns the wheel...

~ ~ ~

Kyle is elated over his success. He returns to Gena, as instructed by Xibnar. The mage is to bring the cat to Xibnar's old magic shop. There he will wait until Xibnar returns. He's been feeling a lot of activity going on inside the bag. "The cat must know it's in trouble; that's why it's squirming so much. Kyle doesn't know the mystery of the squirming. His guess is close, but not on the mark. It's not the future the big cat is uneasy about, but the past.

~ ~ ~

On horseback, Thadden can cover a lot more ground. Even though the price of the horse was high, it is well worth the money. It obeys his every command and does so with great speed and maneuverability. He can feel the muscles of the animal underneath him. It is a strong, powerful animal. By nightfall, he is again in the city of Gena. He slows his horse down as he gets outside Belghar's castle. The thief brings his horse into the cover of the trees. He tethers it to a branch. With an encouraging pat and the command to be on alert, Thadden sneaks back towards the dangerous moat. He prepares himself to pull off either an incredible rescue or the death of him, Menecha, and her father. "Feacon, you stupid cat, where the hell are you when I need you." He yells into the night as he approaches the moat.

Chapter 10

Bolts of electrical current speed into Jake's system; the sensation is not very pleasant. He bites his tongue as his head and body rock uncontrollably back and forth. His arms practically break as they are trying to fly up, but the straps hold them down. He wants to scream but prays that Drekkar will bore of his silence and untie him for the killing stroke. Thus far, however, Drekkar seems to be enjoying Jake's plight. He laughs continuously. Blood pours out of Jake's mouth as his teeth continue cutting deeply into his tongue. "You are very noble. Why don't you just scream and end your agony? Or do you enjoy getting pain, as I do giving it?"

"I'll Anthoy, killing you when I get out ob thith thing." He manages to babble incoherently through his bloody mouth. It's probably the last sentence he'll ever utter. Infuriated, Drekkar grabs a huge carving knife.

"When I finish with you, you'll wish you could scream. You'll be begging me to stop." Jake's last bit of defiance is a glob of spit that splatters into Drekkar's blabbering mouth. "Thunk"! The cleaver cuts off Jake's pinkie of his right hand. Drekkar turns the wheel. More electricity ripples up and down every bone in the prisoner's body. His hand twitching sprays blood out in every direction. With too much strain, the tongue finally gives, and it slices in two by Jake's teeth. It falls to the floor. Jake realizes with numb horror that he will die on the chair unless he does something. He begins to tighten then loosen his wrist muscles while the jerking motion of his body is still going on.

"Maybe I can loosen these bonds enough to break them." The electricity turns off. Drekkar holds the cleaver in the air.

"Well, well, well, which finger shall I cut off now? There are just so many options; I don't know where to begin." He stares at the finger selection long and hard. "Aha!" he replies as he's ready to bring the cleaver down.

~ ~ ~

Thadden takes in a deep breath. He's at the spot on the castle where the dungeon should be. He hopes he is right. Time is of the essence. He hopes that Belghar's guards aren't on double watch after his last visit. "Maybe they'll all be up top. Nobody is going to expect me to enter the castle through the dungeon." He prays for the latter as he dives into the murky, moat water.

~ ~ ~

As the cleaver is on its descent, Jake takes all of his pent-up furies and puts it into one lunge. Whether it's his sudden strength surge or the loosening up of the rope while being electrocuted, he snaps the bonds and steps aside. The cleaver sticks into the wood, where seconds before Jake's hand had been.

"He wasn't going for any fingers; he was going for my whole hand." Jake's thoughts provide him with more adrenaline. He knows that Drekkar is too strong for him. He's losing blood fast. He must end this quickly. Drekkar smiles! He enjoys this part of the game.

"So you finally show some emotion. That's good. I like that a lot. Too bad, you'll have to die because of it." "Crunch"! Jake's left fist hits Drekkar in the nose.

"You bwod by node," Drekkar tries to say as he holds his broken nose in his hands. Blood flows between the cracks of his fingers. Before Drekkar can launch an offensive, Jake sends another fist into the throat of his dark-skinned torturer.

"Kkkhhh" Drekkar tries to utter something as his windpipe crushed. Drekkar will die shortly he is not getting any air. His breath is already starting to fade. Jake, however, is not about to stop. He pushes Drekkar into the chair. He leaps for the wheel. If he could speak, Jake would probably throw in a comment before he had his turn at being the torturer; as it is, he silently turns the wheel. For the first time in his life, the torturer knows pain. As his body rocks back and forth and sharp jabs of pain pulse in him, he admires Jake for not screaming. Drekkar tries to yell but instead just wastes precious breath. Jake turns the machine off. Drekkar sags to the floor. He is about to die. Unfortunately, Jake won't let him die in peace.

Jake grabs the cleaver. A quick yank, and it comes out of the wood. Barely standing, he grabs Drekkar by the hair of the head. He smiles in Drekkar's face. Drekkar spits. Jake takes the spittle and swallows it in mockery. Knowing that his time of existence is up, the torturer lowers his eyes to the floor. "Thummp"! The cleaver embeds itself in the middle of the head. The skull and brains expose themselves partially to the air. Jake drops the weapon to the floor. He rips off a piece of cloth from his tattered pants. He vomits at the carnage he himself has caused. He wraps his hand up in his makeshift bandage and hopes it'll stop the bleeding.

~ ~ ~

Thadden quickly makes his way to the designated spot. Frantically, he begins to pull on a ring. It starts to come loose. Another tug and it moves some more. There is one thing Thadden wasn't sure of; if a creature resides in the moat. One does, and it's only been there for a few days, but it's hungry. Nobody knows where Belghar found the beast. On the other hand, nobody wanted to ask him. It sees the figure in the water and heads for the food.

Thadden turns around as his senses tell him that something's not right. It is a creature with eight tentacles, an oval head, two eyes, and a vast mouth bearing down on him. He knows he's running out of breath, but he can't afford to let the creature kill him either. Very quickly, it covers the distance between them. He does not draw a weapon as he would be too sluggish in using it in the water.

"Maybe I can kill two birds with one stone." He slaps the creature. It gets enraged beyond belief. In a fury, it charges at the thief like a cornered boar would a hunter. It tries to reach him with its tentacles, but he quickly eludes them. The creature spots Thadden and decides to propel itself forward and crush the meal first. As it comes along, Thadden waits. At the last second, he dives down. The creature slams into the wall with monstrous velocity. The wall crumbles, and an opening appears. His lungs feel like they're going to burst, the thief swims for the tunnel. Luckily, he comes for air and the water doesn't fill up the room.

"It is magically protected from flooding." He stares at in awe. He climbs a set of stairs and looks at the door. Breathing a sigh of relief, he opens the door and enters the dungeons.

~ ~ ~

With grim determination, Jake staggers over to the door. He opens it. Two guards stare at him with weapons ready. Seeing all hope vanish. Jake prepares to fling himself at the guards and hopes for a quick death. Just as he is about to commit his suicidal act, there is a sound like steel sliding into the skin. The guards topple forward. A dagger sticks out of one of the guards' back, while a gaping, bloody hole is in the other one. With blurry vision, Jake sees a figure standing in front of him. A sigh of relief washes over him. It is Thadden.

"What have they done to you?" Thadden asks. He receives no reply. Jake's need for energy is no more. He starts to wobble and falls into Thadden's waiting arms. Reaching into his packsack, Thadden retrieves the three healing potions he had gotten from Xibnar in their deal. He pours a bottle over Jake's flayed back. The wounds close up.

"I'm glad he passed out," Thadden thinks. "He won't feel any pain when I have to use these potions." The thief opens another bottle and pours on Jake's bloody mouth. He forces the mouth open and realizes why he got no response from Jake. The tongue is not inside. Hatred, strong, and vicious, wells up inside of him, leaving a bad taste in his heart. He'll make Belghar pay for this one. Seeing the bloody bandage on Jake's hand, Thadden decides to remove it. His anger doubles when he notices the absence of the right-hand pinkie. Using a little more of the potion, he heals the stump. Realizing that there's no time, he takes out his water flask. He splashes a little bit on Jake's face. His eyelids flutter, then he comes back into consciousness.

"We have to get out of here. Follow me; I'll lead us to safety. Then we'll find a place to rest. When I tell you what I'm going to, do we'll both be very busy in the next few days."

Jake nods in agreement as they exit the dungeon. Jake fills up with excitement. He is finally free of jail and his torment. Jake is sure that whatever lies ahead is nothing in comparison to what has just happened. With a smile, he follows the thief.

~ ~ ~

In the darkness, Feacon remembers his last day with Xibnar. Xibnar was mixing his potions, and Feacon was licking himself. The wizard stopped what he was doing, looked at the cat, and then had performed one more act of cruelty onto his familiar. He grabbed the cat and lifted it high over his shoulders. As it scratched him in defiance, he threw it against the wall. Using its body to the best of its ability, Feacon had twisted and turned and absorbed most of the impact on its paws.

"Ha! Ha! Ha!" Xibnar laughed as he returned to his alchemy. Xibner had foolishly believed that the cat had been under his control and was too afraid to attempt to leave him. Maybe, that's why he was so careless and had forgotten to put the leash on his magical pet. Feacon glared at the back of his owner and had decided that it'was then or never. He raced forward,and slashed his claws at the wizard's legs.

"OWWWWWW" Xibnar had howled in pain. As soon as he tried to locate the troublesome cat, Feacon lunged at his face. His claws ripped into flesh as they drew blood. Again Xibnar cried out in pain. The cat lunged off his face, onto the floor, then teleported himself out the door. Trapped in the body of a cat, Feacon was finally free. It had only been a few miles from there that he met up with the thief known as Thadden...

~ ~ ~

Feacon comes out of his slumber. Things are different now. He is no longer free and is again somebody's prisoner. His mind starts to plot out his escape when he feels his prison move down.

"I'm being put onto the floor." The cat notices. With senses on high alert the cat prepares to pounce. Patiently, warily, he waits to escape.

Thadden has no problem when he enters the murky, moat water. The creature seems to ponder for a minute and then realizes who is entering the water. Wanting no part of the human causes it so much pain; the animal jets out a black liquid and disappears into its midst.

"Hold your breath, and follow me, Jake." He dives into the water. Jake follows suit. Before long, both men are on the shore. They lie next to each other, gasping and panting. In the cover of darkness, the two men rest. Thadden tells his story and what he must do next. Jake grabs a stick and writes four words in the sand. "I want to help". With a look of surprise at Jake's courage, he takes Menecha's father's hand and thanks to him.

"I'm sorry, I shouldn't have got you and your daughter involved. I didn't mean to..." Jake cuts him off.

"Thank You". He writes in the sand. Both men hug each other and cry up in the sky.

CHAPTER 11

In the mountains of Naryeq, a sudden surge of activity is occurring. The citizens of Tyrella notice large groups of Goblin patrols outside the city gates. A small but powerful army force is a big city, fear a sudden attack is forthcoming. The queen is the only ruler and is sending out scouts to check out this alleged threat. She plans to wipe out the Goblins before they can even surmount an attack. On top of a horse set the general, who is leading the scouting party. The legends speak of this female General as one of the best generals in this world's history. She can wipe out entire legions, with but a hundred or fewer men. Her name is Magdellaine. Those who know her name also know fear. As a general, she does not need to be with the scouting party, but she is on her secret mission. With cold steel eyes and a nerve to match, she rides ahead, searching, seeking, and hoping.

~ ~ ~

Menecha wakes up from her forced slumber. To find herself staring up at the dirt-packed ceiling. She sits upright as she remembers a kiss, then darkness swept over her. Confused, she looks around her surroundings, trying to make some sense out of her current predicament. She is in a dirt cave. The only light is from a fire. A creature, nasty and ugly, sits in front of it, staring at her. She stands up. The beast watches her closely but does not move. Realizing that she is a prisoner but not sure by whom or by what, Menecha tries to walk past the creature. With surprising quickness, the monster, a Goblin, stands in front of her and bars her way. It grunts and points to the corner; she just came out of.

"So much for just walking out of here,"Menecha replies. She returns to her corner. The Goblin resumes his seat. Looking just beyond him, the female prisoner can see daylight fading. A little piece of sunset creeps into the darkness and shines onto the entrance floor. It isn't powerful enough to disrupt the dark and just remains in place like a beacon. Menecha can see a glimmer of hope at this sign. She has a feeling that she better escape soon; now, all she needs is a plan.

~ ~ ~

Just before the successful rescue of Jake Rebish, Belghar sits on his throne pondering.

"Pontew, there is still no word from that bounty hunter."

"I know, sir; he has yet to report back. He is the best, though; I'm sure it's only a matter of time."

"A matter of time?" Belghar blurts.

"Well, a matter of time until he gets us that thief." Pontew answers.

"Give that bounty hunter another week. If he fails to produce that thief for us by then, well, you'll just have to kill him and hire somebody else. I need that necklace, and I need it soon." His eyes flare up in anger as Pontew bows, and leaves the room.

~ ~ ~

Romeelus watches two figures, on one horse, ride by Fentia. A quick glimpse assures him that it is his intended target. Now the bounty hunter is back in the game. He hobbles over to the horse he just purchased, mounts it and follows Thadden and Jake.

~ ~ ~

The campfire is warm and provides ample illumination for the dark, damp, chilly cave. The sun is just beginning to set, and the last bit of light at the entrance gets swallowed up by the darkness. Menecha's guardian sits with vigil near the fire.

"It's now, or never, girl," Menecha mumbles to herself as she gathers up her courage. She stands up. The Goblin, still sitting, watches her. Motioning towards the fire with her hands, she asks if she can sit next to the fire. The creature sees nothing wrong with the suggestion and allows her to sit directly across from it. The girl sits down. A warm feeling hits her insides, then works its way outside. It isn't until she sits next to the fire that she realizes how cold she is. Patiently, she waits until the chill disperses from her bones then sets her plan in motion. With the presence of her guard's eyes, she slowly begins to unbutton her top. Thinking that he's in for a good time, the Goblins eyes light up. He loosens his grip on his spear. Menecha rhythmically dances, and begins to strip. Her fingers gently undo the last of the buttons. As she is about to bare her breasts to her captor, he drops his weapon.

"Now, you idiot, now," Menecha yells to herself. She kicks sand. It blinds the guard. Reacting quickly, she runs over to the blinded guard and stabs him with his spear. It falls forward.

"Aaaiiiieeeee" It screams as its furry body catches ablaze. Releasing the spear, she runs out of the cave. She sees two paths in front of her. One contains Goblins; the other is clear. She decides to take the clear path, and begins to run. Her only hope is that her pursuers aren't as fast as she is.

~ ~ ~

Thadden, and Jake, pass by Fentia without even a glance. Their destination lies elsewhere. As they travel for miles, Thadden tells Jake the part of Jake's plan to carry out. With a nod for affirmation, they continue in silence. Thadden forgets about his head's price and the bounty hunter that claimed his cat in their haste to complete their task. If he were to look back quick enough, he would be able to see his seeker following closely behind. Thadden is getting sloppy with his mind on other things.

"I know a short-cut, through the woods up ahead. It shall get us to Shondell a lot quicker than the road we're on." A nod is his only response. Romeelus spots Thadden turn off the road and wonders if they saw him. Cautiously, he approaches the area. The sound of branches breaking tells him that no one notices him. The bounty hunter and his horse veer off the road as well and remains in pursuit.

~ ~ ~

The darkness presses heavily on the troops as the scouting party brings itself to a halt. Magdellaine continues forward, ignoring the break of the scouts. Whispers from the troops drift up to her.

"Where is she going?"

"What is she looking for?"

"Is she going to stop?"

She is the General. She answers to no one but the Queen. Nevertheless, she does pause as she questions herself about what she is doing. Somewhere out, there is trouble; she must seek it out. Her intuition tells her that the trouble somehow involves her. The soldiers just stare at her back as she moves away. At times like this, Magdellaine is better off alone. They wait ten minutes until she is out of sight and then go about scouting the area. Unbeknownst to them, they'll be encountering Goblins soon. The livelihood of Tyrella is at stake should they fail in their scouting.

~ ~ ~

"Thoom"! "Thoom"! "Thoom"! Menecha's heart is about ready to leap out of her chest. She is running for her life. Her fears have come true. The creatures are gaining on her bit by bit. She knows they'll catch her again. "Thoom"! "Thoom"! "Thoom"! Her feet run faster. They pump forward for all they're worth—a horn blasts from one of the Goblins. A fear buries itself in her heart and fills it with doom.

"Thoom"! "Thoom! "Thoom"! The sound of her heart is becoming dimmer as fear grabs hold of her heart and tries to block the sound from her

84

ears. It begins to squeeze harder and harder. Her face is dirty, messy, and sweaty. "Thoom"! "Thoom"! "Thoom"! Branches smack into her face. She shoves them aside. The forest sounds seem to revive, as hoots, growls, and horn calls fill the night air. With a snarl, a Goblin lunges for her shirt. He grabs it, but it comes free, as Menecha, in her panic, forgot to re-button it. It Infuriates the creature who throws its club at the fleeing prisoner. "Thunk"! It hits Menecha in the back of the head. The blow knocks her unconscious. Grinning at victory, the Goblin picks its weapon back up. It is about ready to carry the unconscious female, when a calm, authoritative voice stops his advance.

"Grab that girl, and you'll be very, very dead." It doesn't understand the language, so the Goblin charges the owner of the voice.

~   ~   ~

On the outskirts of the remarkable city Tyrella, hidden in the wilderness, is the Shondell Guild. For centuries, Tyrellians, and other folks, have tried to find the famous guild. No one has ever found out the secret whereabouts, although Tyrellians do believe it's near them. They don't realize that it's closer than they think. Just as you leave Tyrella, head north then enter the forest near a big boulder. After walking for two miles, you will enter a valley. In this valley are two cliffs. Should you choose the ridge on the right-hand side, you will have located the guild's entrance. Just walk up to the cliff base, mutter the daily password, and an entry will appear. The passwords change every day of the week. They remain the same, on the same days of the following week. All of this, Thadden explains to Jake, as they are about to enter the valley. He thrusts two things into Jake's hand. One is a silver medallion with an etching of a Panther's face.

"Show this to the guard. He'll recognize it as a clan symbol. He shouldn't bother you once you show it." Jake nods. "And this is a map to the guild. You have to go here." He points to a spot on the map. "When you get there, grab a staff and a robe. They'll be together. It'll be on a table still, as they are still examining them. They do this with all of their newly acquired material. You know what to do once you get there." Another nod tells Thadden that Menecha's father understands.

"Good-luck." He replies as he watches Jake, who has dressed in Thadden's attire, enter the valley. The bounty hunter watches the thief as he makes his way into the valley. Romeelus doesn't care who the person watching is, but he'll kill him if he interferes with his plans. Motionlessly, he watches the back of the thief's friend. Then he slips back into the forest to lay his trap. He is not aware that Thadden has heard him. Now, the thief has two dilemmas. How does he carry out plan one and deal with the bounty hunter who has found him?

"Since the bounty hunter didn't attack me, and he'd plenty of time while he was watching me, it can only mean that the clothes switch between Jake and I is working." This knowledge gives him time to carry off-plan number one before enacting his revenge on the cat thieving bounty hunter.

~ ~ ~

Kyle sets the backpack down, just as Xibnar himself appears.

"Hello, apprentice! I assume that your inferior little mind has completed its task and gotten me the nasty, little cat." Kyle feels his anger beginning to boil at the mention of the word 'inferior.'

"Yes, the cat is in the bag. You know, though, I am no longer an inferior." Kyle replies calmly.

"Well, sure you are. Is it not I who thought up the idea? Is it not I who broke you out of the miserable dungeon? Is it not I who granted you all those powers? There is no question in my mind that you are inferior. Now, I don't want to hear any more on the subject. If I have to teach you a lesson as well as the cat, then I'd be more than happy to oblige. I suggest you concentrate more on where the thief is and see that he is doing as instructed." Xibnar portrays an aura of self-importance that Kyle does not like one bit. Knowing that the time for his revenge is drawing near, Kyle leaves the mage to his cat.

"Enjoy the moment while it lasts Xibnar; for it is I who shall be the only left to be able to laugh." With that, he disappears with a loud, thunderous boom. His power is growing strong. Unfortunately, his hatred is more potent, and that just may be his undoing.

~ ~ ~

The Goblin charges the figure that stands protectively over Menecha's body. Magdellaine stands waiting for the attack. A longsword and shield are her only weapons. Thrusting his spear, the Goblin hopes to take off the female warrior's head. Had it been an ordinary soldier, it probably would have done just that, but this is not a typical soldier. This is a General. Magdellaine deflects the creatures' blow with her sword. The spear snaps in half as she sends the blade into his abdomen. His death cry rings loudly. The sound of horns answering the howl sounds very close. She knows that there is no time to retreat, so she waits.

"My scouting party will be here soon. For the sake of the girl, I must fend off the horde until my army arrives." She narrows her eyes as the first five Goblins come into view.

Chapter 12

Slowly, the group of Goblins advance; they are unsure of the outcome. Even though they have five-to-one odds, they are uncertain of their quarry. Magdellaine waits patiently. She finds it encouraging that they have yet to charge her.

"This will give me more time to stall until help arrives." Finally, one of the monsters moves at her. She blocks its mace with her shield and thrusts with her sword. Her attempt fails, as the creature wisely parried with its weapon. Two more animals come forward to help out their companion. Her odds are certainly against her.

~ ~ ~

Jake remembers Thadden's instructions and manages to get the guild's door open. A pair of eyes stare at him.

"Password?" The guardian of the entrance asks. Jake hopes the sweat that he feels isn't showing on his face. He breathes in to calm himself and then points to his mouth. Seeing no tongue in Jake's mouth, the guard gives him a stick. "Write it out!" Jake grabs the stick then writes the password in the sand. The guard grunts in satisfaction then yells to somebody above him.

"Open the gate." A grinding of gears and the vast gate opens. "You may pass." It is all the voice utters as it again begins its watch. Jake hurries on through on rubbery legs. As soon as he passes through, the gate closes.

"So far, so good," he thinks in his head. It's his only form of a speech he can perform, other than writing. Walking quickly, he forms the map's image in his mind and prays that he doesn't make a mistake. He only has a short time to reach and obtain the items before Thadden works his magic; he must already be outside by then. Fear tries to find a way to work its way to his heart, but Jake is only concentrating on one thing, his love for his daughter. It shatters his fear and sends shards of its life throughout the guild. Other thieves, beggars, and even assassins seem to shrink away from Jake, as he sends the fear in their direction. Heedless, he keeps going to the only thing that will save his daughter.

~ ~ ~

"Clang"! "Clang"! "Clang"! The sound of steel striking steel rings and echoes in the cold air; a fierce battle is raging in the forest. Magdellaine closes her eyes and remembers her training. he always could take on three or more men; why would this be any different. Her thoughts give her an answer.

"It's not any different." She yells as she blocks two maces with her shield and parries another with her sword. Anxiously, the other two Goblins wait for their turn. The path only allows three men to walk abreast, which is a situation that is to the warriors' advantage. She brings her foot around and snaps the knee of one of her assailants. Her sword skewers it, as it falls to the ground dead. Instantly, another Goblin rushes forward. It ignores its falling comrade as it stands on the body and swings its spear. Laughing, Magdellaine parries the weapon and bashes another Goblin in the face with her shield. It drops to its knees and spits out a few black rotting teeth.

One goblin manages to hit her left leg with its mace. This Goblin is female, Magdellaine notes by the noticeable chest difference of the warriors.

"It appears the women are the better fighters." She notes to herself. "Much the same as it is with this world." With a swing of her sword, she cuts off the arm of the Goblin holding the spear. The blood sprays into her face, blocking her vision. Its scream causes an answer by more horns. Time seems to be running out for the heroine. Grimly, she wipes the blood from her eyes and glares at her opponents. The last Goblin's waiting is over. Magdellaine still has three opponents as the toothless Goblin gets back to its feet. Again she laughs madly as the creatures stare nervously at one another.

"Come on, you bastards. Come and get your prize." None seem too eager to answer the challenge.

~ ~ ~

Jake takes a right, heads down the corridor, and then takes another one. Hooded figures rush past him, and Jake arrives at an intersection. His mind tries to draw up the map. It comes to blank at the corner. Letting a sense of calm swarm him, Jake heads left.

"Let this be the right path. For the sake of my daughter's life, please let this be the right one." His thoughts speak louder than his mouth ever could. His mind feels like it's about to burst with such pressure, he continues.

~ ~ ~

Thadden waits for about ten minutes and then heads for the guild himself. His part in the plan is about to unfold. Romeelus watches as the thief's partner begin to follow the thief.

"How odd?" He thinks as his gaze lingers on the Thadden's back. With a sigh, he continues on his trap laying. "I'll get the thief when he comes out. I assume his partner is involved in his escape from the guild. Maybe I'll get to find out what it is they are doing before I murder them." With his injured leg, Romeelus savors the thought of finally capturing the elusive thief and completing his contract.

~ ~ ~

With the ease of putting on a pair of boots, Magdellaine hacks and slashes through two of the Goblins as they stare helplessly at the blood gushing out of them. They fall like wheat to a scythe. The sound of running through a forest, and blazing horns, warn her that the creature's friends are very near. Coincidentally, her last opponent is the female warrior, who has been the only one to strike her. She nods to her opponent then mounts her attack. The creature blocks the sword and the shield, but not the knee to her gut.

"Ooooff"! The Goblin exhales some hair. The shield bashes her in the ears. As it howls in pain, Magdellaine's longsword finds its way into her throat. The howls become a gurgle. The gurgle becomes silent as the creature dies. The foliage erupts, and one hundred Goblins surround Magdellaine. They howl in excitement at the sight of such easy prey. Suddenly, there is another row from behind her—a sigh of relief flashes on her face. The scouting part has arrived.

"Sorry to have taken so long, Lady Magdellaine, but you moved very fast. As soon as we heard the horns, we double-timed it all the way here. It seems as though we won't be getting rest, though." The soldier looks past her.

"Cornelius, you have arrived just in time. Please dispatch of this rabble; I must get this girl to safety. I shall return if you have not."

"It is as you say, milady, and we shall return." He smiles and then salutes. She salutes back then picks up Menecha's unconscious body. Without another word, she leaves. Glad for the action, Cornelius, and his scouts, run forward to the clearing to meet the unfortunate Goblins.

~ ~ ~

Thadden opens the door and encounters the guard.

"Hello, Trowell. Would you be so kind as to let me in?"

"Do you know the password?" The guardian seems not to budge.

"You know that I know the password; just let me in. I must get inside."

"You know the rules as well as I Thadden; now, what is the password?"

Thadden whispers the password into his ear.

"Very good, Thadden, that wasn't too hard. Now, what is so important that you chose to ignore the password?"

"Somebody has just come in here; he stole my map of the guild and my amulet. He knows all of the passwords. Maybe you remember him; he can't speak." Thadden watches the guards' eyes as they widen.

"My god, I just let him in. Raise the gate; we have an intruder." Trowell pushes Thadden through. "If you get that guy, bring him here; I want a piece of him as well." Thadden nods his head. The gate closes down. According to Guild rules, the guard at the gate must stay at the entrance. In case the intruder should try and get back out that way. Also, he must still prevent people from coming in, even if it's the guild master. In any emergency, no-one can go in or out until the problem is taking care of. Trowell now maintains the most important job at this point. Eyes alert. Trowell remains at the gate.

~ ~ ~

With the sound of battle ringing in her ears, Magdellaine carries the body down the path. Her muscles tighten at the load, but she has moved more massive people. It takes her twenty minutes to get to the castle. The guard at the gate stares at her in wonder; her blood-soaked arms carry the girl into the court. One of the servants rushes forward and waits for the instructions.

"Bring the girl to the infirmary. Make sure she is not injured, then place in my suite. I'll be looking after the girl for a while. Report back to me as soon as she awakens. Eyes that immediately say "don't disobey me," flash at the servant as she bows to Magdellaine. Two more servants rush forward to help carry Menecha.

"Time to visit the queen." She replies. Her boots echo off the floor of the exquisite castle; the echo imitates the echo in her sad, sad heart. Soon, she disappears and is around the corner.

~ ~ ~

Walking faster, Jake comes into view. He is at the door. He has chosen correctly. Breathing a sigh of relief, Jake tests the knob. The knob turns. He can hear the alarm dinging and the scurrying of feet. Quickly, he is inside the room. Torches, many of them, provide plenty of light to see. Against the wall are the objects that he is looking for. A book and a stave, both unprotected, seem to goad Jake into action. Joyously, he snatches the book and puts it in Thadden's backpack. With shaking hands, he looks at then refolds the map. With the staff in hand, he opens the door. The sound of running feet can still hear, but none have reached this far down the corridor. As he walks, he listens to the noises ahead of him. He hears a thumping of footfalls. Looking to his left, he spots a door. Menecha's father just gets the door closed when footsteps run by. He sneaks back out and continues. Finally, he steps into a doorway and breathes a sigh of relief when he gets the door closed. "Safe,"! His mind talks to him. Although time is on his side, he still doesn't have a lot to spare. "As soon as the thieves check their treasure room, they're going to start going door to door." Thadden's little room is small. It has very little in it as Thadden takes his stuff with him. "There is no honor even among his kind, it appears." There is a bed in the corner and a mirror, but little else. Remembering where he is, Jake seems to revive again. He heads into the bathroom. There is black, disgusting smelling water in the basin and a fly-infested bucket of dung in the bedpan.

"Menecha will kill him if he ever lives like this around her." Laughing to himself, he feels around the wall and comes across a loose stone. It moves with a slight tug. The sound of earth moving and grinding seems to be a little too loud and suspicious if someone was looking for a thief in their lair. Jake is all in at this point. He enters into the darkness. As he begins to walk away, his brain issues a warning. "Close the door now, you idiot. Are you trying to implicate Thadden?" His hands start feeling for a loose stone that should close the door. He starts to sweat. Voices, loud, and excited are heard right outside the room door. Just as the door opens, Jake's fingers find a loose rock. He tugs at it, then runs for his life. Remarkably, the door closes silently. Torches line his escape route as he runs through the twists and turns of his passageway. Up ahead, he spies salvation. A beam of light, at the end of the tunnel, marks his escape. With a joyous cry, which sounded more like dead air, he runs into the light. The sun beats down, and as it destroys the snow, it gives Jake strength.

"Hello, Master Thief. I'm so glad to have finally met you. And in this meeting, you shall surely die." With the staff in hand, Jake whirls to face his doom. A fighter he is not.

~   ~   ~

Queen Kyrella sits imperiously on her throne. Her beauty, beyond description, is deceptive to the cruel heart that lies within a beautiful breast. She is a fair lady, but her quest for immortality has caused her to be bitter. Rarely does she let a mistake go without proper punishment? A servant fans her, and another washes her feet as there is a knock on the door.

"Come in!" She commands. The door opens, and in steps a servant.

"Your highness, Lady Magdellaine, is back from her expedition and wishes to see you."

"Then let her in, you doddering fool. She is the only one that I allow in here without permission." She waves the servant away as Magdellaine enters.

"Good evening, m'lady." Magdellaine curtseys. "I have just returned from my journey and would like to tell you what I've discovered."

"Take a seat, Magdellaine; I'm sure it's important."

"Thank you, it is important." The servant with the fan retrieves a chair and brings it to bloody general. "Thank you," Magdellaine replies to the servant. "I went ahead of the scouting party, and I heard a little scream. I came across a naked girl running away from a group of Goblins. She was knocked unconscious. I had fears that they would rape her, so I stood over the girl and killed the two creatures. As I did so, five more came to replace them. My thoughts were only for the girl's welfare, and I couldn't possibly run away and leave her to them, so I stood my ground and waited for our soldiers to arrive. As soon as I killed the last Goblin, the remaining force had arrived. I thought I was done for when our troops showed up. Cornelius and the men were fighting the Goblins when I came here with the girl."

"You brought the girl here?" Hmmmmm. "That might prove interesting. When she awakes, let's see if we can train her as a warrior. It'd be good to have another warrioress in our midst. Even at those uneven numbers, Cornelius won't have a problem with that rabble. Is that all?"

Magdellaine was regretting this question, but she must now face it. "I believe the girl that I rescued is my daughter." Her tear-stained face looks up at the queen.

Ha! Ha! Ha! Ha! The queen's laughter cuts into Magdellaine more than any weapon. "This should indeed prove to very interesting. With a final bow, the general, with the blood and tears, exits the room.

"Is my daughter worse off than when I found her?" She asks herself. Only time will tell.

Chapter 13

Thadden can almost laugh as he doesn't see any trace of Jake. All the thieves don't know how or where Jake disappeared. After they check out the treasure room and find it two items less, they run down the corridor—each room they check. There is no sign of the intruder. Thadden's heart speeds up when they get to his, but again there is nobody. They check all the other rooms, and the same result occurs. A quick meeting is underway. After a few modifications to passwords and badges, the meeting adjourns. Thadden is a little alarmed at not one person being suspicious, but he is on a mission. He prepares to leave.

~ ~ ~

Jake prepares for what he is about to face. He knows not why he is under attack, but Jake knows he must try and defend himself. Romeelus lets out a gasp.

"Y-y-you are not Thadden. Where is Thadden, and why do you where his garb?" Silently Jake points to his mouth. "A mute, huh. I see it must have been him who followed you into the guild. Another trick? I do have you, though. Perhaps he'll bargain his life for yours." Again, Jake does not respond. At that moment, a strange feeling comes over the men. It's a feeling Romeelus has felt before. He whirls. Kyle stares at him, with eyes of pure hatred.

"I come here not for a prize, but revenge. You beat me the last time we met, although ironically, it was I who got the prize. After I kill you, I'll kill your friend, and then I'll get that thief. It is his death that I shall cherish the most."

"Then I guess our paths cross again. You see, I have had a contract to kill the thief, as I was the cat. If you continue to compete for my prizes, then it is you who shall die. I have learned a lot from our last encounter. My first lesson was never trust a mage." He easily avoids the hands that push through the snow and try to grasp onto his ankles.

"Maybe you should change your tricks; they're becoming boring and easy to avoid." Romeelus lands gently on his injured ankle. His ax misses as Kyle ducks the swing.

Jake can do nothing but watch; its mesmerizing effect causes him not to leave. He doesn't care who wins, as Thadden will be the winner's next target.

"At least the bounty hunter will keep you alive. You can stall him." His mind pushes him into action. He swings the staff. It strikes Kyle in the back, and electric sparks fly off the armor.

"Aaarrgghh!" Kyle turns around to face his new threat. He sweeps his arm, a gust of wind, or so Jake thinks, picks him up and sends him backward. The padding of snow softens his landing as the mage thuds against the base of a tree.

However, it was the distraction that Romeelus needed as he buries his ax into Kyle's shoulder. A scream of pain releases into the forest. A flock of birds takes flight at the loud disturbance. Romeelus struggles to free his ax out of the bone. Blood runs down the blade and onto his hands. Kyle lifts Romeelus by the throat and holds him in the air. He can't breathe. His face turns red. The world around him is spinning. Desperately he tries to knock the arms away. He only has seconds left. "Thump"! Romeelus sags to the ground. He's gasping for air. Through hazy vision, he can see the real Thadden fighting Kyle. Slowly he gets to his feet. Thadden seems to be doing much better than the bounty hunter ever had. His sword seems alive as it pierces the armor and cuts a leg, an arm, anything that gets in its path. Kyle seems heedless of the pain. "Clap"! Kyle claps his hands together. The sound is creates a sonic boom. Thadden covers his ears and drops to the ground, howling in pain. Jake is covering his ears too, as he tries to scream but is less effective. Romeelus' helm absorbs all the noise. With a clear head, he continues the fight. Kyle turns to face the next threat.

"Why don't you just quit, bounty hunter. It'll make your life a lot easier."

"Because I know that behind all of your parlor tricks, you're just a weakling, waiting to be exposed." Romeelus lunges forward; his hands push the ax into the shoulder even farther. As Kyle screams in pain, the bounty hunter kicks with his splinted leg. The dagger comes out of its hiding spot. "Enjoy this, creep." He sticks his leg and the dagger into the magician's midsection.

"Rraaarrg" The agony in Kyle's voice carries for miles. Thadden finally recovers from the sonic boom and prepares to launch himself at his foes again. "You shouldn't have done that." Kyle rips the ax out of his shoulder with one hand. With a deft grace, he throws it. Over and over, it turns. It imbeds into Romeelus' thigh making Romeelus drop to the ground. His bag of tricks is empty. His life is over. With amazement, the bounty hunter watches as Kyle's shoulder is healing by itself.

"Dung" The bounty hunter utters. Menacingly, Kyle hovers over the helpless man.

"Now, you'll learn what it's like to buuurrnn." There is an evil kind of joy in Kyle's tone. He raises his hands in the air. An arcane muttering begins. Kyle's' eyes flash open. Romeelus envisions his death when he watches a big ball of flame come spiraling towards him.

Suddenly, a figure leaps into the path. ARRRGGHHH! Thadden takes the brunt of the blast. Searing heat singes his skin, armor, and hair. He crashes to the ground and rolls back and forth until the fire on his back is out. Some heat finds its way around the thief and manages to strike Romeelus as well. As he moans from the pain, he can only imagine what pain his savior, his target, is in. Thadden passes out as the pain is too much. Blisters, huge, painful, cover his body. His face is OK, as he protected it with his hands. In a desperate stand of defiance, Jake stands protectively over Thadden's steaming body. Kyle surveys the people with a newfound look.

"It's strange that enemies will protect one another when another threat is present. I could kill you bounty hunter, and this frail human who is standing before me. But the courage you three have shown has opened a new light in me. Maybe, I can learn from this lesson. I shall study this new situation. Should I deem it necessary to come back and kill, then I will? But I fear this will not be the case. Good-bye for now, maybe we shall meet again, as allies." Kyle bows to the men. With a snap of his fingers, he leaves the men together. Jake glares at Romeelus.

"Don't worry; I'm in no condition to take the thief prisoner. Nor do I feel the need to kill him. I admit defeat. I cannot kill a man who has just saved my life. I cannot stay here and I wish that I could help Thadden, but I must go. Give him my regards. Tell him I plan on going to Belghar and canceling his contract." He tries to arise, but a surge of pain, much like a thousand stinging bees, forces him to lie back down. Jake scurries off. He comes back with Thadden's horse. His muscles bulge by lifting the singed thief and lays him across the horse's back. He lashes the staff to the side of the horse. More than he thinks the bounty hunter deserves, Jake, with an act of human kindness, speeds off and brings the Romeelus' horse. Silently he starts to help the man in the black armor to his feet. Weakly, Romeelus pushes up, and he is standing. Jake guides the man to his horse.

"I can make from here." Romeelus replies with dignity. He whispers into the horse's ear. It bends its legs down and lowers itself to allow its master to mount. Painfully, he gets onto the horse. "T-thank you!" He manages to say before his horse leads him out of the forest. Voices loud and near snap Jake to move into action; the guild's thieves have heard the commotion and have come out to investigate. Jake mounts his horse and goes before the thieves can even get close. Their prey is out of eyesight.

~ ~ ~

A soft, damp, cool sensation on her face causes Menecha to open her eyes. She has an image of Goblins applying some oil just before they are ready to cook her in a pot. Her heart fills with fear. "I must escape." She replies. With a start, she opens her eyes and sits up—a beautiful, caring face beams down at her.

"Be still, child; everything is alright. You are safe now." The voice is like a melody that soothes and calms Menecha.

"Where am I?"

"In the castle of Tyrella."

"How did I get here?" Menecha's memory doesn't remember anything but running away from the Goblins.

"You were rescued by our soldiers, who were patrolling the forest. We figured it was wise that you stay here until you got better."

"Who are you?" There is a slight pause. Realizing that the girl raises a question to her, and it needs an answer, Magdellaine replies.

"Just a soldier! I was the first person who came across you."

"Have I seen you before? You seem very familiar to me."

"Of course not, dear. It's just your mind playing tricks. We have never met before. Now, go back to sleep. You need your rest. When you wake up, there will be food waiting for you. You can ask more questions later." The general kisses the girl on the forehead and then leaves the room. A single tear escapes and runs down her cheek.

~ ~ ~

Belghar sits at his dinner table in a sad state. He awaits the return of Pontew. He left the castle to get news of the bounty hunter and the thief. His food is untouched, and by now, it is quite cold. The window is open, and a gust of winter air is enough to freeze anyone. He does not seem to notice, as his body surrounds itself in a red hue. Finally, a raven, black as the night sky, flies into the window and lands in front of the table Belghar pushes his hand forward. The window shuts as if a gale had closed it. The raven undergoes a strange transformation. Its beak moves in, and it begins to grow in height. Black, feathery wings fold in and instead become hands. Sharp pointy claws become legs that are solid yet bowed. Pontew, with his creepy, black eyes, the only thing that remains the same from his raven transformation, stands before Belghar and prepares to report.

A look of misery comes to the surface of his face.

"I have news of the bounty hunter and the thief." He waits for Belghar to begin his questions; "bounty hunter?", "thief?" but no questions come out of Belghar's mouth. With a resigned sigh, he continues. "It seems that it was the thief that rescued Jake and killed Drekkar. They were seen together and got into a fight with Kyle, the sentry who had escaped from the cell. The bounty hunter was there as well. I can only imagine why the bounty hunter never killed the thief. They were helping each other fight Kyle, who is now more than just a night watchman. Romeelus, the bounty hunter, must have just wanted to take your money, then end up helping the thief. I didn't see the necklace, though they did have the staff, and I presume the book. Perhaps, another mage is seeking the same items as you. If that's the case, he will soon be too powerful than even you. I don't see where Kyle fits in unless he just wants to pay the thief back for beating him. But where did he get his magical powers?" Belghar's fingers whiten as they tighten around the dinner fork. None of the news seems to please him. His eyes turn red, and the table catches ablaze. Soon, naught remains of the table except for burnt, smoldering wood.

"The girl, what of the girl?"

"Our nets of spies tell me that she is in the city Tyrella. She was able to escape from a group of Goblins."

"Pontew, I think it's time we showed this world the true meaning of the word power." Pontew has seen the look in Belghar's eyes before. The look will never know satisfaction until some bloodsheds. He shudders at what is to come ahead. "Get the legions ready. You are to be in full battle gear and be ready for a war. We're not going to stop until we have a total submission from every person in this world. They want a war. well now they have one." The window flies open. The ashes that were once a table sail into the wind. A full-fledged war is at hand.

Chapter 14

Feacon writhes on the floor in pain. He is preparing to spring at the opponent, but Xibnar is too fast. He is anticipating this maneuver and instead traps the cat in his old leash. Grinning triumphantly, the wizard's boot thuds into Feacon's head.

"I see the leash still fits on your miserable neck. It'll be a long time before I let you off of this leash again. I'm going to have to teach you a few more lessons about ownership first, though." The feline hero shakes his head to try to clear it.

"Thump"! Another boot finds its mark, and Feacon can only wait for a reprieve. Viciously the assault continues, as boot after boot connects with the cat until it is finally unconscious. Enjoying the spectacle, Xibnar sits down and waits for the cat to awake. He has more pain in store for the traitorous cat.

~   ~   ~

Jake rides non-stop until he arrives at The Smelly Goblin. He manages to help Thadden off the horse while a stable boy brings the horse to the livery. The innkeeper looks up, recognizes Thadden's body, and decides to show Jake to a decent room.

"Don't worry about payment, sir." The innkeeper babbles on as he leads the way. "Mr. Thadden is a frequent customer to this establishment, and his credit is good. I'll just put it on his account." Jake nods to the man, even though he heard not a word. His attention is currently on the badly burned body of his friend, and daughter's protector. A servant helps him carry Thadden into the room and put him on the bed.

"I'll send somebody up to look him over." With that, the innkeeper leaves Jake to tend to his friend. The innkeeper shakes his head at his foolishness.

"Once again, I lost the battle for a room, and this time the bastard wasn't even conscious." He lets out a big sigh. "Well, on the other hand, I've more business since the last time he came here, and my prices have gone up. Maybe it's in my best interest that I will be nice to this thief. It hasn't hurt me thus far. Of course, his friend, who arrived just before him, had just left me a healthy tip. That has helped me make my decision a little easier." He continues to ponder his rich future as he searches for a healer.

~ ~ ~

Just a few minutes before Thadden's arrival, Romeelus had wheeled into the stables. Despite all of his previous warnings, he knew he must rest. With the feeling of lead in his heart, the bounty hunter headed into the inn. He saw the same innkeeper that was there the last time he came looking for Thadden.

"Say, did you find your friend Thadden?" The innkeeper tried to remain calm.

"Yes!" Romeelus replied. His tone indicated that he did not wish to speak of the ordeal. Based on what happened last time, he wisely changed the topic.

"What room would you l-l-like?"

"A room with a bed, no windows, and near the bathhouses," the hunter replies. Romeelus' aching, burned body wanted to just collapse into the dreamy, soft, and warm realm of sleep.

"Here, take room 20. Here's the key to the bathhouse." Romeelus grunted thanks and then dropped two gold pieces onto the counter. He was gone before the innkeeper even realized it. Feeling very happy about the payment, he was delighted to have heard of Thadden and his generous but unusual friends.

~ ~ ~

The Duke of Millings'Dale, Clyde Le Frontaine, is a happy man. His daughter is about to marry a very influential prince. It is a marriage both sides of the family are glad to witness finally.

Having received no reply from Belghar, Clyde sent a request out to other nearby cities. After he waited for a few days, he finally received a response. A distant cousin of the Duke, who happened to be reasonably wealthy, provided the funds for Clyde's daughter's wedding. The happy couple awaits their big day.

Yes, the Duke is a happy man indeed. The wedding is ready for tomorrow. Already, caravans, and wagons, head to Millings'Dale to witness "the wedding of the century." None of the people seem to realize how true that statement will soon be.

~ ~ ~

In the city of Tyrella, there is a celebration of a different sort. After a quick, merciless victory over the Goblins, the queen's soldiers return home for some much-needed merriment. Only two of the soldiers have died, and three more are seriously wounded. The rest suffer from minor scrapes, bruises, and sore muscles. The Goblins are now no longer a threat to the city. As the soldiers drink and enjoy the women's pleasures, Menecha is in the throne room of the mighty Queen Tyrella.

"Good Morning child, I trust that you slept well?"

"Yes, I have your graciousness." She lowers her eyes to avoid staring at the beauty of the queen.

"So tell me, Menecha, that is your name, isn't it?" The queen's perfect eyes seem to see right through Menecha's soul.

"Y-y-yes it is. How did you..?"

"We are aware of a lot of things that go on outside this city. Your name is the least important of them. What is important is how you came to be captured by those Goblins? And why you were being held captive in the first place?"

Menecha briefly explains her situation and then bursts into tears. Magdellaine rushes forward to console her grieving child.

"We shall take care of the matter for you. In the meantime, how would you like to learn how to defend yourself? After all, you can't just get captured all the time. It's time you learned to protect yourself from both the evil creatures in this world and from the creatures that are called men." The queen rises from her throne in an excited flurry. "Magdellaine, see to it that you train her in the use of the sword and shield. In a few days, we shall take care of the upstart Belghar, and she better be ready by then." With that said, she turns on her heels and leaves the room.

"Come, child, there is much for you to learn." She helps Menecha to her feet, and they, too, are gone.

As nighttime falls on The Smelly Goblin, the innkeeper locks his doors. It is a ritual he does every night to prevent someone from sneaking into the inn. It is time for him to go to bed, and he can't watch the door and sleep at the same time. His servants see to it that nobody leaves their designated sleeping quarters. As he blows out the candle on the desk, a sudden chill enters the room. Goosebumps appear on his arms, and his hair starts to stand on end. He sees a shadow on the wall in front of him. The shadow is walking and appears to be carrying an ax and staring directly at the spot where the shadow's shadow belongs; he sees nothing. "Clump"! "Clump"! The sound of footsteps mirrors the movement of the shadows' feet. The shadow heads down the hall. The candles that line the hallway go out as the shadow passes by. "Clump"! "Clump"! The innkeeper runs forward before the darkness can overwhelm him. "Clump"! "Clump"! The shadow rounds the corner, and the innkeeper is suddenly afraid in the dark. "Clump"! "Clump"! Sweat bursts out of his pores, and his heart begin to race. Fear, the terrible beast that thrives on other people's misery, laughs at the innkeeper as he begins to panic. "Clump"! "Clump"! He thinks back to the history of the inn and wishes he had changed the name. "Thump"! "Thump"! "Clump"! "Clump"! The sound of the footsteps seems to be getting closer. Although his eyes have gotten used to the darkness, the innkeeper doesn't know where he can go. "Clump"! "Clump"! "Thump"! "Thump"! "Thump"!

The sound is right in front of him. He turns as if to run. A hand grabs onto his shirt. He turns around to face the creature. A face looms before him, hideous and evil. It has bloodshot eyes and pointy teeth. The nose is big and deformed. The mouth opens up to release a snarl. The innkeeper begins to scream. "Shump"! An ax severs his head from the body. No scream had a chance to escape. The Goblinoid creature grabs the keyring from the lifeless, headless corpse. On the tenth anniversary of its death, the Goblin brother has arisen to begin a new carnage. Death is coming to all that reside in its home. In the darkness, it heads to the first room. It's heavy footsteps precede it. "Clump"! "Clump"!

Chapter 15

Flutes, banjos, and harps make merry music, as the Duke's daughter's wedding to the charming prince gets underway. Children play, and young girls fantasize about their marriage. Visions of handsome princes and stunning dresses weave their way into their imaginations and hearts. They giggle and whisper to one another. A gong, loud, commanding, stops all activity. The children stop playing; the girls stop their giggling. A silence, a hush, cascades over the crowd. The anticipation is heavy.

"Prepare to meet the Prince of Qooshar." Trumpets blare at the name as the prince steps into the vast hall. The crowd lets out several "ooohh's" and "aaahhh's," and one woman swoons at the magnificent sight. With a perfect smile and a debonair wave, he stands before the bishop and awaits his bride. The woman revives and is on her feet when it's the bride's turn to enter. Once again, a hush falls over the crowd.

"Now we present to you in all of her beauty, Brianna, daughter of Duke Le Fontaine." Trumpets blare, voices sing in merriment. The doors swing open. A light shines brightly in the dim room. Brianna steps through the light, like an angel descending from heaven. Her gown is exquisite. Fragments of gold sparkle in the light, the crowd applauds. A tiara, pure silver, encrusted with several diamonds, sends a rainbow of light in many directions. Again the woman faints. With a slight bow to the crowd, Brianna stands next to the prince. They look at each other with love and lust that has never been seen before in Millings'Dale. The bishop opens up his book and begins the ceremony.

"I stand before you today to marry two people. Two people who will enter wedlock and forever stay by each others' side. Before I begin the vows, I must know if there are any rings?"

"Right here!" Clyde Le Fontaine speaks up. He holds out a pillow made out of the most delicate lace.

"And is there anybody who does not want the marriage to take place? Speak up or forever hold your peace." There is no response. A sudden clamor outside stirs the crowd as they look towards the door.

"Don't worry; my men have the situation, whatever it may be, well in hand." The Duke replies with an air of confidence. The crowd relaxes, and the guards take their defensive positions around the couple.

"Very well then, do you Prince Lotham take Brianna to be your lawfully wedded wife?"

"I do." The prince replies with sincerity. The priest speeds up the ceremony. The noise outside gets louder with the sound of men fighting, and the screaming carrying into the castle's silent halls. The bishop clears his throat and then continues the ceremony. A slight murmur escapes from the crowd. The lady who fainted finally comes to once more.

"Do you, Brianna, take Prince Lotham, to be your lawfully wedded husband?"

"I do!" She replies with tears in her eyes.

"Would you put the rings on each other's fingers?" They do so quickly, sensing the need for urgency. "I now pronounce you man and wife. You may kiss the bride." The crowd applauses, but not as loudly as they want to as the noise is right outside the door. The door bursts open, and soldiers run into the room. Soldiers stand in front of the married couple as the Duke tries to rush them out of the back door.

"There will be no escape for thee!" A voice snarls. Part of the ceiling comes crashing down. Belghar glares at everyone as all eyes turn to him. Pontew is at his side. All escape routes are blocked. Although no weapons are unsheathed, he looks very, very dangerous. The wedding is over.

~   ~   ~

In the haunted inn, Thadden lies unconscious on a bed. Jake stands protectively at the door while a healer tends to the thief's burns. The healer mutters a few arcane words and closes his eyes. Soon he reopens his eyes, holds his palms in front of his mouth then breathes into them—a cone of frost forms into each palm. Muttering a few more syllables that Jake can't understand, the healer places his hands over Thadden's body. Suddenly flame leaps off of the thief's body and surrounds the priest's hands. Once his hands are burning, the healer then slams them together. "Whoosh"! The flames extinguish, and no burns remain on Thadden. Opening his pouch, the healer takes out some smelling salt. Thadden's eyes flutter open when the salt reaches his nose. The healer gets up.

"He is fine now. See that he gets some rest. You could use some yourself." Receiving no answer from Jake, the priest leaves the room. Pushing himself into a sitting position, Thadden looks around the room.

"How did I get here? What happened to my burns?" He remembers that his partner can no longer speak and asks no more questions. Jake's look of exhaustion tells him all the answers.

"Thank you, Jake, for everything! You are tired. Please lie down. You deserve it." With a nod and a grunt, Jake hands the staff and robe over to Thadden. When his head reaches the soft, welcoming pillow, he falls fast asleep. Thadden places the wooden staff and the robe onto the floor. He doesn't feel the need to hold onto magic. It always has to give him nightmares.

~   ~   ~

Directly across from Thadden's room is Romeelus. Although he has wounds, he feels fine. His wounds slowly mend. He laughs as he thinks back to his younger days as a beginner bounty-hunter.

"The secret to survival is always to have an edge." His master would always tell him. It was no fluke when Romeelus found out about a great ax that would always return to its master, provided that the master was still alive and that the ax could also provide healing for the wielder. The healing was by far faster and more efficient than

trying to find a healer, especially in the middle of a fight. One of his contracts was the owner of the ax. Romeelus took a month to plan his assassination. It was an easy kill, and ever since that day, the ax belongs to Romeelus.

"I guess I still hold an edge, master." He replies cynically. As he waits for his wounds to heal, he thinks about his adversaries. "I think I may have to cancel that contract on the thief; I do owe him my life. But where do I go from here?" He falls asleep with that question still lingering in his mind.

~ ~ ~

"Clang"! "Clang"! The sound of clashing steel rings in the training yard of Tyrella's castle.

"Not bad! Menecha. I'll make a warrioress out of you yet." Magdellaine encourages as she swings her sword at the novice again. They've been practicing all day. Starting with wooden swords, Magdellaine taught Menecha the basics. After several raps on the knuckles, the young girl learned how to parry very quickly. The queen came in and instantly told them to switch to steel weapons.

"The girl will have to learn with steel, or she won't learn at all. Maybe after you lop off a few fingers, she'll learn to get better." The queen's insensitive remark awakens Menecha from her funk. Since then, the two women have been using steel. Menecha's arm is tired, but she knows she must press on. Magdellaine can sense the girl's fatigue and is slowing down to compensate. "Clang"! "Clang"! "Thump"! Magdellaine's sword bites into the wood as Menecha jumps clear and nicks the general with her weapon.

"I did it, I did it. I finally got you." Menecha starts to jump up and down; she slips and falls to the ground. Cold steel presses against her throat.

"Don't you ever parade around like that again? You do that in combat, and you'll be dead shortly after." Magdellaine nicks Menecha's throat. A slight trickle of blood appears. "I shouldn't have allowed her even to get me. I have to take my mind off the fact that she is my daughter. If I pamper her, she won't get anywhere." Magdellaine painfully reminds herself. She holds a hand out to the girl.

"Ready to go again?" With a feeling of respect and a display of courage, Menecha gets back to her feet and grabs her sword. She nods her head and grins. The sparring match resumes.

~ ~ ~

Chaos erupts in Millings'Dale. At the sight of the blocked escape, panic uses its magic. Soldiers swarm forward. Their objective is to push Belghar and his horde back outside. They hope to allow a pathway for the citizens to flee. With a hollow laugh, Belghar retreats. Blades hack and slash as the sky rains blood. The soldiers fight courageously, but it is in vain. The people that manage to make it into the sunlight die quickly in cold blood. Pontew is a symbol of magnificence; seemingly defenseless, the Duke's charge at him only to meet their death. As the blades descend on Belghar's aide, they are quickly knocked aside by his fists. Two thunderous punches to the soldiers' hearts and they die. A child wails for his mother. An arrow, sleek and fast, strikes the child in the throat. The crying is no longer anymore. Man by man, the Duke's last soldier finally gives one last grunt and then dies. Of the weddings' inhabitants, all that remains is the Duke, Brianna, and Prince Lotham.

"Well, well, well, Clyde Le Fontaine, it has been a while since I have seen you last. Let's see when was it?"

"Two and a half years ago! At the Belgharian Yearly Festival!" Pontew whispers into Belghar's ear.

"Oh, yes! The Belgharian Yearly Festival. Didn't the Duke get himself a little tipsy and make a big fool of himself?" Pontew nods. The Duke's eyes burn holes into his shoes. His complexion is waning. All color drains as he gets white as a sheet.

"Come, come, Clyde. You should be happy. Your beautiful daughter has just gotten married." HA! HA! It is a time for merriment and singing. Why isn't there any singing?" He asks the question teasingly.

"Because you massacred all of my guests," Clyde answers angrily.

"I massacred all of your guests?" He puts on a look of surprise. "You don't think I killed these people, do you?"

"Well, I certainly didn't put a sword in that woman. Or how about that child? He was just an innocent little boy; now he's dead. Now you're going to tell me that you didn't kill them. I think you're sicker than any man I ever met." The Duke spits. Spittle flies and lands on Belghar's cheek. He casually wipes it away.

"Do you want to know who killed them, Clyde? Well, I'll tell you. You killed them, Clyde. You sent your foolish soldiers to their graves by sending them at me, instead of surrendering quietly. I wasn't planning on killing anyone. I was only going to take prisoners. But you decided to play the hero. Well, look where it got you." Belghar points to the mound of dead bodies, which already has flown for tenants. "Look at these bodies, and go to your grave knowing that you murdered all of these people." Belghar raises his hands and pushes them forward. Belghar's powerful magic lifts Clyde off the ground. His body slams into the wall. With his spine broken, he slumps to the ground. Blood bubbles out of the mouth.

"Noooo!" Brianna wails. Tears are flowing down her cheeks; she runs towards her dead father. Lotham charges Belghar with a scream. He almost makes it, but a weird sensation invades his brain.

"Stop!" Pontew commands. Not wanting to but having no willpower to resist, Lotham stops. Sweat pours down his face. Suddenly, with the last scream, Lotham dies, as his head explodes from the pressure.

"You! Soldier! Get the girl. I have some use for her." Belghar grins. At the sight of her beloved dying, Brianna has nothing left to live for. She retrieves her father's sword from his scabbard. Before the soldier can reach her, she plunges her body onto the weapon. In so doing Brianna robs Belghar of a prize and some perverse pleasure, and dies in a bloody heap. Belghar's face contorts with rage.

"Burn these bodies. I want everyone to see my carnage. I want everyone to Beware." With no remorse, Belghar leaves the scene. All that remains is a pyre of bodies.

Chapter 16

A scream, hideous and terrifying, awakes a lot of sleeping individuals at the Smelly Goblin. Thadden and Jake bolt upright, staring into the darkness of their room. In a matter of seconds, Thadden dresses and has his rapier at the ready. It isn't long before Jake is up, and he clenches the stolen staff in his hands.

"That scream was on this floor. I think we better investigate." Jake nods in agreement. Only darkness and a gust of chilly air enter the room. "The torches are out. We must search in the darkness. Be alert; who knows what we're up against now." As he enters the hallway, Thadden can feel the oppressing silence and see nothing but blackness. A smell, foul and fresh, reaches his nostrils. It is the smell of everyone and everything's downfall. It is the smell of Death. After adjusting his eyes to the darkness and keeping his senses on full alert, Thadden turns left and heads down the corridor. Jake quietly follows behind him. The smell gets stronger and stronger as they walk further and further down the hall. A knob turns. Both Thadden and Jake tense and hold their weapons up, ready for an attack. A figure wearing black steps out of the shadows; he notices them and then tries to shut the door. Thadden's foot stops the door. Putting his weight into the door, he enters the room. A very familiar figure stands before him, holding a glowing, green ax.

"I was just going to check on the noise. If you don't believe me, then see for yourself." He gestures for the two men to enter and search the room. "I guarantee you'll find nothing of interest."

"Oh, but we have found something! A person who has been trying to kill me for money is a fascinating thing. How about you, Jake? What do you think?" Jake nods his head, and a row of white teeth flash in the darkness, indicating his pleasure of the find.

"Listen, thief, I had a contract to kill you, but now I've changed my mind. You have proved yourself more than just a great fighter. You have honor, which I, although you might doubt it, do appreciate a great deal. I have no further wish to harm you or your friend. I plan on going to Belghar and canceling my contract. That is something I have not done in my history of bounty hunting. Before you kicked my door in, I was checking out the scream. I still intend to do that. And I don't want to fight you to save someone."

"One question, first! What have you done with my cat? Does the man we encountered have anything to do with it?"

"The man stole the cat shortly after I took it from you. I have no idea who he is and what he plans to do with the cat."

Thadden smiles knowingly; his guess was correct.

"I had assumed so; that's why I took the fireball for you. You were the only man with the information, and I couldn't afford to have you killed." Thadden sheaths his rapier. "I don't want to fight you anymore. I'm not sure who would win that battle. We were also going to investigate the scream. If you would like, you could come along with us. A third person, I'm sure, couldn't hurt." Sheathing his magical ax, Romeelus smiles and joins the two men. Feeling the safety in numbers, the men head out into the hall in search of the murderer.

~ ~ ~

In queen Tyrella's chambers, a conversation of different sorts is going on.

"How is your daughter doing? Has she mastered the art of the sword yet?"

"She is doing well, your grace. Her sword fighting is coming along well. She should be ready for the battle with Belghar. Is there any word on Belghar?"

"You mean, is there any word on your husband and the thief? No, there is no word except that Belghar doesn't have them. However, I did get some disturbing news. It seems that Belghar has other concerns now. He went to the wedding at Millings' Dale and slaughtered everybody, including the Duke.

I guess we shall be at war after all, and it'll be sooner than expected. Now, let's get back to the girl. Bring her in here, and five of your best swordsmen. It's time to see just what your daughter has learned. Have you told her the truth yet?" Magdellaine face pales, confirming the Queen's suspicions. "Well, no matter. I'm sure she finds out from somebody else, sometime in the future." As Magdellaine leaves to retrieve the girl and the fighters, she starts to wonder if that "somebody else" might just happen to be the queen herself.

~ ~ ~

Menecha is enjoying herself as she practices with her sword. A surge of excitement and enjoyment fills her inner being whenever she picks up her weapon.

"No wonder Thadden loves to fight. It makes you feel superior to those who can't fight." At the mention of the name, she bursts into tears. The weapon clatters to the ground noisily. There is a knock on the door, and then it is opened. Menecha does not care who it is; her loneliness cannot be filled by whoever is coming into her room.

"Are you alright, Mench?" Magdellaine's voice asks soothingly. Menecha stops crying, not from the vote, but from what the spokesperson said.

"I'm fine," she puts on a brave front as she wipes away her tears. "I was just thinking about Thadden and my father, and I burst into tears. I miss them both so much." Magdellaine, oblivious to the blunder, speaks up about the reason why she is there.

"The queen wants to see you. I believe she wants to see what you have learned with the sword. I told her you were doing great, and your learning very fast. I, of course, was telling the truth." Menecha blushes as she straps her weapon on.

"Could I talk to you after, Magdellaine? I need to talk to somebody to ease my loneliness. You see, my mother left when I was a little girl, and I've been thinking about her a lot lately."

"Sure, Mench, we'll talk after we see the queen." Magdellaine blunders again but doesn't catch on. "I have to go get some swordsmen, so I'll be right back. When I get back, we'll go to the queen. Just be calm; I know you won't disappoint me." Magdellaine leaves. With a feeling of exaltation, she prepares for both events. The fighting she can handle. It's approaching Magdellaine, about calling Menecha, that will be tough. "Mench" It's a term Menecha's mother always used. The coincidence, Menecha thinks, is too apparent to ignore.

"I am going to have a fun day today, and maybe that missing piece in my heart will finally go away".

~   ~   ~

In the inn, a long-dead corpse is about to commit another murder. Murdering twenty people so far, it has had a productive night. It walks by a room with arguing voices. It will get that room later. The two to one odds it doesn't like, yet. But this creature gets stronger with every kill; it will be back. After all, it has all night. Ahead it sees the door of its next victim. It's decayed, and a rotting hand tests the knob. The door is locked. An evil chuckle and the creature produces the key ring. The locked door becomes unlocked soon, and the filthy Goblin, with an ax in hand, enters the room. With its infra-vision, it has no problem seeing the slumbering guests. They had heard the scream, but like most people, they locked their doors and fell asleep, feeling safe. It creeps up to the bed. A couple, and a one-year-old infant, lay sleeping in the ground. The creature remembers being young once. It picks up the baby and cradles it in its arms. It was young once. The human boys would always tease and bully him. Only until he beat them up did they stop their acts. But they always ridiculed him and laughed when he wasn't around. Even his brother participated in the humiliation. With these terrible thoughts in mind, the creature becomes enraged. It takes the infant's head, and with its strong hands, crushes the head like a hammer would a tomato. It throws the body to the ground, grabs its ax, and swings down onto the male. "Shuummp"! The ax strikes the neck, severing the head from the body.

Gwyninne has a beautiful dream. In it, she sees a big family house with a well-kept garden. There are tomatoes, potatoes, corn, turnip, cucumbers, squash, and plenty of carrots. A big, strong, supportive husband is standing by her side. "Oh, how I love eating carrots." She says in her sleep. She envisions many other kids, too. Their house will get bigger with each kid while she gets older. She can see her grandkids, and tears form in her eyes. Her dream is so vivid, real, and everything she desires, but her body tells her something is wrong. She opens her eyes. A creature hideous looms over her with an ax held high. It is grinning. She lets out a scream. Fear of her some harm coming to her baby saves her life.

"Nothing must happen to my baby." Adrenaline surges into her and helps her roll off the bed, out of the way of the ax. It imbeds itself into the wooden frame of the bed. Alone, she hopes she can save her baby.

~ ~ ~

As the trio continues down the hall, a scream, female, provides them a clue. "The scream came from behind us. Somebody must've slipped by us when we were in the room arguing." Thadden states. With a fantastic burst of speed, all three men sprint back. Panic hits them as there is no more noise. They might be too late to save the person, and they still don't know what room it is. As if in answer, another scream pinpoints the destination.

"Third room on the left," Romeelus speaks. The three men run for all their worth.

~ ~ ~

The creature fights with its weapon as it tries to dislodge it from the bed. It swung too hard and didn't intend to miss the target. Gwyninne stands up and scans the room. Dead eyes from her husband's decapitated head, staring back at her. She can see the creature trying to get its weapon loose. Running by the beast, which is oblivious to her actions, she looks in horror at her baby's crushed head. With a feeling of rage and sadness, she screams. She knows it is too late and must now save herself. Just as she runs to the door, there's a snarl, and the Goblin wrenches the weapon free. It scans the room and spies its victim running out the door.

~ ~ ~

Thadden, Romeelus, and Jake get to the door just as Gwyninne steps out into the hallway. Jake runs to her aid. Thadden and Romeelus, with weapons in hand, plunge into the room. They are appalled by what they see. Blood is everywhere in the room. There is a savage on the creature's face. It wields an ax. With a scream, Thadden charges it. Romeelus, seeing the dreadful sight, remembers the story behind the inn and wishes he had kept his promise about not coming to this inn ever again. Then all fear disappears as he remembers who he is. He is Romeelus, the bounty hunter. With his identity regained, he enters the room to help his new companion.

Chapter 17

An hour after the soldiers' request, and Menecha, there is a knock on the Queen's door.

"Come in!" she replies haughtily. Magdellaine enters with Menecha at her side and six soldiers in tow. "Ah, it is so nice to see everybody here. As I'm sure some of you know, we are going to have a little sword practice. Magdellaine will stand at my side; we must witness this event together and from the same perspective. Now, Menecha, I want you to stand in the middle of the circle that I have laid out." Menecha spots a group of oil lanterns, lined up to form a circle. She steps inside and draws her weapon. "Ahh! It's good to see that you are such an eager child; let's see if you can prove yourself. Guards, kill her!"

"No!" Magdellaine yells. She looks up at Tyrella, horror-stricken. "Are you mad? I can see a little sparring match, but a fight to the death, against so many odds. What was the point of me even teaching her?"

"Does not our entire army base itself on fighting against impossible odds? Do we not pit ourselves against foes twice, or even three times our number, and come out with a few scratches? Besides, I see that these men are not your best. But they'll have to do. Are you going to continue to argue with your queen, or are you going to show that you have some confidence in our warrioress?" The queen's demeanor tells Magdellaine that she better trust Tyrella. "Good! Guards, kill her, or be put to the whip in the dungeons." There is a mad scramble for weapons as the guards start to charge. Standing in the circle, calm, serene, Meanecha waits for the men to come at her. She will not lose. She has too many unanswered questions. Questions that will need an answer when this contest is over. Seeing no threat before them, the soldiers eagerly go in for the kill. But Menecha is no fool. Many times, Magdellaine's face loomed over hers, telling her that there were no fighting rules. With a salute to her weapons teacher and the queen, Menecha kicks one of the lamps. It flies upwards and smashes into a soldier's face. He forgets about his battle as he catches on fire. He drops to the floor and rolls. He manages to get the fire out at the cost of his face. It blackens and is bubbly. He lies still, waiting for the pain to end. The other men hesitate to approach. The soldiers realize they must attack Menecha with caution. Slowly they position themselves around her. Five men and no more tricks, Menecha's odds seem grim.

The thief dives at the slobbering creature. It waits for his move, and with surprising swiftness, it ducks. Thadden smashes into the wall and falls to the floor. Romeelus swings his giant ax. "Clang"! Sparks fly off of the weapons as the two magical axes battle it out. Reacting on their own and not by their master's wishes, the weapons fight each other. Romeelus and the creature do all they can to avoid the other sword when it out-maneuvers its opponent. Romeelus spies Thadden getting back to his feet and knows he must stall. Picking up his foot with the cast, he kicks the creature. The cast shatters and does no real damage.

"I was done healing anyway." Romeelus remarks to himself.

Thadden prepares to swing at the Goblin's back.

"Not the most honorable technique, but it's not an honorable creature that we are facing." He turns the rapier. "Clang", "Snap" His weapon breaks in two. The creature, or rather its sentient weapon, was able to parry the attack. Its speed was phenomenal. Romeelus charges at his foe with murder in his eyes, the Goblin, it moves deftly aside. His charge carries him into Thadden. Together, they fall in a heap. Victoriously, it stands over them and prepares the killing stroke.

~   ~   ~

Meanwhile, Jake stands just outside the room, tending to the girl. She babbles incoherently. Violently, she shakes. He holds her in his arms and comforts her. He wishes he could speak. He wishes he knew what the staff could do. It remains useless in his hands. She begins to cry. His hand grips onto the team until his knuckles whiten. Soothingly, he strokes her back and rocks her back and forth.

"At least her shaking stopped,"he thinks. "If only I could speak. I might be able to find the words to comfort her. Was she alone? Or was she with a loved one? If I could speak, I could find out these answers. Damn it! I wish I can talk". He yells in his mind loudly. His arm goes numb. "How long have I been holding that staff this tightly." He tries to let go of the weapon, but it remains in his grasp. The numbness travels up to his elbow, then his shoulder. He begins to panic.

"How can I help her if I can't even help myself?" He starts to shake his hand, in hopes that the staff will fall. It does not. The numbness travels up his neck, throat and stops inside his mouth. As he envisions his death due to lack of oxygen, the sensation changes to that of tranquility. A voice inside his mind speaks:

"Speak! I have given you the ability to do so when you are holding this staff."

"Maam," to his amazement, she looks up at him. "I could not speak until now. Some magic has allowed me to do so for the time being. We share similar pain. My wife left me to raise my daughter by myself. Now some cruel man has kidnapped my daughter. I was at the mercy of a torturer in the dungeons of Belghar. If you need a shoulder, you can use mine. If you need a set of ears to listen to, you can use mine. I want to help you." With tears bursting out from her eyes, she hugs Jake's hug. In Jake, she saw her husband. Her husband had not died but instead transferred himself into this man's body. She saw a man speak with no tongue; in her panic driving mind, she saw her way out. She sees her husband. He is still alive. Perhaps, they'll have another baby. She knows it'll look the same. With these thoughts in mind, she touches the staff and then falls asleep.

Jake felt her essence flow into him the minute she touched the staff. With her asleep, he can help Thadden and Romeelus. Jake looks inside to see the creature looming over the pair. Grasping the staff with two hands, he lets out a yell.

"Stop!" With a look of dismay, the Goblin turns in time to feel a strong gale of wind pick him up and slam him against the wall. It barely misses the two men, who struggle to disentangle one another and manage to stand up. The creature gets up quicker. It starts to run at him. He waits and then forms his mouth into an "O" shape. With a simple blow and the word "chill," a ball of frost streaks towards it. The creature and its weapon stop in mid-run. The frost strikes it square in the chest and put such frigid temperatures on the heart and body that the body collapses. Thadden kicks the body. It topples over frozen solid.

"Now, can we get out of here?" He asks the pair, who stare at him with disbelief.

~   ~   ~

At the queen's chamber, another battle is taking place. Menecha stands at the ready. None of her opponents dare make the first move.

"I don't have all day," she reminds the guards. The taunt enrages one guard, who makes a swing. She parries it quickly. "I'll wait until they all start swinging. Then I'll make my move. "Come on, you bunch of imbeciles. Can't five of you take on one little, novice girl in a simple sword fight?" With their egos wounded, the men finally go into action. She ducks the high swings, parries two low swings, and then steps sideways out of the fifth man's sword stroke. He pays for this maneuver as she slashes across his stomach. His gut slices open, and intestines fall out. She catches his body as it falls forward, and using its momentum; she pushes it sideways. It falls on top of one of the guards. He tries to catch the body of his comrade; as he does so, his weapon drops, and he leaves himself open. Menecha drives her sword forward; it penetrates through his shoulder and pokes out the other side.

The other two men plan their attack. They come in when she is trying to yank her sword out. She drops to the floor and grabs the guard's weapon. Stabbing where she used to be, one of the guards manages to skewer the wounded guard who has her sword sticking out of him. Both his body and the body he was holding up thump to the ground. The other guard, remembering her last trick, was waiting for this maneuver. He stopped at the last minute of his charge and swung downwards. He nicks her leg as she rolls out of the way.

On her feet, she swings her sword twice. Both hit and one more guard is dead. The only guard left is the only one who has hit her. Staying within her circle, she waits for him to attack. He also is waiting for her to attack. She is planning to hack at him wildly, but then he speaks his arrogance.

"Forget it, wench, you aren't going to win. You can't reach me, and you can't come out of your circle. I'm on to your tricks. If you surrender, you will lose with dignity. If not, I'll attack you with my crossbow and wait for you to die." His arrogance causes his mistake. He is not looking at her when he loads his crossbow.

"There are no rules in a fight." She replies with fury. She leaps at him. Before he can react, she is on his back. She places her sword against his throat. "I'm on to your tricks as well, soldier." With a slight yank, she slices the throat. He staggers forward, clawing at the air. His knees collapse. Menecha stands on the back of his legs and pushes him forward. Using his body as a bridge, she steps back into the circle. He gurgles one last time and then is still. Silence follows for twenty seconds.

"Simply amazing! Her feet never touched the floor the entire time she was out of the circle. I see your student has learned a lot in the time she's been here."

"But why waste six of our guards? Aren't we going to need everyone that we have for the fight with Belghar?"

"If they couldn't handle a simple little girl, what good are they against other men? Besides, she'll be taking over their positions. It's a lot cheaper to feed one girl than it is to feed six men. Think of it as economics. The demonstration is over. I do hope you enjoy your discussion this afternoon. Good-day!"

Magdellaine, and Menecha, exit the room. One holds her head in ecstasy, the other in shame. "How can I explain to Menecha that I could not come back?" Magdellaine does not know, but she knows that she must find the answer in the next few minutes.

~ ~ ~

Elsewhere on the road of Farlairve, a vast, menacing army march forward to their destination. Amid the warriors, a group of men carries their leader, Belghar. On a throne, he sits. At his side is his formidable and mysterious aide, Pontew. Both men stare forward.

"You know Pontew; it makes me feel young again, to be on this war campaign. It makes me think back on the old days when we would go out and slaughter thousands of men on the battle-field. I used to love the thrill of victory. Each sword stroke, and each magical spell of mine, would rip into the enemy and send them scattering. And of course, you were a sight to behold on the battlefield as well. Do you remember those days, Pontew?" He stares down upon his aide and waits for an answer. No answer seems to find its way out from his mouth. Instead, Pontew stares solemnly at his feet, watching each step going forward.

Pontew?" Belghar tries to snap Pontew out of his daze.

"Hmmmm." Pontew responds, looking up at Belghar.

"I said, doesn't this remind you of the old days?"

"Does what, sir?" He asks, still in a daze.

"War! Marching! Killing?" Belghar waves his hands frantically. He seems on the verge of frustration.

"Oh, Yes, I suppose so, sir," Pontew responds. He goes back to staring at his feet.

Belghar's gaze penetrates deep into Pontew's thoughts. What he finds is appalling.

"You don't approve of me doing this, do you, Pontew?" His eyes burn into the back of Pontew's skull, awaiting his response.

"Not sir," is the response.

"Oh! And why is that?" His tone mocks.

"Well, sir, what exactly is the point?"

"The point?" Belghar slips back into his habit. It is a habit that Belghar generally loses once he is at war.

"The point to this whole bloody war? Pontew says incredulously. People are dying for reasons that they don't even know. A thief steals a necklace from you and takes away some young girl, whose only interest you show is for common pleasure. Well, I don't see why a war has to start over something as small as that. If you want pleasure in somebody young, why don't you seek that boy servant of yours? I know he'll gladly oblige you." Pontew has reached his boiling point.

"How dare you!" Belghar's fist slams Pontew to the ground. "What I do is my own business. I don't have to answer to you, nor anyone else. You should do well to remember that fealty oath you took. If you don't follow my orders, then I will have you executed. Do I make myself clear"? The army halts. All eyes stare towards the conflict.

"Yes, you do, sir. Yes, you do." Pontew's eyes glare back as he rubs a sore jaw. Pontew finally sees what madness he was loyal to.

"Good!" Belghar smiles his usual "I have won" smile and continues to go on. The army begins his movement forward. In the mind of Pontew rages an inner conflict so fierce, it makes a thousand-year war seem calm.

"Ganshrag is in our sights, sir," a scout reports.

"Good! Men, prepare for war. Were going to show this realm, what it means to know fear." With a joyous hoop, the men head for the town.

Chapter 18

In the aftermath of the fight in the eerie inn, Thadden, Romeelus, and Jake make time to relax. Gwyninne lies in Jake's arms. She sleeps peacefully and surrounds herself in his warmth. The three men speak in whispers to not arouse the woman who has just lost her husband and child.

"How did you learn to speak?" They stare at Jake in amazement.

"I think it was this staff. I was holding on to it and wished I could speak so I could try to comfort this lady. At one moment, I felt a terrifying numbness start from my fingers and travel up my arm. It didn't stop though, it went up to my neck and throat, and then it was gone when it was in my mouth. A voice spoke at that moment and told me that my wish would happen. As long as I hold this staff, I can speak. Otherwise," he drops the staff and continues to speak, but no words come out. He picks up the team. "See what I mean."

"I wonder what other properties that staff contains. It is worth something to someone. Who did you steal it for?" Romeelus asks, remembering the incident at the thieves' guild.

"We stole it for a man who is holding Jake's daughter hostage. She was the girl that I was with when you took Feacon from me."

"Feacon? Is that the cat's name?" Thadden nods. "I regret having done that now. When someone pays me to do something, I do it to the best of my ability. How did you come about that cat anyway? Was it yours from the start?"

"No, Feacon and I go a long way back. I shall tell you the story, and then we should get going. We must be in Gena tonight. We must strike a bargain with a madman." Letting fatigue seep out of their bones, the men sit back and await Thadden's tale.

~　~　~

As the men listen to the tale, there is another tale about to start in a castle many miles away. Magdellaine and Menecha make it back to Menecha's room minutes after the young girls' glorious victory. As soon as the door closes, both ladies stare at one another. The color drains from Magdellaine's face.

"Please sit down," she gestures towards the bed. Menecha does so. "I have some news to tell you that you need to know."

"I don't suppose it has anything to do with you being my mother, does it?"

"Have I slipped up that much? No matter, since you know, then I might as well start telling you my story."

"It starts way back when you were born. Your father and I were very proud. It was like a dream came true. We cried tears of joy when you were born. We were so happy for the first five years. Then something happened. Jake would celebrate your birth with all of his buddies by going to the bar. Your father started coming home, drunk every night. He would always be loud, and when I'd tell him to quiet down, he'd just yell at me even louder. I could see in his eyes that he wanted to hit me, but that was against your father's nature. His mind, even in that drunken stupor, would always be able to keep your father on the right track. I got tired of seeing him waste his life away, and our money too, so I told him that I would enlist in the Tyrellian army. That, for him, was the last straw. He threatened me and told me to get out of the house. I was frightened. Not just for myself, but you as well. As soon as I gathered my things and went outside, your father came after me. He was crying. He tried to come after me and talk to me, but I was now too angry to listen. I still loved him, but I couldn't live there anymore. That was the last time I saw him, and you."

"Through the network of spies that we maintain, I had been able to keep track of both of you. I heard that he had stopped drinking the day after I left.

I waited and waited for him to contact me, but I never heard a word. I assumed that he wanted nothing to do with the woman who deserted him." Tears form in Magdellaine's eyes.

"That's not the way it was. Dad has always loved you and still does. He would always tell me stories about you. Dad was very proud of you. He would cry whenever he thought back on that night. Over the years, it was obvious you were never coming back. I think he blames himself to this day. My father wished that you would have forgiven him and come back. I realize why you left, and I forgive you. We both just want you back." Hearing words that she never thought she would ever hear, Magdellaine, the fearless heroine, bursts into tears. The two women hug each other and cry. Perhaps, there is always a time when a person faces a new reality, a new light, and a new life can begin.

~ ~ ~

Shortly after leaving Xibnar, Feacon felt the first signs of hunger set in. In its great escape, the cat had forgotten to make sure that he ate. It remembered a time when it could hunt and wished it were big cat again. A small mouse crosses its path. Perhaps a hunt can still ensue. Feacon once again became the king of the jungle. Just as he was about to pounce upon the unsuspecting victim, a mouth-watering smell challenged him to follow. Through the use of teleportation, he made it to the site of the scent in no time. The presence of hunger had overtaken Feacon. Over an open fire, fresh, pink fish seemed to dare him to take it. Feacon leaped and snatched the Salmon. A voice interrupted.

"Where do you plan on taking our fish?" A greasy bearded, yellow-toothed man asked. He stared straight into Feacon's eyes. Feacon tried to back up and sensed other men behind him. His hair had stood on end. With a nasty hiss and an arched back, he tried to scare the men away from his prize.

"Well, boys, it looks like we are gonna have us a little cat meat to go with our fish." The two men, younger in comparison, grinned with amusement. Feacon prepares to teleport away. He hoped it will be in time, as one sword stroke could have killed him outright. "Whooosh"! "Thud"! One of the men dropped dead when a sling stone found its mark and crushed his temple. More aware of a more significant threat, the two men stared into the trees, in the direction of the stone.

"Hey coward, come out here and fight us like men. Don't hide behind the trees. I want to see if you can handle yourself, man to man." There was silence. Feacon had been eager to see the individual as well. His curiosity keeps his feet on one spot. *"Coward"! "Coward"!* He yelled into the trees. *"...ard, ard"* echoed back to him.

"Looking for me?" a voice replied from behind the two men. They whirl and see a man dressed in black. Wearing nothing more than breeches; a hat; sword; a sling; courage; and a cocky smile, Thadden stared at the men. *"Now, what could this little cat have done to you men; that you have to try to kill it?"* Thadden asked. Through glaring eyes, the man replied.

"It took our fish. We just wanted to take it back. Now if you'll get out of our way, we'll gladly get our fish, and the cat, and be out of your hair."

"I think you gentlemen should just fish for some more. The brook has plenty of salmon, and it won't take you too long. The cat is hungry and deserves to eat the fish."

"Get out of our way, or die." The man drew his weapon as he hissed the words.

"So be it. You were giving a chance." Thadden unsheathed his rapier. The fight is over before it began. The two men attack together. Thadden parried both blows and smashed his hilt into the younger man's teeth. Blood trickled out as the man held onto his teeth and tried to put them back into his mouth. He somersaulted, landed on his feet, then kicked the man in the spine. There was a snap, and the man fell to the ground.

"I let you men live so that you can reflect on this incident and remember never again to harm an innocent animal." He knew that the statement had sunk in. Thadden turned and headed back into the trees. The black cat had walked back with him with the fish in it's mouth. *"Purrr" "Purrr"* It said to him, with its head and tail held high.

"What's your name, cat?" He never expected to receive an answer.

"Feacon" was all that it said. There was silence once more.

~ ~ ~

Thadden finishes his story. There are tears in his eyes.

"I think it is time we go and get the girl. Once that is accomplished, we'll then find the cat. I hold myself at fault for whatever may happen to the cat. Should the time come, I shall give you my apologies." Romeelus turns away from the grieving thief. Jake wakes up Gwyninne. After a quick preparation, they head for Xibnar's Magic Shop.

~ ~ ~

Other plans go underway on the road to Ganshrag. At least the town was giving fair warning. An army is ready and waiting for Belghar to advance. It is a small army, but it is at least prepared, unlike the impoverished town of Millings'Dale. Belghar laughs at the pathetic attempt to stop his army. Inside the town gates, the people pray to their gods. They don't know why such evil is out to destroy them, but they wish he would leave them alone. They want to get out of the madman's path. As night falls, Belghar stands before his men. With a blood-chilling, inspiring laugh, he barks out one command.

"Charge"! The men storm the gate. Soldiers on the gate do their best to slow the charge. Hot oil dumps down onto the attackers; oblivious of the attack, the men continue to swarm the gate. Archers line the wall with flaming arrows. "FIRE!" The gate captain bellows. The arrows streak downwards and ignite the oily men. Screams pierce the night. The gate buckles as a ram slams into it. The defenders know they will die, but not until they take some of the enemies with them. As the gate crashes, guards in the interior prepare to defend the entryway. Bodies crash together as hand to hand ensues. Women and children, led by a few soldiers, flee out the back road. They must move to safety until the battle is over. Tears roll down their cheeks as they know they'll never see their fathers or brothers again. Such is the story with war. As dying screams fill their ears, a deep sadness rips into their souls. One question is left to haunt them.

"Why is this gut-wrenching horror invading their once quiet life?" Agonizing screams are the only answering reply.

Chapter 19

Xibnar hums merrily to himself; Feacon lies miserably at his feet, with the collar around his neck. "Soon, I shall have the items from the thief, and once I end his pathetic life, the girl will no longer be his concern. And you, Feacon, you will be the good little cat of the olden days. We will get along excellent, you and me." He strokes the cat's fur. A hiss comes out of the cat, but Xibnar is not afraid. He smiles. Things are going his way, and nothing will stop him from becoming the greatest wizard of all time. As he thinks these foul plans, his hands complete a spell. Smiling, he continues his planning as he waits for the thief, the items of magic, and his incredible destiny.

~ ~ ~

As dawn arrives in what remains of Ganshrag, the cruel and mighty Belghar laughs at his victory. His foot crushes the skull of a hapless soldier, who lay wounded on the ground, helpless.

"It is such a glorious day, isn't it Pontew?" He smiles as he walks.

"It is the sire. It's much too beautiful than to be wasting it admiring one's handiwork." His stomach churns at the gruesome sight.

"I disagree, Pontew. One should always spend time admiring one's handiwork. How else can you get any pleasure out of the day? One shouldn't go through the trouble to do something if they're not going to enjoy it afterward."

Belghar's eyes start into Pontew's, looking for a sign of deception or betrayal. He sees nothing but loyalty from his aide.

"I suppose so, my liege. Are we going to hit the next town, or do you think the people have learned their lesson?"

"I'm sure these people have learned their lesson. However, I'm not so sure the Tyrellians have. They seem to deem themselves independent of my rules. Isn't that where the child that defied me was last seen?"

"It was. The girl is still there at last check."

"Well then, I guess I shall have to take it upon myself to ask the queen to surrender the brat to me at once. Should she refuse then, it is not by my hand that they shall die from. The queen herself shall decide the fate of her subjects." With a swirl of his cape, he enters The Bumbling Drunk. "Prepare the falcons! I want to relay my messages out at once. Then find me, my servant. I need him. Oh, and Pontew, be sure that neither you nor anyone else enters the bathhouse. I am going to be taking a bath, and I do not wish to be disturbed. Of course, I do require my servant, for ah, cleaning purposes."

"As you wish, Belghar" Pontew bows; and then retreats to do his lord's bidding. Without another word, Belghar enters the building. The stride in his step oozes with his confidence.

~ ~ ~

On the road to Gena, four individuals, who have gotten very familiar with the road, ride on their horses. As they ride down the road, a figure stands in the middle of the road. He is someone that the men have already met. Expecting trouble, the group slows to a halt. They can't afford to have this confrontation. It will only deter and slow them down from their appointment with Xibnar. Romeelus and Thadden hop off their horses, and with weapons in hand, walk warily to Kyle. He stops them ten feet away.

"Please come no further. I mean, you no harm. I merely wish to speak to you of urgent business." He holds his hands up in a peaceful gesture. Cautiously the men sheathe their weapons.

"Make it quick." Thadden hisses. "We are pressed for time and wish to be in Gena soon."

"I know of your destination. I bear news of something else that concerns you as well. A wizard by the name of Belghar has waged war. He has massacred every man, woman, and child in Millings'Dale, and has nearly destroyed Ganshrag. Only the women and children remain, and their protectors are hiding in the Five Valley Forest. News has reached me that he is coming back this way and is heading for Kyrella. Should he beat the Tyrellians, all hope is lost. He will continue on this rampage until there is nothing left, or until everyone announces him the overlord of the world. His army is vast, and he plans on calling upon the aid of Demons and foul creatures of other races.

"Someone needs to go back to Fentia and speak to Kram. The assistance of the Gahwarves is greatly needed. We need to warn the towns. Anyone who can fight must bear arms and meet at Kyrella. Those who cannot seek shelters and pray that Belghar does not ravage any more cities or towns on his way to Kyrella. I, too, have a business in Gena. I must stop a madman. When I have completed my mission, I shall meet you at Kyrella. Thadden, come with me. You and I shall deal with Xibnar. Romeelus, talk to Kram; you are the only one with any close ties to him. Jake, you and Gwyninne ride the horse to Kyrella. You must help in the preparations for war. There is a surprise that awaits you there as well. Begone, and be quick. We have so little time." Thadden gives the reins to Romeelus. Jake and Gwyninne ride back the way they came.

~ ~ ~

With a suspicious glance at Kyle, Romeelus decides to trust him. He turns his horse around and follows Jake's dust. He hopes he can convince the dwarf to lend a hand in the war that is to come. Grabbing onto Thadden's arm, Kyle snaps his fingers. Just like his master, Kyle teleports away and takes the unsuspecting thief with him. The road is quiet once more.

~ ~ ~

In the castle of Queen Tyrella, two women lay on a bed. Having spent most of the night crying, they have fallen asleep. Unfortunately, other matters, other forces care not for their troubles. After only a few hours of sleep, a knock on the door forces one of the occupants in the room to wake up and answer the persistent beating.

"What is it?" Magdellaine yells, holding her pounding head in her hands. Menecha stirs, and she too finds herself awake.

"The queen has urgent news. She wishes to speak with Lady Magdellaine and Lady Menecha right away."

"Tell her we will be right there." The sound of shuffling feet and there is silence in the room again. Magdellaine's head gives her some reprieve. "Well, daughter, we might as well see what is going on. It must be important if we are needed right away." Menecha drags herself off the bed. Lashing on her sword and scabbard, she follows Magdellaine out the door.

~ ~ ~

Romeelus makes it back to Fentia and wonders if he is ever going to leave this town. He jumps off his horse, hands the stable boy the reins, and then runs off towards the Kram's blacksmith shop. He arrives at the familiar sound of pounding. Opening the door, he hears the voice of the Gohwarf, obviously upset.

"Now listen here, I do the best work around these parts, and do not haggle for my wares. My prices are as follows. If you think you can get as good a quality as I'm giving you, then you can go right ahead. I guarantee that it is not going to happen. I have half a mind to bang you upside the head with my hammer and see if you caved in the skull will make you believe my words." Romeelus enters the smithy room to see the Gohwarf holding his hammer in one hand and his ale in the other. A human begins to back his way out the door in fear of the Gohwarf. The human turns around and slams into Romeelus. He picks himself up. Seeing no help from the human, he scrambles madly past Romeelus and runs out the door. Kram puts his hammer down and pulls a swig from his flask.

"Humans have no sense of humor." He laughs hysterically. "So, how goes bounty hunting? Did you catch the thief you were looking for?"

"Yes! I caught him. He is a better person than I originally thought. We are allies now. If you listen for a little while, I have some essential news to tell you. I have an even more important question to ask of you as well. Let's take a seat. How about giving me a swig of that ale while you're at it? For the first time in my life, I need it." As they sit down to talk, the flask exchanges hands.

~ ~ ~

The sound of thundering hoofs on the road alert Tyrellians that someone is approaching fast. The Queen sends out her soldiers to await the rider. Jake arrives on his horse with Gwyninne holding tight to his waist.

"I've never felt this alive." She murmurs to herself as she tightens her grip and nestles her head in Jake's back. At the sight of all the people looking at them, Jake reins his horse. A guard steps forward.

"State your business!" Jake releases the reins and grabs the staff. The thought of being skewered because he couldn't speak would not help his cause.

"There is trouble brewing, and it's heading this way. We just came by to warn you, and then we'll be moving on to the other towns."

"What kind of trouble?"

"Belghar has waged war on the entire nation. His force is huge and nearly unstoppable. There is talk of him joining forces with supernatural beings and horrible monsters. This city is his main target. Be ready, for he moves quickly. We must continue. Please don't delay us any longer." He looks at the guard. With a shrug of shoulders, the guard stands aside and lets the riders go forward. Already panic plagues the city. All those who heard the conversation flee home to their families. here is going to be a war. Suddenly the town is alive. The queen has a riot on her hands. Things are not going well.

~ ~ ~

Jake and Gwyninne continue. They pass an occasional traveler but give no warning. The traveler will know of the news as soon as they reach the city. Soon the horse slows down to a walk. As night descends upon them, Jake knows they must stop. The night is cold. They veer off the road and head into the trees that line the roadway. Under a clear sky and a bright moon, he ties the horse to a tree. Gwyninne still sits atop the horse. The moon strikes her face, and in the moonlight, Jake can see her beauty for the first time. Even with signs of fatigue, and her unkempt appearance, her beauty shines through and blocks all other scenery out. She folds her arms across her chest to keep warm, and Jake snaps out of his dreamy state. He rushes to her side and holds out his hand. She takes it, and with his help, her feet are on the frozen, snowy ground.

"I'll get a fire started." He hands her the staff. Knowing it's his only means of communication, she clutches the staff protectively. Once he has his wood, he has a hard time starting the fire. The wood is too cold. Things get worse as the clear sky becomes invaded by snowflakes. Gwyninne approaches with the staff still in hand. It is glowing red.

"This is keeping me warm. Maybe you can use it to start the fire?" He smiles. Their hands touch for a second. Flooding of warmth fills up their insides. The heat lasts long after the touch is gone. Jake notices the chill in the air. Jake grabs the staff. "Light!" he commands. Suddenly, a strong surge of power flows through his arms. They seem to want to rip right out of their sockets. The surge flows through his arms and into the staff. It glows red hot. Strangely, his hands don't burn. Then with a remarkable display of power, a flame shoots out of the staff. The sky flashes for a second, and then all is calm. A roaring fire is at their feet. His eyes spy another strange occurrence. The wood in the fire is not burning. With a warm fire going, the couple sits down on the ground. A twenty-foot diameter circle that was once the snow is now just dry ground. Jake begins to wonder just how much power is he holding in his hands. Wrapping their arms around each other, more for comfort than warmth, they look longingly into each other's eyes. With his free hand, he clasps the staff.

"Gwyninne, saving you has been the best thing that has happened to me as of late. It's been a long time since I have even been near another woman, save for my daughter. I have thoughts that I have never had in a long time. I fear I'm going to lose you soon, and I need so much more time with you. Tomorrow, we travel to two towns then head back to Tyrella. I want you to stay in one of those towns while I go back to Tyrella. I hope you understand. I have to fight in that war, but I don't want to see you get killed."

"It's cold, Jake. I need to be warm. Let's not worry about tomorrow. Let's just live for the moment. Every moment from the minute we met until the end, I shall always cherish in my heart. Just hold me, love me, and keep we warm tonight. All we'll ever need is each other." She turns her face to his. Under a snowy night, beneath the moonlight sky, the pair kisses. All noise is silent except for their fierce lovemaking. Then they curl up in each other's arms and fall asleep.

Chapter 20

Thadden and Kyle arrive in Gena a lot sooner than the thief thought possible. They pass through the market, which is usually alive with people and money. Today, there is nothing but silence. All residents care not for money, food, clothes, jewelry, and other such novelties. There is a war. The men have all gone to fight in Belghar's army, while the women and children stay in their homes and pray. Cautiously, the thief and the former sentry watch the door of Xibnar's Magic Shop.

"You go in first, Thadden. I want him to think that you are alone. Of course, you don't have a bargaining chip since Jake has the items he requested. But we won't need one. I'm the last person Xibnar's going to expect to be allied with you." Thadden nods, and with a sigh, he heads to the door of the shop. His only thoughts are of Menecha and any harm that might befall her. He gets the sense of deja vu as he walks up the stairs; the difference this time, though, he has no advantage. Hesitantly, he knocks on the door. The familiar voice of Xibnar arises from behind the door.

"Come in, Thadden; by all means, do come in." HEE! HEE! HEE! He laughs madly. Thadden opens the door and steps inside. The room is messier than last time. Vials, broken and useless, lay on the floor. The counter is still there, but charred marks indicate a fire of sorts has occurred. Behind the counter is a beaming Xibnar. He stares at Thadden with wild eyes. "Hello, Thadden. It is a pleasure to see you again so soon. I do have a surprise for you.

I know it's too your liking." His smile tells the thief that it is not something he will enjoy. "Don't be shy!" Xibnar seems to be saying to no one in particular. He bends down. When he comes up, he is holding a squirming Feacon by the scruff of the neck. Thadden is about to leap at the wizard but catches himself at the last minute.

"Now is not the time." He warns himself.

"You know Thadden, did like you, and until I found out that you were the one that took my cat from me. Feacon is my cat, and no one will own him except me." He screams. He drops the cat. "Now, I believe we have a little business to discuss. I don't see the staff or the book on you. You need them both if you expect to see the little girl alive again."

"I want you to bring the girl out so I can see her. When I see her, then I shall produce the items you require." Thadden crosses his arms. Xibnar has seen this pose before. It means no business is going to start; I meet the thief's needs first.

"Very Well!" Xibnar lets out a whistle, and a panel opens up from the wall. Menecha steps out. Chains are around her ankles, wrists, and neck. "Now, where are my items?" Xibnar crosses his arms. "Two can play this game." He grins in triumph.

"Wait one minute. I shall go retrieve them." Thadden departs. Once he gets outside, he bends over and picks up a rock. Seeing the signal, Kyle sets his plan into action. Thadden goes back inside. Once he steps inside, his skin prickles, and the hair on his arm stand up. His instincts kick in as he narrowly avoids a crossbow bolt. Xibnar comes out of hiding.

"Well, well, thief. It seems neither one of us will get what we want. At least I'll get the satisfaction of ridding the world of you." He steps forward, and then with a blur, his hand is in motion. Thadden tries to avoid the object, but it homes in on his face. A putty-like substance covers his nose, mouth, and eyes. I shall enjoy watching you as the breath slowly disappears from you, and you try desperately to save yourself. I finally outmatch you!." Ha! Ha! Ha! Ha! As he gloats over his victory, a telekinetic force slams him against the wall. He gets to his feet as Kyle stands before him. "Oh, Kyle, Kyle, Kyle. Why would you turn against me? Do you think that you have gained so much power that you can thwart me? You are pathetic!" A spear of cold arcs toward Kyle; he prepares himself with a wall of stone. The spear shatters the rock and shrapnel of ice and stone and imbeds them into Kyle's armor and flesh. He grimaces in pain.

Meanwhile Thadden struggles to get the paste off of his face. He is having no luck. Feacon notices that Xibnar's attention draws toward Kyle. The leash is on, but it is free of any moorings. With his feline agility, he hops onto the counter. Xibnar has yet to notice him. Quickly he jumps down and hurries over to the fallen thief, whose face is turning purple. Vines erupt from the floor and entangle Kyle. Xibnar smiles at his pre-set traps. "Magic is more than just on the spot casting. It also entails setting timers or triggers. I'm going to teach you a valuable lesson. You are no match for me!" A streak of fire heads over Kyle's head. Vials of oil ignite and drop onto the former sentry's head. The pain from the burning oil and the vines that have now caught on fire is almost more than Kyle can bear. As Thadden struggles for consciousness and his life, he can feel something walking on his chest.

For fear of being eating, he tries to buck the creature off. It digs its claws through his leather armor and hangs on. He prepares to die when remarkably air reaches his lips. He begins to suck in as much as he can. Getting air back revives his senses. He sends his ears out to listen to the commotion. Kyle is screaming in agony. Xibnar is gloating at him in a loud voice. "Purr" "Purr" he hears. He breathes a sigh of relief.

"Feacon," he replies joyously. His nose is free and air homes through the nostril like an arrow. "Master," a dee voice relays in his mind. Finally, he can see. Feacon finishes his licking of the paste and licks him once on the face. Xibnar yet looks to see if Thadden is dead. He gets a surprise. Thadden cuts the leash and gets to his feet just as Xibnar curses and prepares a spell. The battle is far from over.

~   ~   ~

In queen Tyrella's castle, plans are underway. Menecha and Magdellaine get to her throne room. They are amazed at the assemblage of people there. Among them are Cornelius and several of the top soldiers.

"Ahh! I see that the General and Menecha are here. We can begin our meeting. I have brought you all in here because a terrible threat has come into our existence. This threat comes in the name of Belghar. Already he amasses his forces and destroys two towns. Millings'Dale was the first and the most brutal. No one knew of his oncoming army, as the duke's daughter was getting married. They killed every man, woman, and child. Their blood still stains the snow red. Ganshrag was the next town to be taken. They gave some advanced warning and got their women and children out of the town and into the forest. In his butchery, he has decided that we are the ones to perish. Some falcons have arrived today, with the message that he is going to attack. He wants us to be ready so that we can give him a good fight. He thinks he is going to win this war. Of course, he gave us an alternative, and that is to give Menecha over to him. Now, normally I would do it just to minimize the bloodshed." Magdellaine stands protectively in front of Menecha. She dares somebody to try to take the girl. "But I'm not going to in this case. First of all, the girl is now one of my soldiers. I do not give any of my soldiers to anybody. Second, I don't think it would be easy to get the girl. Both her mother and she would kill more of my men; then, it is worth it. Third, Belghar and I have had this war coming to us for a long time. I think it is time for the confrontation to be over with. Lastly, I don't like it when a man does what he does, expecting everybody to bow down to him. We are Kyrellians, and we bow down to no-one." There are a cheer and a stamping of feet after her speech. She puts up her hands for silence. "I want every soldier practicing every day. All weapons are to be cleaned and sharpened. Hot oil, ballista, and catapults are to be properly aligned and in good working order. We are going to show them just how Tyrellians fight." As everybody leaves, she hails her messenger. "I have prepared a message to send to him. Put copies of these messages on his falcons, then send them out."

"At once, your highness," he bows then leaves. Of the crowd, only three figures remain beside the queen. She addresses them individually.

"Cornelius, I want you to tell your soldiers not to utter a word of this war. We don't want to start a widespread panic. I shall prepare a speech for my people tomorrow." He salutes and is gone. "Magdellaine, you are in charge of all the weapons. Make sure that everything is working, clean, and sharp. Start putting your soldiers through drills. We must be ready for this war." Magdellaine salutes and leaves. "Menecha, you must prepare yourself for war as well.

Keep your weapons sharp, and keep practicing. A sharp blade is no good if you forget how to use it."

"T-t-thank You, your highness. I would've died if I had to go back to him."

"Don't thank me. You are one of my soldiers now. Had you not been, you would already be gone. Now go, and get ready. The next few weeks aren't going to be very kind." Menecha salutes the queen as well and then disappears out the door.

~ ~ ~

It isn't until later that evening when two strangers ride into town and relay a message that the queen has a riot to deal with. The ugliness of war is already rearing its nasty head.

Heedless of war, for now, two individuals and a cat concentrate on a battle. Xibnar punches his hands through the wall. Turning around, he mutters a word then throws the stone slab. It sails through the air, and as it does so, it enlarges. By the time it reaches Thadden, it is wide as he is tall. He ducks and rolls out of the way as it shatters against the wall. Once more, Xibnar's attention diverts as Feacon teleports into his face. His claws and teeth do little damage, but it blocks his vision enough for Thadden to hurl a dagger into his stomach. Feacon drops to the ground from the thunderous punch and teleports away in time to avoid being squashed by Xibnar's foot. Blood soaks the wizard's robe. Kyle puts the fire out and, with a scream, shatters the spell that controls the vines. The burning vines go out when they hit the floor. Though badly burned, Kyle was able to put up a protective barrier to limit the damage from the heat.

"Now it's my turn Xibnar. I have learned a lot about the workings of magic, as you will well see. Having lost enough this week, I don't plan on losing again. Earlier, you stated that I'd be the "darkness and the light." I've already been the darkness; now I'll be the Light." Xibnar tries to prepare his defensive spell. Thadden leaps forward and thrusts his rapier into Xibnar's emerald eye. Xibnar screams in pain; he loses his concentration. Kyle closes his eyes, slams his hands together. There is a look of triumph and power in his eyes when he opens them. Holding his hands in front of him, he aims at Xibnar. A ball of light, immense and bright forms, and streaks towards Xibnar. Unlike Xibnar's rock spell, however, the light decreases in size. It shrinks down to the size of Xibnar's heart and slams that exact spot. A hole creates where the ball of light entered. Thadden and Kyle watch as the light invades the mage's cruel, mad heart. Holes appear in the heart, which stops beating. He falls to the ground dead. The heart turns solid white, and then the opening closes. Xibnar is no more. Thadden retrieves his rapier. As he does so, the emerald eye that was once a necklace pops out. It clatters to the floor and then shatters. Thadden manages to scoop it up and pocket it.

~ ~ ~

Feacon recovers from the punch and stands next to Thadden. Thadden is left to wonder what happened to Menecha as they prepare to leave. Before he can get the last look of a dead wizard, Kyle snaps his fingers, and they are gone from the scene. Once they leave, the building starts to shake. Cracks form in the wall. Vials fall off the bathroom shelves and shatter. The cracks grow more significant, and the building creaks. As the noise gets louder, there is a final creak, then an explosion. The building tumbles down and covers Xibnar. As a last respect to its owner, the building provides a tomb for Xibnar's corpse.

CHapter 21

As daylight wakes up from its temporary slumber, two figures start to stir. Jake opens his eyes and smiles. The snow is gone, and a warm fire is crackling. Gwyninne's beauty and grace cause the facial expression that he has not used since the night before his arrest.

"It has been too long since I've felt this happy," he thinks to himself. His fingers gently stroke her cheek. She smiles and opens her eyes.

"Hi!" she purrs. Gwyninne gives him a quick kiss. Jake jumps up with a new spring in his step. Amazingly enough, the fire had kept the snow from falling on them and kept going all night. Pointing the staff at the fire, he utters one command.

"Douse!" No sooner do the words leave his lips, and then the fire leaps into the air and arcs towards the staff. It spirals as it enters the staff. When all of the fire is in the staff, a feeling of warmth hits his fingers. It is gone seconds later. Jake's amazement shows that he was not expecting that event when he chose the word douse. He shakes his head and never vows again to underestimate magic. A feeling of warmth surrounds him. He turns just as Gwyninne hugs him.

"I love you, Jake." She says sweetly. Tears sneak out of his eyes.

Hugging her fiercely, he responds, "and I love you, Gwyninne." They embrace for a few moments more, and then sadly, they remember their duty. Jake gets the horse. Soon they are on the road again and are heading for Mist

Hallow. Fresh snow kicks out from underneath the horse's hoofs as it gallops up the street. She smiles as she hugs him tight. Cold wind blows against them but neither notice the temperature, warm by love.

~   ~   ~

Elsewhere in Fentia, a bounty hunter tells a tale to the attentive ears of a Gohwarf. Kram Ironjaw takes another swig from his mug and then passes it on to Romeelus. It is the third mug that has been drunk so far. As the tale comes to a close, Kram's fist clenches and unclenches.

"So you see, Kram, we desperately need your help and the help of your fellow Gohwarf's. If we all don't take a stand at Kyrella, Belghar and his minions from hell will control the world. Our lives will plunge into darkness and despair under his iron-fisted reign." He takes a swig of ale.

"I shall help you, Romeelus. I will leave immediately for the mountains. You can expect us to be at Kyrella in five days. That is the best I can do."

"Fair enough! I shall alert the queen and pray that we can hold them off for that long. I don't know when Belghar is attacking, but I know it'll be in the next few days. Good-bye, friend, and thank you." He shakes Kram's hand vigorously, and then they bump fists. Taking one last look at the Gohwarf and his shop, Romeelus leaves Kram to his preparations. The stable boy greets Romeelus when he arrives.

"You spend an awful lot of time in this town for a stranger."

"Yeah, kid, I know." He grabs the reins and jumps onto his horse. "There's a war coming, kid, and you should be in hiding."

"Oh, I know. My father and I aren't afraid. We do the most business when there's a war. We'll be fine."

Sadly, Romeelus shakes his head.

"Greed is the death of everyone," he mutters as he rides out of the stables. He thinks about his past and remembers the price of greed as he rides towards Tyrella...

Young Romeelus walked toward the forest. This day marked his second mission as a bounty hunter, and he was eager to make the contract. A second rate magician had made a habit out of cheating peasants. He used grave threats to take the money if a problem arose. Unfortunately, he cheated an individual who happened to be somewhat influential. The relative contacted the bounty hunters guild and put out a contract. The guild commanded Romeelus to kill the magician. He could keep any money found by Romeelus as the price for his assignment. Romeelus had agreed.

The bounty hunter quickly tracked the wild mage. He followed the tracks into the forest. Before long, he saw the wizards abode sitting atop a hill. Smoke billowed out of the chimney. Some birds chirped. Other than that, there was no noise to be heard. Cautiously, he crept up to the house. A man snored inside. Quietly, he turned the knob. It was unlocked. He entered the home effortlessly and noiselessly. The bounty hunter was in a small room. It contained a stove, which was still warm, a table and some chairs, and a sofa pushed against the far wall. It smelled strongly of herbs and sulfur. A kettle was on the stove. Steam lazily arose out of the kettle. The cup on the table and spices' smell indicated that the mage had just drunk some herbal tea and went immediately to bed. There was nothing else interest in this room. The sound of snoring came from a door on the left. Another entrance to the right of the kitchen/living area was closed. He took out his bastard sword. The time for his mission was at hand. The sound of snoring had gotten louder as he got closer to the door. Before long, he was in the room and grinned triumphantly down at the sleeping figure. He believed that the victim should always know why he would die, so he woke the mage up. He kicked the mage in the ribs.

"Wha?" the mage opened his eyes.

"You have been sentenced to death by the townspeople of Byyr. Never again will you threaten and rob innocent people of their hard-earned money. I am your executioner. Good-bye," he swung his sword down. It cleaved into the breastbone, went down to the abdomen, and then ripped the crotch out as he finished his stroke. The mage died quickly. He searched the room but found nothing of interest. Romeelus left that room but knew he had one more to go. This door was locked.

"Jackpot!" he cried. Before long, he had picked the door. It was ready for his entry. "Now, we shall see what you are hiding, Mr. Wizard." He opened the door.

His eyes lit up at the treasure he found. Heaped into the corner was enough money to equip him with weapons and armor fully. "The mage had hit more than one town and more expensive towns at that." Something attracted his eye. He looked, and against the wall, he found a glowing ax. Instantly his mind raced. "A magical ax! Just what a beginning Bounty Hunter needs," he smiled at the thought. He picked the weapon up. It molded to his hand perfectly. There were also trinkets, baubles, and jewelry, but there was nothing of real importance. Romeelus knew that he couldn't possibly carry all of the treasure. "I must dig a hole and put what I can't carry in it. With enough time, I'll have the best armor and equipment my money can buy." Satisfied, he left the room. Something strange happened at that point. The floor burst, and a pair of hands pushed itself from beneath the boards. A green scaly creature with huge fangs stood directly in front of him.

"The treassure belongsss to my massster, put it back, and leave peassefully." It carried no weapon, but its teeth had an ominous color. Saliva dripped down its chin as it spoke. Romeelus noticed that it had no legs. Instead, its lower body consisted of a tail, much like that of a snake. Unlike the snake, it did have arms, and the arms came directly at him. Fear tried to take Romeelus at that point, but the bounty hunter shrugged it off and swung his sword. It bit into the creature's scales. Green puss mixed blood gushed out and covered his sword. Its arms tried to grab him, but he managed to avoid them. He yanked his sword free.

More blood splattered out and hit the floor. The blood hissed as it struck the wood. The wood smoldered. The bounty hunter started with dismay as the creature's blood was dissolving his sword. "Acid," guessed. The arms grabbed him as he got lost in thought. They started pulling him towards the gaping mouth of the snake-like creature. It was then that he guessed at what was wrong with the teeth. They were laced with poison. "Must not let this creature bite me," he thought to himself, as the teeth came near. As if summoned, the ax went out of it's sheathed and landed in Romeelus' hand. Wasting no time with his surprise, he reacted. He swung the ax. It lopped off one of the creature's hands. The teeth still came at him.

Romeelus reversed the ax and used the pommel to smash the teeth of the creature. For the first time, it howled in pain. Just as he was about to celebrate his victory, another strange thing occurred. The beast opened its mouth. A stream of green acid poured onto Romeelus' face. He writhed in agony as the burning sensation was too much too bear. Blindly he struck out. The weapon pierced the creature's heart. However, not before it could grab onto him with its one good arm, and with its tongue lash itself to his head. The creature toppled on top of him. Two pincers popped out of the tongue and punctured his skull. With its last dying breath, the creature let one dribble of spit roll down the tongue, which then goes into Romeelus' brain. Romeelus passed out as the creature died.

~ ~ ~

"Yes, sometimes, the price of greed is too high." He whispers in the wind as he feels his cowl, which he has worn ever since.

In Ganshrag, an assemblage of forces awaits the speech of Belghar. The queen's falcons arrive with word of her answer. As always, Pontew is the one who brings the news to Belghar.

"Sir, I have the news of the queen's response."

"Response?" He picks up his habit again.

"Yes, you had asked if she would give up the girl to you."

"Girl?" Belghar seems lost. Pontew rolls his eyes. He knows it's going to be a long day.

"Menecha! The girl that ran away. Her father was the one in the dungeons."

"Oh, yes, that girl." As always, when he's not at war, Belghar's mind seems to wander. The boy servant, Belghar's favorite, comes out of the bathhouse carrying a smoke pipe. Pontew remembers that these memory lapses usually occur after Belghar spends some time with the servant. He now knows the reason for Belghar's forgetfulness.

"Do you want to know the response?"

"Huh! Oh, Yes, Pontew. What was her response?"

"She says that she will not give up the girl to the likes of you. Furthermore, if you wish to obtain her, then you are going to have to take her. Your threats are idle, and she feels that it is time you learn the true meaning of power." There is a pause—Belghar's facial expression changes to a scowl.

"Well, Pontew, she can't say I didn't warn her. Prepare the army for a speech. We shall begin our march tonight. Before this month is over, there's going to be a new world. And I'm going to be the one who rules it." He chuckles sinisterly. Pontew stares at his lord.

"Sire, have you been smoking those leaves again? You know they cause you to have excessive mood swings."

"So what if I have. Your only concern is to do what I say. Is that understood?" Pontew nods his head. Silently he leaves. War is at hand.

Chapter 22

In Tyrella, there is a sense of urgency. Any available carpenter, masoner, and such are hard at work constructing the additional defenses for the up and coming war. The people in the city, who have not fled for safety elsewhere, have locked themselves in their homes. The sense of doom invades them like a deadly plague. Queen Tyrella does her best to calm her people and dissuade them from leaving. Her speeches fall on deaf ears. Magdellaine is like a whirlwind. One minute she is watching the soldiers; the next, she is checking out the defenses. Every available minute is taking up. As the day progresses, she feels pleased with the rapidness and expertise of the preparations. Occasionally she checks up on her daughter practicing with the rest of the soldiers. A feeling of dread drenches her from head to toe. "Oh, Mench, I hope we make it through this war. I don't want to lose you after finally getting you back after all of these years." She turns and heads back to the defense preparations. Two tears travel down her face.

The guards at the gatekeep their eyes focused on the road ahead. Their hands and knuckles turn white as they nervously grip their spears. In the sky, the clouds darken. Seeing the sign of an oncoming storm, the sentries swallow hard and grasp their weapons tighter. It is a bad omen before a war. Suddenly, there is a shout, and the gate comes alive with the sound of running and shouting soldiers. Arriving out of nowhere and heading towards the entrance are two figures. One of the figures is wearing black clothing and armor. A rapier in its sheath is on his side. His eyes have a haggard and worn look to them.

155

Even though he looks pale and haggard, the guards sense a feeling of toughness and cunning in the man. Walking next to him is a black cat. Its head is held high in pride. The other man with him is wearing robes. It covers his entire body. A hood drawn over the head provides enough shadow that to hide the man's face. The two men and the cat approach the gate. The gatekeeper, under the protection of many soldiers, addresses the group.

"State your business!"

"We are here to talk to your queen. We wish to help you in your fight with Belghar." Thadden keeps his voice even and neutral.

"And what kind of help can the two of you provide?"

"Well, we know what Belghar is capable of. I am quite capable in the fighting department, while my companion here is a powerful mage. You will need our help in defeating him."

The gatekeeper gives a slight nod. "And what are your names?"

"I am Thadden, and my friend's name is Kyle."

"Meow"

"Oh, and this is Feacon." Feacon rubs against Thadden's legs.

"I see," an odd expression surfaces onto his face. "You! Soldier! Go and find the queen. Tell her that a Thadden, Kyle, and"… "their cat Feacon wishes to be let in and aid her. And be quick." The soldier dashes off. There is a sound of hoof prints, and a rider wearing black plate mail, and carrying an arsenal of weapons, rides into view. As the guards tense up, Thadden speaks up.

"He's with us; another person that you will need to help you defeat Belghar and his unholy army. The gatekeeper shakes his head. Romeelus joins Thadden and Kyle.

"Gentlemen, I give you the mighty Romeelus!" Romeelus gives a slight nod and folds his arms across his chest. There are a whistle and a flurry of mumbling from the soldiers. A small breeze comes by. It comes by long enough to cause everyone to shiver, and then it's gone. Once it is gone, the soldier runs back. He does not seem winded, although the sweat on his face indicates that he ran all the way there and back.

"The queen says that she will be down to check out our guests. They must not be allowed inside until she arrives." The gatekeeper glances down at the three figures.

"Well! You heard the man; ya can't come in until the queen comes down." Folding his arms, he glares at the men as if they were a group of commoners. Silently, the three heroes wait for Queen Kyrella.

~ ~ ~

Beyond the first gate, there is a second, more robust, magically protected steel gate. This gate leads to a huge moat. This foul-smelling, dirty green water, probably guarded by some creature, goes one hundred feet wide and surrounds the city. There is a huge drawbridge lowers only for-trade merchants or expected visitors. To get into the castle and the city, one must first find a way to span the moat. It is a task that many have tried but have yet to succeed. The drawbridge opens up into an elegant courtyard, with a scattered array of trees, colorful flowers, and lavish water fountains. In here, anybody who comes in must wait until a Paige or squire can call their name before they can enter. When they state a person's name, he then goes to either the castle or the city. They are taken away through one of the two massive steel doors. A visitor taking a glimpse of the castle's detail and its surrounding defenses would shake their head in awe at the amount of power it would take to overwhelm Tyrella.

~ ~ ~

Meanwhile, somewhere on the road, an army with sinister plans is on the move. It comes to a halt. They stare up at the black cloud-filled sky and relish in its foreboding message. Only such weather as this can inspire foolish men to follow an evil man. The very crazy man who is now sitting atop a boulder, his arms in the air waging his insane war over a necklace that got stolen. As his voice bellows into the dark sky, there is a sudden rumbling noise. His voice lets loose a hideous howl. Feeling the excitement of the moment, the soldiers decide to join in the revelry. Before long, the source of the rumbling comes into view and halts. The creatures stare at the group of soldiers with the same bloodthirsty look that the soldiers are portraying. Their mouths turn into a snarl, and their pointy, sharp teeth snap at the air. Finally, the leader steps forward and approaches the boulder. He turns his nose into the air and starts to sniff. Belghar's scent carries through the cold air. When it reaches the Goblin leader's nostrils, he lets out a yelp of pain and then bows its head. Belghar, his arms outstretched, takes the creature's hand in his.

"Succumb!" Belghar commands into the wind. There is a thunderclap, and a lightning bolt shoots from the clouds. It streaks downward and slams into Belghar, who absorbs the impact without swaying. Electricity swarms around the magician then shoot through his arm. As the blue bolts enter into the Goblin's weak hands, there is a slight grimace of pain. All is still a strange expression that comes across the Goblin leader's face. Belghar lets go of the creature's hand. With nothing to hold it up, the leader sags to the ground. Two Goblin soldiers rush forward and help their leader to his feet. When he regains his senses, he pushes his soldiers off of him and barks some orders in Goblin. The creatures go into formation and start to march. With a look of total sub-servience, the leader bows to Belghar and then disappears into the woods. Sucking in their breath at the amazement of their master's powers, the soldiers prepare to march again.

~   ~   ~

In Mist Hollow, two figures on a horse sense an oppressing feeling of doom. Have they already heard about the upcoming war? Or is this the way the town always is? Jake's thoughts hammer him with the questions. Feeling uneasy, Jake halts the horse and dismounts. Gripping onto the staff, he whispers in the horse's ear.

"Stay!" he commands. Gwyninne starts to dismount; Jake stops her with a glare. Looking down at the ground, then back up at him, she looks like she is arguing with herself. Finally, she notes the determination and finality in Jake's eyes and gets back onto the horse. "If anything happens to me, or some-one starts to harass you, take the road back to Kyrella. Do not stop! You will seek safety there, at least." Looking at the desolate looking town, Jake heads towards it's center. His eyes on the alert for anything suspicious, or just any-thing that will lead him to people, so that he may give the news and head back to Kyrella, where Thadden should be with Menecha. The thought of his daughter brings a terrible jolt of pain. His hands wrench the staff. Tears roll down his cheeks at the thought of losing her. With a tearstained face, Jake delves deeper into town.

~ ~ ~

Inside the Castle of Tyrella, Menecha Rebish is hard at work trying to keep two soldiers at bay with her sword and shield. She laughs as sweat drenches her body. Effortlessly, she parries with her sword, and then with all of her might and weight, she pushes her shield forward. It pitches the first guard backward. He staggers into his partner, and they both fall to the floor. As they stare at the ceiling, they see Menecha's face beaming down at them. Her sword is hanging inches from their faces.

"Do you yield?" Wasting no time, the two soldiers nod vigorously. Menecha helps them to their feet.

"Thanks for the practice; maybe next time we'll get you." They all laugh together. The female warrioress shakes her head as she watches the two men walk away with both a bruised rump and a bruised ego. The door to the training hall opens up, and a messenger comes in.

"I need to speak to Menecha Rebish!" Menecha turns at the sound of her name.

"I am Menecha; what can I do for you?"

"The queen would like for you to meet with her at the gate entrance. She said something about a thief, a cat, a bounty hunter, and an unknown." He scratches his head at the message. He leaves. Menecha's heart struggles to remain within her chest as an image of a thief wearing black and his companion, a black cat, flashes into her mind. Sheathing her sword, she walks swiftly to the door.

"I must remain calm in the presence of these soldiers. A true warrioress will not show emotion so quickly." Once she is out of the training hall and out of sight of the other soldiers, she can deny her feelings no longer. She runs down the hall to lay eyes on the man that has captured her heart and destroyed the key.

Chapter 23

A chilly breeze sweeps into the midst of the figures waiting outside the castle gates. All but Thadden seem content to wait patiently. The thief, however, is not one to stand still for very long. His impatience fits, the constant walking in circles, cause the guards at the gate to watch him cautiously. As they finger their weapons nervously, a trumpet blares.

"Make way for the beautiful and powerful Queen Tyrella!" All the guards drop to one knee and bow their heads. A hush falls over the crowd of warriors as the queen walks towards the gate with Menecha in tow.

Menecha's face is flushed. She starts to smooth her legs and then realizes that she is not wearing a dress. She is a warrioress now, and the armor and weapons that she is carrying brutally remind her. Her eyes try and probe past the gate to see a certain rogue with a cat by his side. Her heart begins to jackhammer. It pounds and pounds at her insides and begs to free. With grim determination, she can keep it in its cage. As she nears the gate, she spots the thief named Thadden. She restrains herself from running to the thief and burying her face in his chest, forcing all emotion down. She must be beside the queen. Holding back the tears, she stares numbly into Thadden's eyes. Menecha has come to know patience and knows that in time, the right time, she will be able to run to Thadden. A smirk somehow finds its way onto Thadden's face. Perhaps,he approves of her armor and weapons. Clenching her fists nervously, they approach the gate.

~ ~ ~

Elsewhere in Mist Hollow, Jake's eyes search amid the shops, taverns, inns, and townhouses. There is no movement. The hairs on the back of his neck stand up as a series of goosebumps invades his skin. Feeling bored and just a little bit useless as well, Jake starts to turn around. It is then that he hears the rumbling of the ground. As the earth shakes and trembles, Jake heads in the direction of the noise.

"Might as well check it out. I've been through so much at this point it doesn't matter." Clutching the staff tightly, Jake continues. He travels beyond the small town and catches a glimpse of a vast cave. "Is this where the townspeople have all fled?" Before he has time to explore the cave and receive his answer, someone roughly lifts him off the ground. When it registers just how high off of the ground he is, he thinks to look back. Before him stands a giant of a human-made entirely of stone. The giant examines him and then lets out a hearty laugh. Jake falls to the ground hard, as the man of granite lets him go. His booming voice assaults Jake's ears as he tries to get to his feet with the aid of the staff.

"Hello, stranger! What brings you to Mist Hollow? " The granite humanoid finishes. Still trying to catch his breath, Jake responds.

"I came here to warn this town of the impending doom known as Belghar that is sweeping its way here. And to relay the message that any who wish to fight Belghar can come down to Kyrella, where the battle for freedom or slavery is ready to start. But I guess the inhabitants have already fled." Jake stares up at the monstrous man to see a reaction.

"The inhabitants of Mist Hollow are dwelling in the cave. They are under my protection. Should this Belghar person come this way, I doubt that he will survive much longer? I thank you for the warning, but it was unnecessary. I must go to them now. Leave this town to its fate!" Jake shakes his head at the stupidity of the granite man.

"If you should happen to change your mind about the help, go to Tyrella. We are going to need every person that we can get to destroy the man named Belghar." With those parting remarks, Jake leaves the people to the cave and their protector. Gwyninne was still where he left her. "Let's get out of here. We have done all that we can. It's time for us to ride back to Tyrella. We must rest before the war. With a final look at the Mist Hollow, Jake turns leaves the people to their fate. They gallop back into the mist, heading for Tyrella. A figure made of granite watches them go with troubled eyes.

Cold wind bites into the army that moves along the road to Tyrella. Despite this weather, they move along at an increasing pace. Perhaps it is the adrenaline that is pumping through their veins. Or maybe it is the sheer thought of the butchery they intend that warms their guts and pushes them forward. It could also be their insane, power-hungry leader who is spurring them on with promises of glory and wealth. Whether it be one or all of these reasons behind their determination, one thing remains unchanged; there will be a lot of blood spilled at the end of this conclusion. Floating above the legions in the middle of the army is Belghar. He notes the toughness and resiliency of his army, and he is pleased. A shimmering wave of heat surrounds him, obliterating any cold that approaches him. The dark cloudy sky still hangs fatefully over their heads. Pontew is directly below him, awaiting any instructions. Belghar mentally orders all of the commanders in the legions to halt the troops. With a few pleasing mutters of gratitude, the men begin to relax. When the men settle themselves, Belghar levitates higher and begins to speak.

"Men are progress is great. I suspect that we shall be in Tyrella by midafternoon tomorrow. But until then I wish to ask you a question. There is complete silence. The sound of hundreds of heartbeats lets Belghar know that everyone is listening. "Is there any brave soul among you that would love to serve your master in the highest way?" Instantly all hands come up, and they all cheer as his evil smile surfaces. "Well, I say that I am a little flattered that all of you are so eager to serve me, but all I need is one single, solitary man. Perhaps, I should rephrase the question. Who among you wishes to war with Tyrella?" Again all hands go up in a flurry. "Good! Now, this person that I need is not going to be fighting with Kyrella. They will be serving me in a more suitable service. It is a special service rendered to those who would rather do something else rather than fighting." His smile broadens. "Who among you would rather not fight and serve me instead?" There is a sudden murmur in the crowd, and fifteen hands, all from the same legion, wave into the air. Belghar floats over to the group of hands.

"Ahh! I see I have some volunteers. I only needed one man, but I suppose I have a purpose for the lot of you. Are you sure that you all want to volunteer and not fight the Tyrellians?" Fourteen heads nod. The fifteenth man didn't like the tone in Belghar's voice and wisely backed out of the group. A slight chuckle comes from the back of Belghar's throat. Mumbling under his breath the arcane words of magic, he swishes his cape in the direction of the "volunteers." A fierce, razor-filled wind gusts into the men. Their screams slice the air as razors cut into flesh and bone. Blood drenches the white snow as the men die horribly. At the last man's final death rattle, Belghar continues his mutterings. For the second time this day, Lightning erupts in the sky. Fourteen bolts come down from the sky and entwine themselves around the fresh carcasses. The bodies twitch and float in the air. When they land back on the ground, the lightning bolts untangle themselves from the bodies and merge with the ground. Seconds later, twenty-eight hands burst through the earth and pull the bodies down. When the last body disappears, Belghar's voice speaks up.

"That is what happens to all cowards who do not want to fight in this war. But don't worry, men; I'm not one to waste men. They are a sacrifice for the glory of our war. The unholy alliance from the undead are ready to fight. We now have skeleton warriors who will come to our aid and help us crush those who oppose us, starting with those foolish Tyrellians. Prepare yourselves, men. We march tomorrow. Only by marching in the morning can we expect to reach them by midday. Soon, we shall be the rulers of this world. And to those of you who survive, there is great reward. Sleep for an hour. For tomorrow brings great salvation." Seeing the butchery of their fellow mates, the men come to realize just what kind of situation they have gotten themselves into. Sleep does not come too quickly, and when it does, it comes too late to do any good.

CHAPTER 24

Outside the Tyrellian castle, near the gatekeep, a critical encounter is underway. All heads bow in obedience as the beautiful queen makes her way to the gates. At her side, wearing armor, a sword, and a shield, is Menecha. Thadden recognizes her instantly, and his heart seems to dwindle, like wax under the presence of heat. Painfully, Thadden feels an elbow in his ribs. He looks at Romeelus, who has always been so defiant, bow his head to the queen. Feeling stupid and ashamed, Thadden quickly drops to his knees and pays her tribute. Menecha stifles a giggle as even Feacon has bent down to the queen. Seeing the cat's intelligence in its every action, Menecha feels the tears start to fall. She manages to bite back the remaining tears with a feeling of duty and perseverance and lets the two escaping tears roll down her face and splatter on her boots. Looking past the beaming thief, she spies Romeelus. Instantly, her hand goes to her hilt and prepares to defend the queen if Thadden decides to do this. The third man, she does not recognize. Mysteriously, his face hides behind his hood. She makes a mental note to keep an eye on him. Kyrella motions for everyone to rise; they do; she walks up to the gate, with Menecha at her side.

"So you are the infamous thief that I have heard so much about. It is a great honor to have finally met you, and an even better one to hear that you have come here to help us. We'll take any assistance they offer. And who are these other two men that are with you?"

165

"This here is Romeelus. He's a bounty hunter. He was supposed to be handing me or my head to Belghar but has since changed his mind. Next to him is Kyle. He was once a sentry, and after I knocked him out and infiltrated Belghar's castle to retrieve the necklace taken by Belghar. Kyle was rescued by the man that I stole the necklace for. That man is now dead beneath his shops. Without Kyle's help, I would never have been able to defeat the wizard. Kyle's ability with magic is strong, and we will need his help to take on Belghar and his minions." Thadden finishes. The queen studies the three individuals for a few moments. Then with a shrug of her shoulders, she responds.

"Desperately times call for desperate measures! You three are an unlikely alliance for us to have normally, but I can see your usefulness. Welcome to Kyrella. Menecha will show you around and introduce you to Magdellaine. She is who you will be taking orders from. I hope neither of you has a problem with working. We have much preparation to do still." As she turns to walk away, Thadden's voice fills the air.

"There will be two more people coming still. Menecha's father, Jake, will be arriving along with his female companion Gwyninne. Perhaps you could let them in without hassle or delay. They have been sent to warn the neighboring towns and will be too tired to argue with your gatekeepers." The queen turns around sharply.

"It will be done. Varl, be sure to let the man known as Jake and the woman known as Gwyninne when they show up. Is that all?" She glares at Thadden. He does not cower as she expects. He flashes his smile and replies with a bow.

"That is all, your grace." Noting his sarcasm, but she needs him too much, the queen turns on her heel and is gone from sight. Thadden, Romeelus, and Kyle enter as the gates open. Menecha hurries forward and hugs Thadden. It isn't until she is out of sight from the guards that she starts to weep. Thadden holds her in her arms and hugs her until she is ready.

"Your father will be here soon. He has been through a lot. His tongue is gone. Through the use of staff, he can speak and use magic. If we have time, we will sit together and talk. However, let's worry about where we are staying and what work needs is left to do. I have seen enough bloodshed that I wish to get this war over with and retire from active life. I think it's time for me to concentrate on settling down." Holding Thadden's hand Menecha leads the troupe to their respected quarters. To each, she says.

"Rest for an hour! When you awake, there will be a servant ready to take you to Magdellaine. She will assign you her duties." The female soldier salutes each one as she drops them off. Thadden salutes back sarcastically. She smiles, shakes her head, and walks away with a new stride in her step.

~ ~ ~

When Thadden arrives at the training hall, he notices that Romeelus and Kyle are already there. "I must have gotten the slower servant," he complains under his breath. He approaches his companions.

"How long have you been here?"

"I got in here not too long before you," Kyle replies. With a mischievous smile, Romeelus speaks up.

"I had my servant bring me here as soon as Menecha was out of sight. I just had to check out our allies. These females are outstanding. I could handle maybe two, but any more than that and I'd be dead. Never have I seen such speed and skill with a sword. The men that are here could use a few pointers or too from the women. I think I'm going to have to talk to the men's instructor and help him out. We don't need to have the women make our entire men look bad on the field." Thadden watches the female soldiers practice. He has to agree with Romeelus. He contemplates the bounty hunters' words and realizes that Romeelus doesn't impress easy. Despite the bloody, cold, sadistic side to Romeelus, there is a soul and a fair man. He gazes at the helm that Romeelus always wears and wonders what kind of scars the man has. He follows the gaze of the bounty hunter. A woman fierce, proud, with beautiful shimmering hair; parries a blow from a sword. For the first time, a smile filled with love, hope, desire, and passion attacks Romeelus' face. Thadden's heart reaches out to the warrior who has probably never known love. In that smile, he sees Romeelus as the man he truly is. The thief will never look at Romeelus in the same light again. He puts his hand on the bounty hunter's shoulders.

"She sure is a beautiful sight. Isn't she Romeelus?" He baits him.

"Uhh...Yeah! Her mastery of the sword is truly an uhh...beautiful sight." If Thadden could see the man's face, he knows it would be blushing. He continues his persistence on the shy, flustering man.

"It looks like she could use a little work on her attack. Maybe you should go and see if she needs any assistance?" He throws the question like a master would throw his dog a bone.

"Uhh...I think we should wait for Magdellaine to uhh... show up first. I doubt if that woman would want me to uhh... help her with her swordplay." He gulps and buries the bone. Thadden nods.

"You're lucky you're wearing that damn helm and cowl because I know you're blushing," he thinks to himself. Just as he is about to persist in his tormenting, Magdellaine arrives. Romeelus stops fidgeting his nervous feet. Kyle remains silent and awaits his instructions.

~ ~ ~

Darkness falls on the Mountain of the Gohwarves. Inside the mountain, a rumbling and grumbling of feet and raised voices shake the mountain. It is in the great hall that the origin of the noise comes from. The hall is massive. The Gohwarves had to carve this stronghold out of the mountain with a pickaxe. Through the years, the Gohwarves have got the gallery to be just the way they want it. Occasionally, progress begins to add another section to the already colossal hall. Long, stone tables and short, stone benches fill the room. The rugged, reliable figures of the Gohwarves are currently sitting at the tables, drinking ale, banging their fists, and stamping their feet. There are a slightly elevated slope and a stone platform.

Standing on top of this platform is a Gohwarf with an enormous double-bladed ax. Besides this, Gohwarf is Kram IronJaw. Who, despite the yells, is keeping himself calm. He prepares his speech to either win his fellow Gohwarves to his side or make him an outcast. The leader of the Gahwarves, Vlim axe-wielder, hefts his ax and swings it twice over his head. He rests the ax upside down while holding onto the pommel. The noise silences the deafening crowd. No one wants to incur the great Gohwarf's wraith by speaking now. His command to silence does just that. Kram drains his mug. He waits for Vlim to let him say. As is custom, Vlim begins the meeting ceremony.

"This meeting was called by Kram Ironjaw. As is the custom, he is entitled to give his speech. There is to be silent while he talks to us on the matter of Belghar and our involvement. I already know what to do, but our civilization is that of unity. What one decides, we all decide. There is no blame for any actions once we make a decision. We live and die as one. I now give the floor to Kram Ironjaw." Standing impressively to the side, Vlim stares into the crowd for any signs of discontentment.

Kram stands on the platform and stares at his silent comrades. Gathering up his courage, he begins his speech.

"Friends, I stand up here with a sad heart. A war is about to begin, and a close friend has asked me if we could help battle an evil man. The man's name is Belghar, and he will stop at nothing to achieve world domination and become the supreme ruler. Should he claim this title, we will be living in a world of demons and ultimate savagery. I am standing with a sad heart because it has been years since we have been at war. Our race has become too involved in other races' cultures. As the years dwindled, we became lazy. I came up here to try to convince you to go to war. If you decide not to go, then we shall sit idly by and await our fate. Mayhaps, the humans will win the war against the lord mage and his alliance with the Goblins. There are rumors that he will have undead legions by his side, along with demons. I'm sure humans can handle this small matter. But if you don't want to rely on the tall people, grab your weapons and march with me. We will destroy the evil once and for all." Kram unsheathes his ax and holds it in his hand. As soon as he finishes, there is a thumping of a pair of boots. The one team turns into two, then three. Soon, the whole room fills with the sound of loud thumping boots. Visions of past legends and adventures pull at the Gohwarve's souls. The sounds of battle, cries of pain, and shouts of victory flood their small frames. Vlim and Kram stand side by side with tears in their eyes.

Chapter 25

Riding out of Mist Hollow, Jake and Gwyninne elate as they head towards Tyrella. They realize that the weather has gotten progressively worse—fierce winds belt at them from all sides coming out of the fog. The snow thick, swirling, obscures their vision. As a cold numbness ensnares Jake, he desperately clutches onto the staff. It's the only salvation that the man and woman have left. The wind picks up in an attempt to rip hope out of Jake's hands. He remembers his hell at the hands of Drekkar and how he overcame those odds; Jake grits his teeth and yanks the staff into his chest.

"Noooo! I won't let anyone or anything defeat me now." A yellowish aura surrounds Jake and Gwyninne. He laughs hollowly as the wind, cold, and snow stays outside the atmosphere. Female hands wrap themselves around Jake. Again he is safe. His one thought as he rides towards Tyrella is of Belghar. "You have put my daughter and me through enough. When I get my hands on you, I'll squeeze your neck until your eyes pop out of your skull. Before they stop rolling, I will squish them beneath my feet. There is no hope for you, Belghar. Be prepared to meet your doom Belghar for I am coming for you."

~ ~ ~

Inside Belghar's camp, more vengeful thoughts brew. Stefan, Belghar's favorite servant and leader of the pike infantry, arises from his nightly slumber. It is the morning of the upcoming war. Seeing no-one else awake, he remembers and broods...

He was a young lad. At ten years old, he was as active as any other boy. The only difference was that he had acres and acres of farmland to play on. Stefan loved his farm and his parents. Being the only child, he was pampered and doted on. Life was good for him; until the fateful day that changed his life. His father was out hunting. His mother stayed home as usual and had just finished cooking breakfast. It was a beautiful sunny day. He wolfed down his food so he'd be able to enjoy the day. Before long, Stefan had finished breakfast, played, and ate lunch. When it was time for dinner, he began to get worried.

"Mother, shouldn't daddy have been back by now?" Trying her best to hide how much she was worried, she responded:

"He probably just lost track of time." This answer didn't satisfy Stefan's question. As darkness fell, heavy, thumping footsteps pounded on the steps.

"He's here!" Stefan exclaimed. He ran to the door, excitedly. The door opened, and Stefan's father fell to the floor. Throwing him out of the way, Stefan's mother ran to her husband's side. Wounds covered his body. Blood drenched his shirt. Horrified, she noticed that any animal's injuries were not made but by the beast known as man.

"Stefan?" the dying father cried for his son. Stefan stood beside his mother, terrified. "You are the man in the family now. Promise me you'll look after your mother and that you will avenge me. Before you die, you must kill the man named Belghar. I love you both. Farewell!" He died as his wife cradled his head in her arms. Salty, wet, anguished tears spilled out of the faces of Stefan and his mother. Another sound of footsteps snapped what was left of the family out of their saddened haze. Defensively, Stefan rushed to the door. It opened. Four men with weapons entered the room. Stefan lunged forward; Belghar caught the young boy and backhanded him.

"Thanks for the invite!" he responded. Four men strode boldly into the house. Stefan wiped the blood from his mouth and nose while his mother stood protectively in front of him.

"Get out of my house!!" She tried in vain to stop the men; it was of no use. Belghar stepped forward. The men let out a cruel laugh.

"I am sorry about your husband." He tried to sound sympathetic. "But he shouldn't have tried to hunt the deer that we were already hunting. I'm afraid he was mistaken for a deer. The arrows were already shot before my men realized the error.

He wasn't too happy and decided to attack us. We merely defended ourselves from his onslaught. I offer my deepest regrets and humblest apologies." He smiled.

"Slap"! In a furious rage, Stefan's mother started to beat on Belghar's chest. Strong hands grabbed hers. Two of the men held Stefan down while the third man held her from behind.

"It seems you won't listen to reason. I guess my men and I will have to make you see the light." Belghar licked his lips. At the same time that his henchman held Stefan's mother, Belghar un-strapped his belt and unsheathed his weapon. She struggled against the man, but it was a useless motion. "Keep that boy's eyes open. I want him to see what we are going to do to her." Belghar grinned. Long, sharp nails pierce her flesh through her clothing. "Rip"! Her clothes fell off her body. Her pink flesh ignited the flames of desire that coursed through his twisted veins.

Belghar raped Stefan's unwilling mother. When he was finished, his henchmen repeated the same to her. Stefan was forced to watch this grisly sight. It was then that Belghar committed his most insidious act. With weapons in hand, he carved at Stefan's mother. He gouged out her eyes and cut out her tongue.

"Now, my dear, I saved your ears so you can hear what we are going to do to your boy." Sheer terror grasped her. Each scream boomed into her ears. She couldn't see but only hear Stefan scream as Belghar and his men raped her child. Sated, the men finished with Stefan. Belghar hovered over the boy's mother.

"Now, you can join your mate, at the threshold of Death's door." His sword plunged between her sore, swollen breasts. She died silently. "Now, boy, you have two options. You can die like your parents, or you can join my men and me. I guarantee that you will like the latter." Stefan couldn't imagine life without his parents. As he was about to choose death, another thought surfaced. It was a promise of more than an idea. It was his father's dying wish. revenge! With a smile, he replied.

"I will stay with you my lord." Belghar and his men welcomed their newest member. It was a long time ago.

~ ~ ~

Blinking his eyes, Stefan comes out of his old memory. He forces the tears back.

"When this war is over, I shall get my revenge on you, Belghar. Then I can die and meet up with my long-dead parents." He swings his Bec De Corbin

173

angrily. Walking over to his pike squad, he kicks one of his men awake. "Arouse the troops. We will be marching to war soon. Be sure the men are ready by the time Belghar comes out of his tent." Scowling, Stefan turns his back on the saluting soldier.

~ ~ ~

Back inside, Tyrellian Castle, Thadden re-continues his goading of Romeelus.

"Hey, Romeelus! There's your redheaded friend. Perhaps you should see if indeed she is as good with her weapon as you are." Romeelus remains silent as Thadden buzzes around his ears like an annoying fly that just won't quit. Romeelus reaches his breaking point.

"Okay! Okay! I will do it. Just quit, you prattling." Gathering his courage and shaking his head, the bounty hunter shuffles over to the red-head. He gulps. With his fingers shaking, he taps the warrioress on the shoulder. "Excuse me!" he speaks. She turns.

"Can I help you?" Her eyes scan him. Her mouth shows a hint of a playful smile.

"I was just curious as to how good you are with that blade of yours." Nervousness gone, Romeelus finds his confidence returning.

"Well, prepare yourself, gladiator. I shall have to prove to you just how good I am. I only hope you don't waste my time. Let me explain the rules to you. First, as this is only a contest, and we are not enemies...yet, only small nicks are allowed. Second and lastly, the first one to win is the one left holding the sword." Neither of the combatants wants the other to win.

"Sounds fair enough to me!' Romeelus has a playful grin of his own. The two fighters unsheathe their weapons and circle one another.

~ ~ ~

Inside Belghar's camp, the troops await their leader. All is quiet from inside his tent. It isn't until the snow begins to fall and the wind picks up that Belghar finally steps outside his tent. Imperiously, and impetuously, he approaches his legion. "Men! Today marks the day of the greatest day of our lives. For today, we march towards a new era, a new stepping stone for us, Belgharians. Today marks the defeat of arrogance and the victory that we will obtain. We will be arriving at Tyrellian castle, and once we storm it, with, of course, the help from our allies, we will rule this world. Prepare yourselves, men, for now, we ride for ultimate domination of this realm." A chorus of cheers follows his speech as hundreds of men rush for their weapons and march towards Tyrellia. Under the rulership and guidance of a madman, can there indeed be any hope for the Belgharians?

Chapter 26

A crowd gathers around the two fighters. With the shield in one hand and her broadsword in the other, she waits for Romeelus to attack. He wastes no time in pleasing her. His ax arcs down. She bats it to the side with her shield. Sasha, the red-headed fighter, thrusts her sword. Romeelus parries. With speed and style, the two combatants fight. An ax nicks Sasha's arm. She grits her teeth and bashes with her shield. The bounty hunter dodges the shield but does not prepare himself for her rolling attack. Diving to the ground, Sasha rolls sideways and sends her shield into Romeelus' legs. He falls to the ground. Getting to his feet quickly, the bounty hunter blocks her sword blow, just in time. Faking a kick, he swings his ax and then throws an ax. She dodges his kick, blocks his ax then snags the throwing ax out of the air. With her quickness, the ax comes down at Romeelus. She surprises him with this move, and he can deflect most of the weapon, but part of the blade glances off his side. Not wanting to underestimate his opponent, the bounty hunter decides to let the redhead come at him.

Still furious at him getting the first cut on her but enjoying the competition, Sasha swings her sword in a figure-eight fashion. Romeelus backs up, studying the pattern. Patiently, he waits for his opportunity. Thinking she has him on the ropes, she continues her pattern while preparing a dagger. Romeelus makes his move. He swings his ax sideways. The blunt side of the ax hits Sasha's wrist. Her sword flies out of her hand. Catching her weapon, Romeelus grins and hands her sword back to her.

"I believe I've won the contest." With a grin, she takes her weapon from his hand. Their fingers brush for but a second, but to Romeelus, it seems like an eternity.

"Maybe we will continue this another time?" her eyes match her smile, wicked and delightful. Romeelus nods in agreement.

"See you on the field, soldier." She walks out of the room with a noticeable and obvious swaying of her hips. A hand slaps Romeelus' shoulder.

"Well, Romeelus, it looks like you've made an impression on her. I bet she asks for her rematch later on tonight. HA! HA! HA!" Thadden and Kyle laugh at the silent, sheepish figure. Finally, a short, quick laugh escapes from the bounty hunters' mouth. It is the first time that he has displayed this emotion. Once again, Thadden's heart reaches out to the man who never knew love, happiness, and feelings. Before the men have time to continue their conversation, Magdellaine makes her presence known.

~ ~ ~

"Hello Gentlemen! I am Magdellaine."

"Thadden," the thief comments.

"Kyle," the former sentry mumbles.

"Romeelus," replies the last voice. She stands back to study the heroes.

"That was quite a display of swordsmanship. You bested one of my best warriors. I feel honored to have you on our side." Romeelus bows slightly, giving her due honor.

"I have come to give out your instructions as our situation is bleak. With Belghar coming with a massive army, we need to prepare. There is a rumor that he has potent allies with the Goblins, Undead, and Demons. I understand that we have the iron-willed Gahwarves on our side, but even they cannot fully fathom what is at stake. This war determines who will rule the empire. Should we win, we will have fair and just rulership. Should Belghar and his forces defeat us, much evil and horror will plague the lands. The Empire will be lost. Thadden and Romeelus, you are to stay up among the catwalks and discourage any attempts to storm the castle with ladders and such. Should you hear a bell, then you will hurry down to the courtyard. If that happens, then Belghar has made it past our moat and has penetrated the gate. We will need you both to confront him. "They nod without comment." Kyle, thus far, you possess the only magic. We will have you so that you can see the entire battlefield an important advantage. From this vantage point, you will cast your spells not to get any harassment from the enemy. Is it true that a man by the name of Jake Rebish is on his way?"

"He is coming with a female companion and a staff that grants him magical powers. He has suffered much in the dungeon of Belghar's castle. He is eager to confront Belghar. With thoughts about the man she once knew as her husband, and his "female companion," she forces back the tears that build up in the back of her eye.

"If you'll excuse me, I have other places I must be. Feel free to wander around. Just be ready when you hear the gong. When the hourglass flips twice, the gong will sound, and everybody must re-converge back here. War will soon follow." Her long, flowing, blonde hair whips around as she exits the training room. Immediately after her departure, two servants enter. One whispers into Thadden's hair, and the other does the same to the bounty hunter.

"Friends, it seems that I must leave. I am uh, needed elsewhere. I'll meet you both later." Thadden and Romeelus both reply in unison. As they depart, Kyle shakes his head in disbelief.

"Well, Feacon, it looks like it's just you and I left in here." A white, very female cat pounces into the room. Green eyes stare up at Kyle, blink, and then Feacon heads towards the fluffy feline. Soon, they, too, are gone from sight.

"Hmmphh!" Kyle says in disgust. "I'm surrounded by traitors." Shaking his shoulders, he leaves the room; perhaps, looking for more reliable companions.

~   ~   ~

On the road to Tyrellia, a rider urges his horse forward. Blowing, blinding snow billows around the man. He is unfazed, as is his companion. The castle looms before them. They know that they will soon be safe. They approach the gate.

"Halt!" a voice bellows. "State your name and your business,"

Jake mutters his name. "Was that Jake Rebish?"

"Yes!" he seethes—his annoyance of the gatekeepers and the weather grates on his nerves.

"Raise the gate! Raise the portcullis! He is o.k." There is a grinding of gears as the gate and portcullis rise.

Jake sends his horse forward for one final spurt. Gwyninne and Jake dismount and collapse to the ground. Fatigue sets in on the couple. Soldiers carry them off to rest in a room. They did all they could for the war. Only time will tell to see if they enlisted the needed aid.

~ ~ ~

In Menecha's room, she is preparing herself for Thadden's arrival. Humming softly to herself, she combs her hair, she thinks about the moment she has been preparing herself. Carefully she slips into her nightgown that shows just a hint of cleavage. Spraying on some of her newest and best perfume Menecha smiles to herself. A knock on the door jiggles her heart. Smoothing her dress and lay herself down on her soft comforter.

"Come in!" Menecha tries not to squeal with delight. The door opens, and in walks Thadden. Staring numbly at his shoes, he mumbles, "hello."

"Can you shut the door, Thadden?" She stifles a giggle. Portraying a sheepish grin, he closes the door.

"Oh, Thadden, it has been so long since I saw you. I thought that Xibnar had killed you, or Belghar had caught up with you. It wasn't until I lost you that I realized how much I care about you." Tears start to build. He moves over quickly to comfort the woman he swore to protect; the woman who now dons armor and carries weapons. It is at this instant that the thief realizes the extent of his feelings towards the woman.

"So much has happened to us since we first met. I'm sorry that I didn't keep a better eye on you. You have grown up so much. Look at you! Weapons, the armor you are not the same girl that got kidnapped at the inn. You are a woman." He loses all control of his emotions.

"I've missed you too, Thadden. I have never loved and missed someone more than I have with you. I-I love you, Thadden. When the war is over, I want to spend the rest of my life…with you." Slender arms wrap themselves tightly around Thadden's neck. Like magic, her dress finds itself on the floor. Fingers start undressing the thief. Feeling love tugging desperately at their heart-strings, they giggle. Their lips lock together. Thadden's fingers lightly brush down her backside. Slowly he eases her down onto the bed…

~ ~ ~

In another part of the castle, the usually grim and confident bounty hunter finds himself in the desperate, un-familiar territory. With a laugh, Sasha undresses Romeelus. As she tries to remove his cowl, he shudders and backs away.

"What's wrong?" She asks.

"I, I was in an uh, accident once, and became disfigured. I have not been able to take it off since. If I were to take my cowl off, I wouldn't want you to be horrified and run away. I can leave and will understand if that is your desire. I just can't remove it at this time." He turns away in shame. Strong fingers dig into his shoulders.

"Wait, please!" Sasha pleads. He turns. "It has been a long, long time since I have met somebody like you. Someday I would like to hear your story. You can keep the cowl on." The bounty hunter turns around. His eyes roam her body. She smiles. Her lips part and beckon him. Heeding the call, Romeelus experiences the strange and fantastic art of lovemaking.

~ ~ ~

On the road to Tyrellia, the sinister army with sinister plans marches hastily towards their destination. With an insane smile, Belghar watches his troop's movement.

"Pontew, the moment that I have been waiting for has finally arrived. My army's progress is both fast and impressive. When we arrive and storm the castle, and rid this world of those Tyrellian bitches. All I have left to do is contact my spy, and he will lower the drawbridge and open the gate. It will be so easy." Heh! Heh! Heh!

Closing his eyes, Belghar concentrates. He chuckles again and opens his eyes.

"It is done, Pontew. When we arrive, the gates will be open and the drawbridge lowered. When you have power Pontew, nothing can get in your way." Belghar focuses his eyes back on his troops. His aide ponders the last statement.

"I just wonder if this power just isn't going to get us all killed." Smiling inwardly, he thinks about the power that he has. "If it weren't for me, you wouldn't have the power that you do."

As the army travels toward their "destiny," his own heart sings a new song to Pontew. It is a tune that leaves a bad taste in his mouth. Only time will tell which side he will inevitably take.

~ ~ ~

Inside the castle, a bell is ringing. Many pounding footsteps shake the castle from the inside out. They are all heading for the room. When the sound of footsteps subsides, there is a hush in the room. On a marble the throne sits the beautiful queen Tyrellia. Staring at her loyal subjects, the queen prepares herself for her "uplifting" speech.

"Soldiers, it is time for us to ready ourselves for a vicious and bloody battle. The numbers are highly against us, but I believe that we will; we must prevail. However, the rugged Gohwarves will be aiding us in our fight against the evil known as Belghar. This is our greatest battle in this world's history. If Belghar should win, the darkness that will plague the land is inestimable. Demons, undead, and foul creatures of the night will infest themselves onto the denizens of this realm. If you die, you might just end up being the lucky one. But I say to you that we will not let this happen. We will win! We have one advantage over the enemy. We have courage. We have faith. We have the superior fighting ability that will allow us to even the odds. Also, we have the aid of some strangers who will be eager to fight with us. When we meet the enemy, we will vanquish them and give this world the light and goodness it needs. We fight for what is right. We fight for the respect we deserve. We fight to be the champions for this realm!". Cheers follow her speech. Everyone drops to one knee in honor of the queen.

~ ~ ~

A gong is heard throughout the Castle.

"To your assignments, warriors; we are now at war." Soldiers rush to their respected stations. Jake and Kyle get word of their positions and leave. Sitting alone on her throne, the queen sheds her tears of prayers.

Chapter 27

Watching the fighting from above, Romeelus and Thadden see the gate come down. Remembering Magdellaine's instructions, the thief and hunter race down to join in the action at the gates.

Magdellaine barks her commands at her troops. "Move forward and protect the gates. We must not let them get inside here. As soon as one of our soldiers falls, another must push forward to take their place. Push the attack, and drive them back. I will deal with the traitorous Cornelius." With a scowl, she heads towards the gate controls. Before she gets there, she spots two figures running in her direction.

"Ahh! Thadden! Romeelus! I'm glad you came down. Cornelius, one of my most trusting soldiers, has betrayed me and opened the gates. I am on my way to deal with him. I want you both to help push the invaders back. If you can make your way towards Belghar, if you can kill him, the war will be over." They nod in understanding.

She stares at the backs of the running heroes. Their confidence instills an extreme calmness within her. Un-sheathing her longsword, she prepares to do battle with her one-time friend.

~ ~ ~

Surveying the battlefield, Belghar grins satisfactory.

"I love it when my plans work. This is too, too easy. I might not even have to use the demons. Not too much longer now, and I'll be able to put my undead legions into play. Pontew! Any word on the Goblins? Are they to be arriving soon?" His aide stands quietly, and then with his air of all-knowing importance, he replies.

"They are on their way. I suspect they will be here shortly." Belghar nods happily at the news. As screams from his legion erupt into the air, he looks for the source. Men are rolling on the ground, covered in fire. A second ball of fire streaks towards another infantry group; it swirls and arcs and finally finds its target. More men scream and fall to territory ablaze.

"So, they have magic on their side. I guess we will have to show just what kind of magic we have on our side, eh Pontew?" Pontew nods his head in agreement. The battle is steadily progressing into the makings of a full-fledged war.

~ ~ ~

Stefan and his pikemen lead the way over the bridge and towards the gates. With war cries and screams, they engage the front rank of castles defenders. He was wielding his Bec-de-Corbin Stefan swings at a soldier. The man easily parries the more powerful weapon but nearly loses his grip on his sword. Stefan continues his attack again, but this time he slips past the man's sword. Stefan's weapon fulfills its purpose, to puncture the most massive armor. With a resounding grind, the armor gives, and the Bec-de-Corbin sinks into flesh and bone. Stefan provides yank, and blood splatters everywhere. In a final attempt at defense, the man swings his sword. Stefan parries and turns the weapon around and hits with the huge hammer. The soldier falls to the ground with a caved-in skull. Admiring his handiwork, Stefan barely has time to parry a sword stroke. Reminding himself to be more careful, he concentrates on his current fight. This time the spear fighter is facing a female warrior.

"Looks like I get to slaughter me a bitch now," he remarks out loud. Unresponsive, the female swings her sword and waits for Stefan to make his mistake.

~ ~ ~

Thadden and Romeelus push their way through the throng of soldiers and make their way close to the defenders' front. Still too far away to engage in any hand to hand, they resort to missile weapons. Romeelus starts loading his crossbow, while Thadden sends sling stones into the enemy. Arrows from both sides still ride the air currents. In the early stages of this war, the body count is considerably high. Romeelus aims and presses the trigger. A crossbow bolt embeds itself in a soldier's hand; he drops his weapon. Before he can retrieve it, Thadden follows Romeelus' lead and sends a stone. It glances off the man's forehead. A chunk of flesh comes out. He gropes around for his dropped spear. Just as he reaches it, another crossbow slams into his midsection. He flies backward and is dead before he hits the ground.

~ ~ ~

Near the gate controls, Cornelius kills his second soldier. He is about to engage in the third when a voice yells.

"Leave him to me!" The soldier quickly steps back and salutes the general. Gulping in fear, Cornelius grips his sword. He hadn't expected Magdellaine's army to respond to the surprise so quickly. Belghar's military has not penetrated the courtyard yet, and the traitor alone. The idea of betrayal suddenly seems so stupid because now Cornelius has to face Magdellaine. Vowing not to die quickly, he waits for Magdellaine to approach...

~ ~ ~

Viewing the battlefield from afar, Jake grips the staff. Staring at the front rank, he sends a blast of air. It starts small, and by the time it gets to the enemy, it becomes a massive tornado. Belghar's troops go in a backward direction. Some try to resist, but the tornado sucks them in. After spinning around inside until they run out of the air, the tornado spits their lifeless bodies onto the field. Enemy arrows rebound backward. Some strike the archers with such force that they die instantly. Finally, the tornado loses its power and dissipates into the air. Its damage took its toll. As soon as Belghar's troops fled from the front

187

rank, Magdellaine's soldiers surge forward and enter the field. The battle takes place outside the castle. Belghar laughs at his troop's demise as Pontew silently watches the carnage. With the battle taking place onto the field, Pontew and Belghar can now act and aid their army. "It is time for the dead to rise again and fight for my cause," Belghar replies confidently.

~   ~   ~

Stefan is having a hard time landing any strokes on the female defender. Just as he finds an opening and is about to exploit it, the tornado slams him back twenty feet. He lands on his back with a thud. The breath leaves him. Slowly, he gets back to his feet and reclaims his weapon just as the army pushes forward and enters the field. Looking back at his "fearless leader," he notes the smile and prays that Belghar knows what he is doing.

Inside the courtyard, a fierce battle between a woman and a man is going on. The betrayer just barely parries Magdellaine's powerful strike. With his shield, he attempts to bash her. She easily sidesteps and slams him on the head with her shield. Stepping back, he shakes his head to clear the cobwebs. Growling, he hacks vigorously with his sword. She parries each thrust, and then with a flick of her wrist, slices his chin. His blood oozes out of him, faking with his sword, he swings his fist. It connects with her cheek. Shaking it off, Magdellaine thrusts with her sword; he blocks it with his shield. He feints again with his sword and attempts another punch. Waiting for this, Magdellaine puts her shield in front of her, ducks beneath the punch, and plows forward. Body and shield slam into Cornelius. She pins his body between her shield and the wall with the controls on it.

Trying to regain his breath, he stares at his general of old. "You will die for your act of treachery. You are a disgrace of the Tyrellian uniform and a maggot. I send you to your death, just as I will send Belghar to his. Be grateful for one thing; you will die quickly." With the last bit of courage, he spits. With a final thrust, her sword slices through the breast bone and pins him to the wall. Eyes wide, he stares unbelievingly as the blade sticks out of him. With a yank, she takes her longsword out and swings. His decapitated head rolls along the ground and finally comes to a stop. Giving it a final kick,

Magdellaine smiles at her army's ability to push the enemy force back and heads to rejoin them.

~ ~ ~

He was feeling the essence of Cornelius' life dissipate; Belghar chants under his breath, letting out a silent curse. Making arcane movements with his arms, he continues chanting. His soldiers rally and resume the fight with the queen's protectors. As the swords and shields clash, and clang, Belghar finishes his last word and completes the spell. Suddenly, boney, skinny fingers attached to a boney hand rise from the ground. All of Belghar's dead soldier's bodies sag under the pressure of the fingers. With weapons raised, the living-dead soldiers remember their purpose. Grinning boney smiles, the soldiers join in on the attack.

~ ~ ~

"Damn him!" Magdellaine curses the evil Mage-Lord. "He summoned his undead creatures. With his dead soldiers back to life, it has us at a loss. He still has all of his soldiers now. I hope those Gohwarves arrive soon. If they don't show, I fear our fight is for naught."

"They'll come." Romeelus replies over the din of the fighting. "My friend Kram will rally them up. They have the techniques needed to deal with the undead soldiers." Scowling bitterly, he glances at his next opponent. It happens to be undead. With his bloody magical ax, he laughs at his foe. Feeling an adrenaline surge comes on, Romeelus laughs hungrily; the blood lust is upon, time for him keep count.

~ ~ ~

Somewhere else on the battlefield, a lone female warrioress battles against two enemy soldiers. Her situation looks grim, but with a heart of pure courage, she refuses to give ground. Her blonde hair billows out of her helm. Her sword, armor, and shield are already bloody, but the blood has yet to start flowing. Her assailants gloat at their advantage.

"As soon as you are unable to fight, my brother and I will have much fun with you. But don't worry, princess; you will be alive to enjoy it." They laugh as they swing in unison. Deftly, she parries both attacks with her sword.

"You're brothers, huh? Well, that would describe the same stink of dung that is coming out of your mouth. Your mother never believed in bathing you." She goads them on. "The angrier they are, the more likely they will make a mistake." She thinks to herself. She swings idly. It glances off one of the brothers' shields. At the same time, the other brother launches another attack. Menecha ducks beneath his thrust, effortlessly.

"You'll have to be quicker than that, Pig!" With a swing that would've felled a tree, the angry brother swings again. She parries with her shield, swings with her sword, and slams her shield into her other opponent. Rolling his eyes back, the man squeals as his sword cuts the groin and half of his midsection. Before his body hits the ground, she hears the satisfying "thud" of her shield hitting the helm of the remaining brother. She looks as the man tries to stop the ringing in his ears. Yanking her sword out of the first man's abdomen, she spins half-way around and stabs backward. The sword skewers through the stomach and comes out the back. All thoughts of future pleasures gone, the two brothers die together. She has little time to celebrate her victory. No sooner does she retrieve her sword when a lot more soldiers arrive. Seeing she hopelessly outnumbered, she mutters a prayer. It is then that she spots three figures running in her direction. Thadden, Romeelus, and Magdellaine, the three finest fighters in all the land, rush to her side.

~ ~ ~

"Do you mind if we cut in, or is this a solo act?" Thadden asks.

"Well, if you think that you can keep up with me, by all means, do join in. But Thadden, do stay out of my way." Laughing at her new cool manner, the lovesick thief dives into his enemies.

"For victory!" he screams. The fighters all join him. It is over quickly.

~ ~ ~

190

Once again, Belghar's troops hack away at the defenders. More and more of Queen Tyrella's forces are dying under the new army of dead soldiers. They fail at many attempts to dissuade the unholy warriors. With Stefan in command, the pikemen, joined by a few of their "born again" soldiers, prepare themselves for the Tyrellian cavalry. It is a cavalry of the most sufficient reputation. They hope that they are up to the task. With lances and arrows ready, the cavalry ready their horses and charge. As the horses gather speed, the riders rip arrows into the hapless pikemen. By the time the pikemen and cavalry clash thunderously, the pikemen have already lost a quarter of their men.

~ ~ ~

In the tower, two men yearning for battle watch longingly from afar. They have each done their share of spell casting but ache for the hand to hand combat that they see going on before them. Kyle unleashes another fireball, this time on a force of skeleton warriors. It is successful; they disintegrate on impact. Never again do the bodies rise.

"Interesting!" withstanding his curiosity no more, he leaves his hiding spot and heads onto the field. Kyle heads out onto the field with the same mystical armor he used to confront and beat Romeelus.

~ ~ ~

Seeing his friend head out onto the field and having the same longing, Jake ponders his options. From his vantage point, he can see Thadden, Romeelus, his beautiful daughter Menecha, and his ex-wife, all joining in on the splendor of battle. He wishes he can be there to fight alongside his companions, his dear Magdellaine, and his daughter, who was once a little girl and is now a woman. This yearning pulls out his heartstrings. It tugs fiercer and fiercer, but somehow he manages to regain control. Warm, loving fingers caress his cheek.

"Gwyninne," he croons. Turning to face her, he hopes she can't see what is in his eyes. She touches the staff. Like a shockwave, she gets hit with an unknown force. With great strength, she fights back the power. Slowly, the essence ebbs, and she sees a path before her. With a hungering curiosity and a need to know, Gwyninne follows the path. The course starts broad, and then bit by bit, it begins to narrow until it is precisely her breadth wide. A forest looms before her. It is dark, creepy. Ignoring the goosebumps on her arms, she continues to follow the trail. She picks up speed, and blackness engulfs her. Not wanting to stop, she continues walking. *Images flash through the blackness. Pictures of Jake growing up and Jake being beaten by his drunken father; while his mother watched fearfully. Then another image surfaces; of Jake when he killed his father with a knife, ending the tyrants rule. There is his beaming smile. As he looked upon the face of Magdellaine; they were a happy couple so long ago. Another smile, another face. This face belonged to Menecha.* Gwyninne is running now; she wants to get past the images. *Jake is drunk now, just like his father used to be. He yelledt at Magdellaine.* Tears well up inside Gwyninne; they are trying to explode out of her eyes. She chokes back a sob. "Where is this leading?" she screams. Another image appears; *Magdellaine left her family. Jake's heartbreak opened his eyes to his mistakes, and he stopped drinking. His only love now was for that of his daughter. Jake opened his tavern. He kept him and his daughter afloat with the money he had made from the bar. His heart was lonely. His face was forlorn. Belghar's face leered at him. Menecha is naked.* "Oh my god! What did he do to her?" *Menecha cried on Jake's shoulders. Jake was crying too.*

~ ~ ~

Thadden arrived. Menecha left with him. Soldiers! Jake was arrested! Drakkar's cruel and twisted face sneered at her. "My Jake! Why is he being tortured so?" Tears pour out of her eyes as she tries to run as fast as she can. Her feet move, but she does not go forward. She tries to close her eyes. Her eyelids stay open as if caught in a spell. Gwyninne realizes that she's here for the duration. Thadden rescued Jake. More misery, as now he cannot speak. He retrieved the staff and book. Finally he went to the inn and rescued Gwyninne. Jake smiled.

Gwyninne is moving again. A light, the end of the forest, is almost within her reach. The path begins to widen. *An image of Magdellaine, blurry, indecipherable, comes up quickly and is gone. Gwyninne stares in awe at the last picture that is enlarged. It is from Jake. With the sun shining beautifully upon it, underneath her image, are the words I Love You!* She makes it into the light and stumbles into Jake's waiting arms. The tears gush out of her. Body wracking with emotion, she replies, "I love you, too Jake." Knowing all that he has been through in his life, she can only look at him with wonder at how nice he has turned out.

~ ~ ~

Despite the tearful reprieve that Jake and Gwyninne share, other men, all on the battlefield, don't have the same fortune. Stefan and his brave pike men set their spears into the ground just as the Tyrellian cavalry bear down on them. Some of the most skillful riders jump over the line of spears and kill the owners with a sudden stroke. As they turn around, the less adept riders find their horses skewered on the barbed shafts. As they try to dismount, the pikemen run forward. They attack quickly and yank the soldiers to the ground. The hapless cavalry soldiers die as others of their squad prepare their second charge. With a pleasing smile at the outcome, Stefan barks his orders and awaits the second charge.

~ ~ ~

Watching the carnage unfold, Belghar seems displeased. "Despite my undead legion, the Tyrellian forces are still winning. Pontew, is that Romeelus over there fighting beside those three other people? Am I to believe the infamous bounty hunter has failed on his quest and is working with the enemy against my soldiers?"

"Well, sir, we did not receive any reports on his actions, and with the plans for the war, I never really thought he was a concern to you anymore."

"I did not hire you for your incompetence. I want you to take our mounted unit and intercept that group. Perhaps, I can end this battle quickly. And Pontew," Pontew looks at his liege and knows what is coming. "Do not fail me again!" Eyes glaring, Pontew yells in a fury and unleashes a cloud of gas. As Pontew disappears, Belghar sends the noxious cloud towards Tyrellian soldiers. The unsuspecting soldiers slaughter an entire infantry of Belghar's elite force and wave their swords at the victory. As they cheer and seek out their next encounter, the gaseous vapor passes over them. They begin to cough. Then without warning, their throats constrict. Dropping their weapons, the men claw in the air. Soon, they are dead of asphyxiation. Belghar's dead soldiers spring back to life. The walking dead now number in the hundreds. It won't be long until even the Tyrellians are hard-pressed to fight this horrible army.

~   ~   ~

From behind Belghar, there is a loud beating of drums. The madman turns and smiles sadistically—the sound of the drums booms in the atmosphere. What follows is the presence of the ugly and bloodthirsty Goblins. Belghar's second and deadly ally has, at last, come to his aid. The eager soldiers barely stop when their leader orders them to. The bloodlust is upon them. Approaching the leader with confidence and oozing of power, Belghar speaks!

"I'm glad you maggots have finally decided to arrive. Your enemy is stopping us from entering the castle. Dispose of them. Take no prisoners." With a chorus of howls, grunts, and slobbering, the Goblins race onto the battlefield. If ever evil could outnumber good, it is now. The Tyrellian soldiers have proved themselves to be the fighters that legends are born.

Chapter 28

As the heroes finish off the soldiers, they see the wave of Goblins descend-ing upon them.

"Kram better gets here soon with some help, or this war will soon be over." Romeelus hisses. The others nod. Scanning across the field, the bounty hunter looks for red hair billowing out of a helm. He almost gives up hope when at last, he spies a warrioress fighting off two undead warriors and two infantry. "That's my baby," he remarks with a grin. "Excuse me, guys, but I hear my duty calling me elsewhere." Putting his heart into his strides, the bounty hunter runs between skirmishes until he reaches Sasha's side.

"Could you use a little help?" A gritting of her teeth is his only response. A stroke that Sasha doesn't see arcs towards her. Romeelus' ax intercepts it. As the odds begin to swing into the lovers' favor, a wave of new Goblins steps forward to replace the dead; it'll be a long time before they will see a break.

~ ~ ~

The cavalry spurs their mounts forward. Stefan and his group try frantically to reset their spears. They are not on time. Stefan dives out of the stampeding horses' way. The rest of his division gets cut to ribbons. He avoids getting trampled beneath the hooves. The riders set their sites on the lone figure lying in the dirt. Stefan sees the moment of his death before him.

"It's not fair!" He yells into the sky. "I haven't fulfilled my promise to my dead father. I cannot die until I have enacted my revenge on Belghar, the murderer of my parents." As the tears stream down his face, the cavalry charges; he braces himself for the impact that never happens. Just as the riders bear down on him, they see the Goblins swarming onto the field. Seeing the effect, the Goblins have the cavalry avoids Stefan and ride toward the more significant threat. Stefan, the last remaining pikeman for the Belgharian army, is given one more chance to fulfill a promise.

~ ~ ~

On top of the castle, Jake finally let's go of his embrace with Gwyninne. His hazel eyes stare into hers.

"I must go out there and fight. I can't stand to be this far away from Belghar. My duty and death link as one. A promise to you I will make. I promise to return to you. After all, I have lost; I will not lose this battle. I will not lose you." In a heartwarming yet lonely gesture, their lips touch, and the kiss provides the strength that Jake will need to fight and destroy, Belghar.

~ ~ ~

Steadily and calmly, Kyle walks onto the field. Ten Goblins spot him and advance quickly toward him. Paying them no heed, he claps his hands together. Muttering softly, he makes the motioning of parting water with his hands. As the Goblins advance, the ground opens up. The ugly, brainless creatures fall in, he claps his hands again. The ground closes. A quick scream and then silence, as blood bursts out of the creatures' ears, nose, and mouths. Warily, three undead soldiers approach. Taking out his scimitar, Kyle waits for the dead. He knows that soon, the dead shall rejoin with the dead.

~ ~ ~

Leading his group towards the heroes, Pontew notices that the bounty hunter is no longer among them. He sighs and rolls his eyes.

"I suppose it is my fault that the bounty hunter isn't here now. I shall just have to deal with him myself. Men, join up with those Goblins and attack those five. Do not stop until they are dead. There are only three of them now. You should be able to dispose of them with the help of those smelly beasts that Belghar allied himself with." They nod with confidence. "Now, where is that bounty hunter?" Walking off in search of Romeelus, the aide to Belghar leaves the soldiers to their fate.

~ ~ ~

Slowly, the odds start to overcome the mighty Tyrellian soldiers. Like an hourglass that is continually turning, the sands shift toward Belghar's favor. The victory is so close; he can almost taste it. With revelry, he watches the defense slowly begin to wane. It is only a matter of time.

~ ~ ~

Thadden, Magdellaine, and Menecha stand side by side and hack away at the enemy that surrounds them. Goblins and skeletons swing at them in mockery. As one or the other falls to the ground, there is always more to take their place. Fatigue starts to set in on the heroes.

"I'm not sure if I can keep this pace up much longer!" Menecha responds to her companions.

"Just do your best. Kram and the Gohwarves have got to be arriving soon." The thief strikes down a Goblin. When it falls, he notices a black shape darting in and out of the enemy's legs from the corner of his eye.

"Feacon!" the thief exclaims happily. "Where have you been hiding?" The cat trips up a skeleton, which in turn falls into three more of its group. They fall to the ground in a heap. Holding his head high, Feacon struts behind the trio. Goblins rush forward to fill in the gap. The sound of breaking bones fills the air as the Goblins walk on the skeleton bodies.

"Look! Behind the line of Goblins, there is a cavalry approaching. Luckily, for us, they can't charge us unless they want to plow through the Goblins that they are allied with." She parries a thrust and cuts off the offending arm. Covered in small nicks and gashes, the three heroes seem to be doing well enough, considering the odds. An arrow flies over the heads of the Goblins. It imbeds itself into Menecha's leg. She grits her teeth from yelling out. The arrow shaft went straight through and is poking out the other side. Letting out a whistle of amazement, the thief moves quickly to her side. He cuts off the arrowhead. Grabbing the feathered shaft, he yanks it through quickly. Menecha lets out a murmur of pain. As Menecha and Magdellaine concentrate solely on parrying all attacks to Thadden, he rips off some cloth from his arm sleeve. Making a tourniquet, he gives the paling Menecha a quick kiss, then resumes his fighting.

~ ~ ~

Pontew steadily progresses his way to the bounty hunter. With the bounty hunter in his sights, he does not see the figure that is only a few feet away, watching his movement.

"I have you now, Romeelus" Pontew raises his hands. Before the monk can strike with his deadly hands, a staff blocks his efforts. Pontew looks up to see the man responsible. Standing before him is Jake. With a scowl of determination, Jake stands in his way.

"To get to my friend, you must first get through me." Pontew fails to recognize the man before him.

"And who are you, to be so foolishly attempting to stop Pontew, Belghar's aide and bodyguard." He replies imperiously.

"Belghar's bodyguard, huh! Well, it looks to me like you are doing a miserable job. How do you intend to protect Belghar if you are over here, and he is way over there?"Jake points behind the monk. "I am Jake Rebish, a former prisoner of Belghar, killer of Drekkar the torturer, and the inevitable ruin of Belghar and his bodyguard Pontew." Grasping the staff tightly, Jake keeps his eyes focused on the next best substitute for Belghar.

~ ~ ~

As battle after battle rages throughout the land; the lightning disappears from the sky. Darkness descends upon the combatants. They seem not to notice as more arrows fill the sky. Bodies and blood litter the earth. All night, the war rages on. By morning the battlefield is nothing more than a bloodbath. Belghar sits on a wooden chair and watches the scene with glory. "I am enjoying what I am seeing. Where is that fool, Pontew? I do not see him among the cavalry sent to destroy the bounty hunter and his allies. But then again, I do not see the bounty hunter among the allies right now either. Oh, well, I'm sure Pontew is taking care of that situation."

~ ~ ~

As the sun reaches the noon position, there is the sound of a horn. It is loud and bold. For a moment, all fighting ceases. Everyone glances around to find the source. From atop a hill stands Kram Ironjaw, and beside him is the leader of the Gohwarves; Vlim Axe-Wielder. Staring at the carnage, the Gohwarves feel the anger within them begin to boil. When they see the undead and the evil Goblins, they know that Kram was correct. It is this evil that the Gohwarves have sworn to rid the world of. Feeling the rage overwhelm them, they storm down the hill; with the coming of the Gohwarves, the sands of the hourglass shift towards good.

~ ~ ~

At the sight of the Gohwarves stampeding towards them, the Goblins shriek in fear, and they see no way out. With eyes wide, they make themselves ready for the charge. The Gohwarves split their troops. Half of the army searches out any Goblins, while the other seeks to vanquish Belghar's steadily growing horde of skeleton warriors.

"This is how you vanquish the undead," Kram yells to any who will listen. With a swing of his mighty hammer, the Gohwarf crushes the skeleton. Its bones scatter.

"You use blunt weapons, fools; that is the only way to harm these foul creatures." Hoisting his mug into the air, he drains the last of his foamy ale. The enemy surrounds him. Throwing his empty mug to the ground, he grips onto his hammer. Like the Gohwarves of ancient lore, he begins to cleanse this world of the darkness.

~ ~ ~

As Kram fights his battle, another battle wages between two people. All night the two have combated. Neither has gained a significant advantage, although both are badly bruised, scratched, scarred, and sliced. Jake can feel the energy pour into him from the staff. He knows that it will be a long time before he will have to worry about getting tired. His time has come to make himself better.

"I will get to Belghar," Jake says to himself with determination.

~ ~ ~

Pontew is thinking otherwise. He, too, seems not to tire. Instead of a staff feeding him energy, he is feeding off the bodies' energy near him. He closes his eyes and goes into a trance. All around him, he can feel can see the aura of power in the air. With this much too feed off of, he is sure he can outlast even Jake.

~ ~ ~

"That staff is what is supplying him with the magic. It holds a lot of energy. When the time is right, I will start to suck the energy from the staff, and quite possibly his soul with it." Opening his eyes, he comes out of the trance-like state and ducks under Jake's staff's swing. Turning his fist into fire, he punches. Jake can't dodge it in time and feels the pain from the searing heat. Grinning with satisfaction, Pontew wonders why he is suddenly feeling malicious and cold-hearted.

"I resent the ways of my king, but yet he and I are much the same. Why am I fighting? Why am I having thoughts so evil that even Belghar himself would cringe at them? Am I becoming a thing of evil?" As feelings of uncertainty cloud his mind, Jake makes good use of this distraction. Whirling his staff, he connects into Pontew's groin. Pontew is coming up out of his fog. He looks up and sees three balls of fire spiraling towards him. Just as they are about to converge on him, he opens his mouth and begins to suck. Jake watches in amazement as the three fireballs enter harmlessly into the aide's mouth and disappear. Pontew grins. Instantly, he blows, and a stream of fire jets out and heads for Jake. Reacting, just as quickly, the man who has had enough surprises in the past few weeks sticks his staff into the ground. A geyser shoots out and puts out the flame inches from Jake's face. It seems the battle between these two is hardly over.

~ ~ ~

Feeling shame at the loss of his troops, Stefan quickly decides to get over it.

"I am glad to be still alive. Perhaps it is time for me to approach Belghar and kill him where he stands." With a firm jaw, he begins his trek towards his leader.

~ ~ ~

As the Gohwarves come onto the field, Belghar once again knows that he has not won the war yet.

"They think they can defeat me at every turn. I have anticipated the coming of the Gohwarves. Although their timing is quite early, I have been waiting for them. Let's see if they have a solution for the Demons that I am going to summon. Yes! They have not seen much of my magic yet, but once I summon the demons. I no longer need to conserve my magical energies. I will enter the battle and take the head of Queen Tyrellia myself." HA! HA! HA! As death surrounds him on the battlefield, he closes his eyes and begins to summon.

Chapter 29

As the struggle for power resumes, Belghar decides that he will not lose
on the battlefield. Retrieving his staff, the mad wizard king pitches his
voice into the sky.

> *Oh, hear me, creatures of darkness.*
> *I summon you to this humble plane.*
> *I need your powers of cruel harshness.*
> *To conquer our foes, who are inane.*
> *My call to you is for evil deeds.*
> *I seek your wickedness this bloody day.*
> *It seems we share the same needs.*
> *So come to me now, and do things your way.*

As soon as the words leave his mouth, the sun disappears into the clouds. A
wind whips up out of nowhere. Heedless of the sudden blackness that has
overcome them, the fighters continue to fight. The staff in Belghar's hands
catches aflame. When Belghar tries to release his magical summoning staff,
he realizes that he can't. Searing hot flames lick at his hands. Holding back
his scream, Belghar pays the price of summoning such powerful, evil creatures. In the sky, a black, octagonal doorway appears. From the opening
leap out six horrible demons, the vast, deformed creatures land onto the

ground. The staff finishes burning. Belghar looks at his black, scarred, burnt hands and laughs.

~ ~ ~

Fighting by Sasha's side, the bounty hunter glances up just as the demons arrive upon the field. Seeing his call to duty, he nudges Sasha and points. She drops a goblin. Looking at the atrocities, she nods. Cutting their way through the enemy, they stand before one of the demons. Six eyeballs attached to eyestalks stare at the two heroes. Its oval head has a mouth with rows of giant teeth; two eye stalks rest on the skull's top. Thick reptile skin protects its torso. Two arms, with nasty long claws, and two legs give it a humanoid appearance. It is wielding a double-bladed sword; this nine-foot demon stares down at the two challenging figures. With a grin of razor-sharp teeth, the terror awaits their deaths. It attacks.

~ ~ ~

Grinning at his newest band of allies, Belghar barely spots the figure coming behind them. He turns in tie to see Stefan creeping towards him. Stefan instantly adjusts his walk, smiles, and bows before Belghar.

"Why aren't you with your troops?" He demands.

"I have no troops left, sir. They have all sleeping with the worms courtesy of the Tyrellian cavalry. I am all that remains of the pike squad." Feigning sadness, Stefan waits for his opportunity. Turning his back on Stefan, Belghar continues to watch the war.

~ ~ ~

On another part of the battlefield, Jake and Pontew combat one another furiously. Having no weapon other than the staff, Jake manages to keep Pontew's busy hands and feet at bay; while at the same time keeping himself ready for any spells that Pontew can whip up out of thin air. Being at his wit's end, he remains on the defense until he can think of a way to trick his adept opponent into making an error. He looks away from Pontew for a second to see the arrival of the demons. It is a costly second. Two bone-crunching punches slam into his ribs. With the same grim determination that helped him get through Drekkar's tortures and out of the dungeon, Jake keeps his focus.

~ ~ ~

Menecha, Thadden, and Magdellaine finish off the last of their foes. No sooner do they do so when two of the demons, licking their lips, decide to join in the foray. It has two heads and a thorny body! It stands on its four legs and has no hands. Except for its spiked tail and vicious thorns, it possesses no other visible weapons.

"Stand ready and strong, Menecha! I'm afraid that this is where it gets difficult." The female general gets into fighting formation. Her longsword is out in front of her and her shield high and to the left.

"The rest was easy?" Menecha thinks to herself with astonishment. She mimics Magdellaine and swings out her bloodstained weapon. The evil creature swings its thorny tail in her direction.

~ ~ ~

In his black armor, the thief stares at his demon opponent. Although it has pinkish skin, with visible green veins lining its body, this demon lacks originality. At the sight of its opponent, the demon transforms itself into an exact duplicate of Thadden. With one exception, it still has its pink skin and green veins. Holding onto a sword and a shield, it grins wickedly at the unimpressed thief and waits for him to attack.

~ ~ ~

Letting the bodies of the Gohwarves, Goblins, soldiers, and Skeleton warriors clash, Kyle makes his way towards one of the demons. He can spot the danger in it before he even gets close to him. A sickening smell of rot and decay floats towards him. It is a demon of death and destruction. Its body comprises various arms, legs, heads, tails, and other past victims' organs. It seems to move sluggishly and oozily. A black trail of tar or oil seems to fall behind it. It instantly spots him and makes its way towards him; as it gets progressively closer, the stench gains more potency. A Goblin keels over, vomits, then dies. A soldier clutches at his throat, and he too drops dead. Just before the creature can advance upon him, Kyle holds his breath.

"I can't hold my breath forever. I have to find its weakness quickly, or the stench will be my ruin." As the sludge demon looms before him, he starts with the basics. Swinging his weapon, he is not surprised to find it pass right through the liquid-like body. A piece of goop falls off, and Kyle's weapon disappears into the body. One of the hands reaches for him, but he back peddles out of reach. "If that hand would have grabbed me, would it have been strong enough to pull me in?" Formulating a plan, Kyle begins to see a way to destroy the creature.

~   ~   ~

Nearby, two battle-weary figures continue their struggle for victory. Feeling tired of Jake's battle, Pontew decides to finally use his knowledge of Jake's energy supply. Entering into his trance once more, he prepares to leech the energy off of the staff and give it to himself, while at the same time, giving Jake the foul, poisoned air from the bodies of the undead soldiers.

"By the time he realizes what I have done, he will be unable to stop me." Outside the world of energies, Jake is carefully studying Pontew. He knows that the monk is in a trance. Feeling a strange pull on the staff, Jake lets his mind enter into the staff. As soon as he does, he realizes Pontew's plan. Quickly, Jake releases his mind from it, and it gives him his idea. With a victory smile, he heads towards the monk's entranced body.

Somewhere else on the battlefield, Romeelus welcomes the charge of the Demon. Sasha, too prepares herself but feels a powerful surge of air slam into her and sends her flying. She lands on the ground and lies still. Swinging the giant double-bladed ax, the Demon attacks ferociously at the bounty hunter. His shield intercepts and shatters from the blow. So does Romeelus' elbow. Wincing in pain, he lets loose a savage cry and buries his ax into the chest of the enormous creature. It cries in agony as the magic oozes out of the weapon and invades its evil, Demonic system. Huge teeth lash out at him in return and bite deeply into his collar bone.

There is another snap, and pain wracks his body. Never privy to such agonizing pain before something unusual starts to happen to Romeelus. He begins to grow taller. His six-foot frame extends to that of the demon's nine. His hands grasp the cowl. With a mighty yank, he throws to the ground. Romeelus' deep, dark secret reveals itself at last. Memories of a magician, treasure, and demon guarded it come back to him once more. He has become the thing that he defeated a long time ago. Quickly the wounds heal as the demon stares in confusion, Romeelus leaps. With strong, scaly arms, he puts the demon into a bear hug. Using its strength, the Demon tries to resist. The savage bounty hunter clamps onto an eye-stalk with his teeth and rips—green ichor spurts out of the spot where the stalk once was. The Demon howls in pain. It is learning too late that it is no match for Romeelus.

~ ~ ~

Fighting side by side, Kram and Vlim behead some more Goblins. They see the fifth Demon, look at each other, and storm after it with intense bloodlust. Haughtily, it looks down upon the two small, hairy men coming after it. Cleaning its claws, it stands erect and prepares for combat.

~ ~ ~

The last remaining Demon glares at the field. It can see no worthy opponent. As it waits for one of his "brothers" to fall, it does not see the large shadow behind it. A strong, vise-like grip latches onto its throat and gives a yank. "Crrrkk"! The Demon's carcass collapses onto the ground. A pair of big feet makes its way onto the field.

~ ~ ~

Belghar watches the progress of his Demons and feels victory slowly slipping away. As he gazes, he spies a form that arises from the ground like magic. The huge stone man-like shape snaps one of his demon's neck like a twig.

"Hmmm! What kind of creature is that?" Curious, he watches its progress. Behind him, Stefan uses the time to regain his courage.

"Soon!" he thinks with glee. He positions himself behind his leader, his oppressor.

~　~　~

Sasha comes out of her unconsciousness to see demons fighting each other. One Demon, however, is dressed very similarly to Romeelus, her new lover. Shaking her head to clear her vision, Sasha discovers that the reptilian creature overbearing the demon is her lover. Thinking back, she remembers the conversation she had with Romeelus.

"This was his accident, the red-headed fighter shudders at sight. Fighting a hard-fought battle with her heart, she knows now if she must give up on love or love the beast that Romeelus has become. Sadly, she sits down on the ground and cries tears of pain.

Chapter 30

The two Gohwarves storm towards the Demon, its bat-like ears twitch in anticipation. Small eyes sunken into its face stare Kram and Vlim down. Its green claws dripping with an unknown black substance await the two Gohwarves rush as soon as they are in front of it, a wall of rotting flesh blocks their path. Vlim and Kram's eyes get teary from the smell; both resist the feeling of nausea. Wielding their weapons, the Gohwarves hack away at the wall of flesh. Chunks of meat disappear as the wall starts to dwindle. The Demon chuckles out loud. With a loud, piercing scream, it attacks. Through the wall, a claw rips through Vim's armor. He screams in pain. The blood on his skin begins to bubble. He knows that it is a poison that is now racing through his bloodstream. Blocking out the pain, he goes into a berserk frenzy. It is a form of rage that only Gohwarves experience. When they take an excessive wound, the Gohwarves go into a rage that only stops as soon as the anger offender is dead. Should anything or anyone get in the way of the Gohwarve's intended target, then they will destroy the obstruction as well. Kram waits for the claws to come his way. When it does, he ducks under it and swings his ax. The sharp weapon slices deep into the demon. As the demon howls, Vlim destroys the wall of flesh and streaks towards the Demon in his frenzy of repeated blows. Kram steps out of the way and waits to see the demon's fate.

~ ~ ~

Quickly, Jake makes his way towards the meditating Pontew. He is aware of Pontew's intentions and can already feel the draining take effect. With the image of Gwyninne in his mind, he struggles onward and now stands in front of Belghars aide.

"If it's the power you want, Pontew, it is power you shall get!" With all his might, he shoves the staff into the monk's chest. Pontew's eyes awaken as he realizes it's over. The energy he was transferring came into him all at once. The staff's energies, magic, and essence flow into the monk.

Jake watches as Pontew's head begins to expand. The eyes fly out. The nose and mouth burst as blood, phlegm, and teeth land at Jake's feet. Finally, the brain and head can withstand no more and bursts. Grey matter and brain parts scatter onto the snow. Jake grabs onto the staff, but there is nothing there. Its magic is gone.

"I guess I'll have to remain a mute again," he thinks. With a sigh, he grabs a sword from a nearby fallen soldier. Eyes focusing, he sees his next victim. "I'm coming for you, Belghar!" He says in his mind. With a smile that would make even Belghar cringe, he starts to walk towards cruel ruler.

~ ~ ~

Running out of breath but not out of options, Kyle waits for the sludge Demon to approach. As it gets close, he un-straps his wooden shield.

"Burn!" the mage commands, and the shield catches on fire. Seething from the heat, he waits for the shield to be ablaze. The intense heat begins to smolder his clothes. Thinking that it is time, he thrusts the shield at the Demon. As expected, a pair of hands reach out and grabs the shield. They pull the shield into the Demon. Thrashing uncontrollably, the Demon starts burning from the inside out. The black oil bubbles out and melts the blood-covered snow. Kyle runs away as the Demon gurgles out a liquid scream. With no way to put out the fire, the Demon becomes engulfed by the flame, and as a final farewell blows up—oil showers the sky and lands to the ground with a hiss. Kyle smirks as a few skeletons disintegrate at the drenching from the oil. Several soldiers get hit, too but suffer no effects. Murmurs of thanks go out to Tyrellian armor. Seeking further skirmishes, Kyle helps the Gohwarves finish off some Goblins.

~ ~ ~

Thadden fares the worst of the Demon encounters. He can see no way to defeat the duplicate Demon. If he thrusts, it parries. If he leaps, it rolls. Like lightning, the demon's rapier slashes at his legs. Blood seeps out. Again the thief attacks. This time he kicks. The Demon blocks it with its shield. Feeling frustration rears its head, Thadden attempts a different ploy.

"It seems to do the opposite of what I do. I wonder if..." He leaps backward. The Demon rolls forward. Extending his hand, Thadden thrusts his rapier outwards. Moving forwards, the Demon has no choice but to impale its chest onto Thadden's weapon. Instantly it recoils and rolls backward before further damage can reach him. The blood gushes outwards, it strikes Thadden. Hot boiling acid burns through his armor and his skin. Releasing his weapon, Thadden falls to the ground in utter, unbearable pain. The creature moves in for the kill.

~ ~ ~

Concentrating on their battle, Menecha and Magdellaine fail to notice the thief go down. The demon's tail lashes out at the women. They jump aside. Menecha strikes the tail with her longsword. It rebounds off the tail doing no damage. Magdellaine tries the same move to the creature's back with the same result. Cursing to one another, they continue to fight and wait for an opening. They figure out a way to work in unison as the Demon circles.

~ ~ ~

Belghar watches as, one by one, his Demons start to waver and fall. His grip with reality was fading fast. Summoning up his magic, he targets a group of Gohwarves. "Ice Spears!" he commands. From his fingertips streaks ten slivers of ice. The fragments stretch out and resemble the shape of spears. Before the unsuspecting Gohwarves know it, the spears skewer them. Some of them die instantly, becoming a block of solid ice. The ones that remain conscious slowly watch as their bodies turn to ice. Their transformation is painful. Before long, they, too, are like their companions. Belghar begins to recite another spell.

~ ~ ~

Vlim wastes no time in finishing off the Demon. It tries to scurry away, but the Gohwarf is quicker. In three short strokes, the product of evil falls to pieces in a bloody heap. Kram remains behind his leader and waits for the frenzy to dissipate. Surprisingly, Vlim is quick to return himself to his normal condition. As he does so, the effects of the poison start to affect him. Kram watches his leader. Writhing in pain, Vlim begins to shake. Rushing to his leader's side, the Gohwarf realizes that poison must be deadly.

"Kram," Vlim calls to his favorite warrior. "Kram, listen to me! This poison is too strong for my body to resist. I know that my death is drawing near. Take my ax, shield, and the amulet of leadership. I bequeath them to you. They are yours now. I won't need them where I'm going. You are the one best suited for leadership in our clan. I know the others won't have a problem following you. Remember my death, and honor this war. I see the war going in our favor. Finish it for me, and take care of the clan. Farewell." The eyes close, and his body gives a final shudder. Tearful, sad, and angry, Kram puts the amulet around his neck. With Vlim's ax and shield in his hand, he seeks out the nearest band of Goblins, goes into beserk mode, and single-handedly wipes them out.

~ ~ ~

Thirty undead soldiers throw themselves upon the stone creature. Their weapons shatter on its stony hide. Having no other option, they flail their arms wildly at it. With a mighty sweep of his huge fist, the stone creature pounds them to paste. The victory is short and sweet. Having no trouble finding the enemy, the stone man surrounds himself with them and continues the fight.

~ ~ ~

In a furious rage, Belghar witnesses victory sliding entirely out of his reach. As he contemplates his next move, he catches movement out of the corner of his eye. He follows the movement.

"A figure, courageous, daring, and stupid, is attempting to attack me". It isn't until Jake gets closer that Belghar recognizes he would-be assailant. "At last, the man who killed my torturer and escaped from my dungeon is getting visions of grandeur. Well, little man, when I fry the skin off of your bones, you will no longer want to be a hero. Maybe, I'll rape you as I did your sweet, sweet, daughter." At that comment, Jake feels the recessed memories and emotions and lets the rage take him. He blocks out everything. Belghar is the only image that Jake can see. Belghar taunts him with a laugh as Jake charges forward with his sword swinging.

~   ~   ~

When Thadden falls, his doppelganger moves in for the kill. Before it can get there, a small black cat intervenes. Uncertain as to the cat's motive, but sure enough of its own ability to defeat the obstacle, the Demon sets its eyes on the small, four-legged cats. Sword in hand, the Demon prepares to kill the cat. As it swings, Feacon teleports behind it and out of reach. The Demon turns. Suddenly, it is no longer a cat that the demon is fighting. A huge black panther roars and leaps at it. The Demon has no time to prepare for this unexpected change of events. Razor-sharp claws tear at its body and pin it to the ground. Feacon's jaws go for the Demons throat; helpless, the Demon can only gurgle a scream as Feacon enjoys a feast.

~   ~   ~

The Demon swings its tail. Menecha manages to jump harmlessly out of the way, but Magdellaine catches it full force. She breathes out just as the tail hits. Because of this maneuver, she can maintain her breath. It does not, however, prevent her from falling to the ground. Quickly, Menecha moves over to stand protectively over her falling mentor/mother. The Demon tries to bite. She blocks the teeth with her tail. Pushing forward the shield forward with all of her strength, she can hold the Demon's forelegs in the air. The underbelly, unlike the outer shell, is soft. Keeping the Demon in the air, she prays that Magdellaine will recover from her blow quickly. Just as her strength begins to wane, she yells!

"Mother, hurry, strike at the belly, it is the only soft spot on this Demon's body!" No sooner do the words leave her mouth when a sword, sent flying, sticks into the creature's stomach. Holding the Demon up, Menecha dives to the side. Gravity, and the weight of the Demon, send it spiraling to the ground. The impact causes the sword to plunge into it's brain. It dies instantly. After getting up, Menecha stands beside her mother. The two stare at the dead monstrosity and breathe a sigh of relief. That's when they hear the roar of a panther and look over to where Thadden was fighting.

~ ~ ~

Belghar waits until Jake within range, then casts his spell. Bees, hundreds of bees swarm towards Jake. As they start to bite him and die, he continues on his course unwaveringly. For the first time in his life, fear invades Belghar's heart. He starts to back up from Jake's forward progress, then Stefan strikes. The Bec de Corbin penetrates Belghar's backside and sticks out of the belly. He looks down at the weapon and then looks for the owner. Stefan stares back at him proudly.

"Stefan? Why?"

"You killed my father, raped and killed my mother, and raped me. I promised my father that I would avenge him. Now it is time to fulfill that promise."

"I killed them a long time ago. I could've killed you too, but I let you live. Is this how you treat my generosity? I may die tonight," he looks down at the weapon, but not before I kill you!" From Belghar's hands emerges an electric whip. Stefan stands and awaits his fate. Crack! The whip wraps itself around Stefan's neck. Electricity pours through his body. Slowly it starts to strangle Stefan.

~ ~ ~

Romeelus' bear hug still grips the Demon tightly. Despite its efforts, it cannot shake free from his strong hands. He finishes biting off the last of the stalks, and with a final demonstration of strength, he breaks the demons back. It dangles limply in his hands. Throwing the body to the ground, Romeelus turns around and sees Sasha. Her expression is enough to tell him what she is seeing. Covering his face with shame, he turns away. The lust for battle sated, he walks off the field, with tears streaming down his face.

Through the bodies of the buzzing, biting bees, Jake can see Belghar's back; a weapon, big, and dangerous sticks through it. With running strides, Menecha's father grabs onto Belghar. Belghar releases the whip and turns. Jake's bumpy face glares back at him. Faster than Belghar can react, Jake swings his sword. He cuts off an arm. Blood spurts out of the stump, drenching the ground. Belghar starts to go into shock. Jake continues and cuts off an ear. Sagging to his knees Belghar can feel himself fading away.

"I'm dying" he says with numb horror. Holding himself up with one arm, he tries to die with dignity. Jake drops his sword and holds "the mighty" Belghar's head in his hands. He thinks back to a promise and squeezes. Perhaps, it is magic, or a sudden burst left over from the staff, but Jake feels strength pour into his hands. Both eyes pop out of their sockets. Blood cascades down his wrists. Throwing Pontew's body to the ground Jake beheads the would be conqueror. With a final farewell to the time spent in the dungeon, Jake fulfills his promise and stomps on Belghar's head. Stefan, now sitting and shaking, stares at his savior with wonder.

"You have helped me avenge my father's death. I go to join him now. Perhaps, someday, we will find a way to repay you." Yanking his weapon out of Belghar's body, Stefan sticks the end into the ground and falls down on it. His body twitches, and then is still. Shaking his head, Jake ignores the chaos around him, and falls to the ground in total exhaustion.

Shortly after Belghar dies, so does his war. His soldiers fought well, but upon seeing their leader die, they quickly lose interest, and give up. The Goblins seeing themselves outnumbered, decide to quit fighting, and try to run back the way they came. Wanting no part of this, the Gohwarves mass murder them until none remain. With no-one to control them the undead skeleton warriors quickly lose substance and simply shatter. Belghar's magic can no longer sustain them. The war is over—Tyrellian soldiers, Gohwarves, and even the granite man head into the castle.

~ ~ ~

Still, on the battlefield, four figures and a panther surround another figure on the ground. Menecha, Magdellaine, Kyle, and Jake, who was wakes from his episode, stand watch over Thadden. Feacon, the panther, watches and waits too. The acid has taken its toll on the thief. It has almost made its way to his bones. Propping himself on his elbow Thadden starts to speak.

"I want to say something to all of you. When I am through with each of you, I want you to return to the castle. When I die, I want it to be in peace. Kyle, I wish to speak to you first. May we speak privately?" Kyle nods. Everybody backs out of hearing range. I hardly know you. I know you used to work for Belghar and Xibnar, but I am glad you switched sides. We could not have won this war without you. Always remember your part in the war, and always fight for the cause in your heart. You have a pure heart now, and I know that it will stay that way. Good luck in your future and always remember me." Hugging Thadden fiercely, Kyle steps back and prepares to leave. "Kyle! One more thing! I notice that Romeelus isn't here. Can you see if you can find him and tell him that I wish to speak with him?" He nods. Wiping the tears on his sleeve, Kyle glimpses at the heroic thief for the last time and walks away.

~ ~ ~

"Magdellaine! You are next." Hearing her name, she appears at the dying thief's side. "I thank you for taking care of Menecha and training her to protect herself. I'm afraid she was left in my care by Jake, and I quickly lost her. I have never forgiven myself for the carelessness. I love your daughter a lot. It just saddens me that I won't be able to spend any more time with her. May you live long and become the next queen of Tyrellia. Goodbye, and good luck." Grieving for the man she barely knew, Magdellaine kisses him on the forehead and departs.

"Jake!" the thief yells. "My friend, Jake, come here! It is your turn." Slowly, sadly, Jake comes forward to see his dying friend.

~ ~ ~

In the forest just outside Tyrellia a black man, carrying an ax, walks away from Tyrellia. With slumping shoulders and a sad face, he says goodbye to his companions in his mind, and with his heart, he says one special one to a red-headed soldier named Sasha. He loses himself in thought that he fails to notice the man behind him.

"Hello, Romeelus. If you are planning to say good-bye to your friends, you're going the wrong way." Romeelus doesn't turn around.

"Mind your business Kyle he hisses. "I have nothing more I can say now."

"Ahh! I see. Well, I guess it doesn't mean anything to you that Thadden is dying from his battle with a Demon. He has requested to speak with you before he goes. Friendship isn't a quality that you concern yourself with." Kyle doesn't see the fist coming. The punch knocks him to the ground.

"I do admire friendship! I just can't face anyone after... after what happened on the battlefield." Kyle gets up.

"Do you think that anyone cares that you have become a part lizard, or whatever it is that you are? I am just delivering a message. You can do as you please." Having said his peace, Kyle snaps his fingers and is gone from sight.

"Goats udders!" Romeelus curses. "That does it. After this, I do not have anything to do with friends. They are a weakness that a bounty hunter of my reputation cannot afford to have." The bounty hunter heads back to Tyrellia with a heavy, ladened heart. There is a chuckle from behind the bushes, and Kyle steps out.

"I knew I could convince him." With a final snap of his fingers, he is finally gone from sight.

~ ~ ~

At the sight of Thadden, Jake burst into tears. He could say nothing and hoped that his tears would be enough when he stood next to the thief, two hands reached out to hold his. Jake began to cry some more.

"Jake, although you cannot speak, I know what you are going to say. After your ordeal in the dungeon, and from the looks of you, your ordeal on the battlefield, you wish you could put yourself where I am." Jake nodded. "For that, I am grateful. But it is unnecessary. It was your courage and willpower that kept you alive in the dungeon and on the battlefield. When I found you in the dungeon, you were about ready to escape. I wish that I would have been half as strong and brave as you had been in the same situation. You are a proud man and have been through enough. Your daughter is the most beautiful woman I have ever laid eyes upon. It grieves me to know that I am going to die. I will never see Menecha again. It grieves me not to have you as a father. She is lucky to have you, as you are to have her. I love Menecha! All I ask is that you keep an eye out for her, and if she marries, make sure it's to someone that I would approve of." Thadden chuckles; the acid starts to dissolve a part of his lip. "Remember me!" Thadden finishes. Giving Jake's hand a squeeze, he nods to the castle. Slowly, painfully, Jake leaves the thief to his pain.

~ ~ ~

"Menecha!" Thadden's voice is barely able to get out. Nonetheless, she hears and comes running to his side. "The acid is dissolving my face, so I don't have a lot of time left."

"That's o-okay, t-tell me w-what you c-can," She blubbers.

"You are the only woman who has ever been able to affect me. Before you, I did not know what it was like to love. My heart aches at the thought of not having to kiss you again. It saddens me to know that we could have had a wonderful life together, but now, we will separate. I love you, Menecha. I wanted nothing more than to be the father of your child. Good-bye!" Not wasting a moment, Menecha kisses him on the lips.

"I love you too, Thadden!" she replies as she smothers his face with kisses.

"Thank you, Menecha. Now go! I must die alone." Giving him one last kiss, she runs to the castle sobbing the whole way. Summoning up the last of his vocal cords, he cries out one last name.

"*Romeelus!*" He was about to try again when he heard the familiar voice reply in his ear.

"I'm here." Thadden's voice becomes a whisper.

"I just wanted to tell you that you are a magnificent human being. Despite what you became on the battlefield, you still have a heart. Sasha loves you, dearly. I'm sure if you go to her, she will accept what you have become. I have nothing to pay you, but I want to ask for a favor. It's a job I want you to do for me."

"Name it!" the bounty hunter replies without hesitation.

"Keep an eye on Menecha for me. Don't let her know that I want you to because she'll insist that she'll be fine. Women do that sort of thing all the time. Do your best to make sure no harm befalls her. Can you do that for me?" Feeling his heart turn over and forcing back the tears, Romeelus watches as the flesh on the cheeks become bone.

"I will do that. No harm shall ever come to Menecha while I am alive."

"G-good! Bye!" Thadden manages to complete the farewell before his lip disintegrates. As Romeelus heads for the castle, wholly shaken from the ordeal, Feacon approaches his old companion.

Giving a final farewell lick to the master he loves, the big cat walks a few feet away and stands guard. Feeling the lick, Thadden smiles, then slowly meets his death.

~ ~ ~

After the thief's friends head into the castle in a gloom state, a figure arrives at the scene. The figure stoops down and notices the green necklace on the ground. "The Necklace of Zedan!" He exclaims. "At last, my uncle's treasure is now back where it belongs.!" With a smile on his face, Kram leaves with his family heirloom in tow.

Epilogue

Eight months later:

Menecha is taking a walk through the forest trails near Tyrellia. As she walks, she looks down at her round, full belly. "Now, Khaden, as you grow up, you will learn all about your father. He was a magnificent man. If he were alive today, he would be so proud to know that you were on your way." She is so absorbed in her conversation; she does not hear the snapping of the twigs. She continues talking. As she talks, she rubs her belly. "It was an adventure that your father was always seeking. His last adventure is where he met me. Unfortunately, the adventure ended up turning into a war, and that war claimed your father's life." A kick, big and prominent, seemed to answer her question. In the bushes, five figures are hiding. The thieves are from the guild and are planning an ambush.

"She will fetch a fine price when we hold her for ransom." One of the thieves gloats to the others. As they prepare to jump at Menecha, a stone hits one of them. Turning in surprise, they notice a man and a woman watching them. Not wanting to alert the woman they plan on ransoming, the thieves creep towards the two people.

"Get out of here before you find yourselves bleeding in the bushes." The leader of the group tries to intimidate the people. The man steps forward and stands in front of the leader.

"You are from the Shondell guildhall, right?" Romeelus asks.

"Yes! And if you leave now, we promise we won't hurt you or your woman. Maybe, we'll give you some of our money from the huge ransom that we are going to get."

"I'm afraid we are not going to let you do that," Romeelus states calmly.

"What!" the leader replies, stunned. He waves with his hand, and the other thieves fan out to surround Romeelus and the woman. "Have it your way then," he replies. He takes out his short sword.

"Before you strike, let me inform you of the mistake you are about to make. That woman you were about to waylay is carrying Thadden's child. You remember Thadden, don't you? He was the finest thief to ever come out of your guild. If he were alive, we wouldn't need to be here to save her. Perhaps, you boys should make yourself disappear before you find yourselves bleeding in the bushes." The thief scratches his head.

"I remember Thadden. He was the cocky one that always made everyone look bad. I'm glad that he's gone. Now, I can finally replace him and be the guild's favorite."

"You could never replace him." Romeelus' acid tone makes the leader flinch.

"Men! Get them! Quickly!" the leader barks beginning to panic. His men move in with poison daggers. The leader swings his sword. Romeelus easily parries and notices the man's ineptness with the weapon. He strikes. Barely parrying, the leader begins to back up.

Two of the men attempt to stab at the bounty hunter from behind. He knows they are there but waits for the element of surprise. There is a roar amidst the foliage, and Feacon, in panther form, swings his mighty paw. It snaps the neck of one of the rogues. The other tries to flee. In one mighty leap, Feacon is on top of his back. Before he can scream, jaws clamp on to his neck, and the fight is over.

The woman with Romeelus is faring just as well. One brigand thrusts with the poisonous dagger, but she moves out of the way, and he ends up stabbing his ally. The poison, although average, was enough to send the man to his knees. Sasha swings her sword and watches as it cleaves her attackers first in half.

Feeling bored of the man before him and still wishing to enact the proper justice to the thief who slandered Thadden's name, Romeelus waits for the attack. Not wanting to risk a lengthy encounter, the leader sees what he thinks is his opening and attacks. Romeelus blocks the swing spins 180 degrees, and swings backward. The ax rips through the leather armor and shreds the heart. Not quite finished with the man yet, the bounty hunter takes the shortsword from the man's dead fingers and slices up through the legs. The weapon slices various genitalia off. Removing his bloody ax Romeelus lets the body fall with a thud. He turns in time to see poison tear a man apart. The last of the thieves try to puke up the poison before it can do any damage, but he is too late. As the last of the foam comes spitting out of the convulsing man's mouth, Romeelus knows that the man is dead.

"Nice work, Feacon! Sasha!" A slight smile plays onto his face at the mention of the last name. It is the name of the woman he loves so dearly. A woman who, despite his "side-effect" or "shape-change," she stands firmly beside him, loving him all the more. Feacon admires his handiwork. Making his way over to the paths, he stares at Menecha, who is slowly fading down the path, heading back into the safety of the castle. To him, she and what she is carrying is one of the few things left to remind him of his former master. When she is out of sight, he preens himself contentedly. The couple ignores the cat, stare at one another, and smile devilishly. Well! Since we don't have to fulfill a promise for a couple of hours, why don't we find something to do to occupy our time?" The bounty hunters' fingers pull on Sasha's hair. She falls backward onto the forest floor. Their mouths meet. With a look of disgust, Feacon walks away, leaving the couple alone.

The End
For now...

Author's Notes

Hello reader!

I wanted to introduce myself and also let you know a little about my novel. The novel you will notice is graphic in a lot of ways. I feel it essential to let you know the makeup and purpose of it.

It began because I have a love of writing, and at the time, I loved the medieval/fantasy era. With that in mind, I will say that the novel represents my entire childhood and early adulthood. It is a project that helped me deal with a lot of emotional, mental, and physical issues that had occurred in childhood. Upon writing the novel, I got to deal with each problem and reflect on the people involved; the result is, I have had a healing that goes beyond what I thought it would have. Life itself is harsh, cruel, and often confusing, so I held no punches in going into some of the detail that I have. The entire novel contains characters that represent people or events in my life. These characters have traits, mannerisms, and acts that reflect events that have happened to me. There is a little of me in each one of the good guys found in the novel. As I got older, I developed different understanding forms, so I felt it necessary to include those in my characters. Also, of note at the time of the writing, I know that I incorporated such creatures as Demons. If you are a Christian and think it will offend you bear in mind, they are merely reflections of the Demons that every individual has to shake off. I am a baptized Christian and have had a hard time with the thought of keeping demons in here. But in consideration, I know that I love the Lord and deem it necessary to keep them in as they represent part of me. To take them out would mean I would have to take away the part of me that had overcome these personal Demons.

I had felt such a weight and burden lift off of me when I finished this novel. I want to express to others who have had physical, emotional, or mental abuse done to them. Writing and communicating your feelings is a great way to start dealing with your trauma. I hope whoever reads this novel will enjoy it and have some personal reflection as they glimpse into the window of my life.

Thank you for reading my novel.

Sincerely,
Mark Greenlaw

Glossary of Terms

Rapier: Weapon of offense and defense in personal combat, con-
                     sisting of a blade with a sharp point and one or two cut-
                     ting edges, set in a hilt with a handle protected by a metal
                     case or cross guard.

Scimitar: A saber with a much-curved blade having the edge on
                     the convex side.

Dagger: A short pointed weapon with sharp edges.

Magician: One who practices magic, a sorcerer, or magician.

Fireball: A type of spell a wizard could cast that creates a big ball
                     of fire that can engulf about 10-20 people depending on
                     the wizard's power.

Silver: It is the equivalent of a fifty dollar American bill. This is
                     in coin form.

Gold: It is the equivalent of a hundred dollar American bill.
                     This is in coin form.

Healing Potion: A healing potion is a vial of liquid that will cause an individual's wounds to heal when drank or poured. They are a quick fix and good to use when in combat.

Guild: This is an association of men belonging to the same class, or engaged in kindred pursuits, formed for mutual aid and protection. In this case, The Shondell Guild is a guild that house thieves who have meetings on how to steal and kill and what hot or unique items are in the area for the taking.

Spell: It is magic that someone uses (cast) offensively or defensively. It is a word, formula, or incantation believed to have magical powers.

Pommel: A knob on the hilt of a sword or similar weapon

Bounty Hunter: One who pursues a criminal or fugitive for a reward. Unfortunately for people in this era, they aren't necessarily a criminal. Bounty hunters hunt for money pure and simple. Innocent or guilty is not essential, just the size of the reward.

Net: This type of net is a mesh net with weighted balls on the outside fringe to enable a person to throw the net and entangle or capture an individual.

Plate Mail Armor: Plate mail is a combination of chain armor with metal plates covering the vital areas such as the chest, abdomen, and groin. Similar in construction to bronze plate mail, plate mail contains chain and leather and is more resilient to damage.

Crossbow: A bow fixed transversely on a wooden stock grooved to direct the arrow (quarrel).

Looby:

My twist on the word "lobby" It's the same thing.

Cowl:

This is a metal face covering that protects the neck and mouth.

Mace:

A massive medieval war club with a spiked or flanged metal head, used to crush armor.

Short Sword:

It is a cutting or thrusting weapon with a small blade.

Tunic:

It is a loose-fitting garment, sleeved or sleeveless, extending to the knees and worn by men and women.

Ale:

Medieval beer!

Breeches:

It is a garment worn by men, covering the hips and thighs.

Long Sword:

This is a cutting or thrusting weapon with a long blade.

Stave:

A staff or cudgel.

Helm:

A helmet.

Ballista:

This is an ancient military engine, in the form of a cross-bow, used for hurling large arrows.

Catapult:

An military engine for hurling missiles, such as large stones or spears.

Goblin:

A grotesque creature of folklore, thought to work mischief or evil.

Bec de Corbin:

A French weapon, also known as "Raven's Beak." With a top spike, back spike, a four-pronged hammerhead, and langets, this was a fearsome weapon. It attaches to an ash shaft; it was well suited for hand to hand combat. It is for blocking, striking, and using the butt to smash feet. It is a weapon that knights would use. It is used for foot combat and particularly effective against full plate armor.